Spank Me, Mr. Darcy

by Jane Austen
& Lissa Trevor

Riverdale Avenue Books
5676 Riverdale Ave., Suite 101
Riverdale, NY 14071
www.riverdaleavebooks.com

Printed in the United States of America.

First Edition

Cover by: Scott Carpenter
Layout by www.formatting4U.com

Print ISBN: 978-1-62601-022-2
E-book ISBN: 978-1-62601-023-9

Chapter 1

It is a truth universally acknowledged, that a dominant man in possession of a good set of cuffs, must be in want of a much younger, submissive wife.

However little known the feelings or views of such a man may be on his first entering a neighbourhood, this truth is so well fixed in the minds of the surrounding families, that he is considered the rightful property of some one or other of their daughters.

"My dear Mr. Bennet," said his lady to him one day as she removed the ball gag from his mouth, "have you heard that Netherfield Park is at last under new ownership?"

"No M'Lady," Mr. Bennet replied.

"But it is," returned she, untying the leather restraints that bound her naughty husband to the bed post;

Mr. Bennet made no answer, as he was took advantage of his freedom to pin his wife beneath him.

"Do you not want to know who has taken it?" cried his wife, impatiently thrusting her hips up to encourage him to enter her hard and fast.

"You want to tell me?" Mr. Bennet groaned, feeling the tight muscles of her quim clamp down on him. He ravaged her like a man teased beyond his endurance, his posterior red and burning from her use of the riding crop. "I have no objection to hearing it – as soon as you come for me."

This was invitation enough.

"Why, my dear, you make me ache," Mrs. Bennet said, sighing her pleasure as he thrust in and out. They had been married twenty years and were raising five daughters, but he still made her feel like a wanton. She dug her nails into his shoulders as the sweet oblivion threatened to have her caterwauling her pleasure to the household. Settling for screaming into his mouth, his lady met his plunges eagerly until the sparks danced before her eyes and tremors threatened to rip her apart.

He grunted and finished shortly after, collapsing on top of Mrs. Bennet. He kissed her shoulder and rolled off to stare at the ceiling while he tried to catch his breath.

"Mrs. Long says that Netherfield is taken by a young man of large fortune from the north of England; that he came down on Monday in a chaise and four to see the place, and was so much delighted with it, that he is to take possession before Michaelmas, and some of his servants are to be in the house by the end of next week."

"What is his name?" Mr. Bennet said, turning on his side to admire her pert form.

"Bingley."

"Is he married or single?"

"Oh! Single, my dear, to be sure! What a fine thing for our girls!"

"How so? How can it affect them?" He danced his fingers over her breasts, watching her nipples tighten and bud. He tugged on them, rolling them between his fingers.

"My dear Mr. Bennet," replied his wife, " You must know that I am thinking of his marrying one of them."

"Is that his design in settling here?" He trailed his fingers down her ribcage and belly. He tangled his fingers in the curly hairs at the juncture of her thighs and tugged."

"Design!" she cried out, her hips lifting in response to his caress. "Nonsense, how can you talk so! But it is very likely that he may fall in love with one of them, and therefore you must visit him as soon as he comes."

"I see no occasion for that," he said, combing his fingers down to her slick wet heat." You and the girls may go, or you may send them by themselves, which perhaps will be still better, for as you are as handsome as any of them. Mr. Bingley may like you the best of the party and I'll not share you with him." His fingers languidly stroked between the soft folds of her core.

"My dear, you flatter me," she purred, arching into his caress. "I certainly have had my share of beauty, but I do not pretend to be anything extraordinary now. When a woman has five grown-up daughters, she ought to give over thinking of her own beauty."

"In such cases, a woman has not often much beauty to think of, or talent. You are definitely both beautiful and talented" He tickled her until she was insensate, her body tightening on his fingers. Mr.

Bennet flicked her to another orgasm that had her clutching his shoulders. Her lovely mouth a perfect "O" of surprise and joy.

He picked up the riding crop and teased it over her buttocks.

She pressed into him as the warm leather tingled against her sensitive skin. "But, my dear, you must indeed go and see Mr. Bingley when he comes into the neighbourhood."

"It is more than I engage for, I assure you."

"But consider your daughters."

"I'd rather not, while I am abed with you."

"Only think what an establishment it would be for one of them. It will be impossible for us to visit him if you do not."

"You are over-scrupulous, surely. I dare say Mr. Bingley will be very glad to see you, especially if you wear your blue gown. You may tempt him, but if I find out he has taken liberties, it is you I will punish." He tapped the riding crop against her nipples.

She shivered at her husband's dark tone. It was almost as if he willed her to disobey him.

"However, I will send a few lines by you to assure him of my hearty consent to his marrying whichever he chooses of the girls; though I must throw in a good word for my little Lizzy. She is so quiet and obedient. She'd make a lovely wife."

"I desire you will do no such thing. Lizzy is not a bit better than the others; and I am sure she is not half so handsome as Jane, nor half so good-humoured as Lydia. But you are always giving her the preference."

"They have none of them much to recommend them," replied he; "they are all silly and ignorant like other girls; but Lizzy has something more of quickness than her sisters. She has a hidden core. A mystery that might stir a man into obsession – quite like her mother." He took her mouth in a rough kiss, but she pushed him away.

"Mr. Bennet, how can you disregard your other children in such a way? You take delight in vexing me. Letting me pretend at dominance, then taking it away with your harsh words and greater strength. You have no compassion for my needs."

"You mistake me, my dear. I have a high respect for your needs. They are my old friends. I have heard you mention them with consideration these last twenty years at least."

"Ah, you do not know what I suffer."

"But I hope you will get over it, and live to see many young men of fortune come into the neighbourhood."

"It will be no use to us, if twenty such should come, since you will not visit them."

"Depend upon it, my dear, that when there are twenty, I will visit them all." He then bent to his task of whipping his wife into a frenzy of sensation. Striking her thigh, the bottom of her feet, he smiled at her pleasure. And when she launched herself on him, he allowed her to have her way with him.

Mr. Bennet was so odd a mixture of quick parts, sarcastic humour, reserve, and caprice, that the experience of three-and-twenty years had been insufficient to make his wife understand his character. He liked to be bound and whipped, but in the end he was the dominant one in the relationship.

Mrs. Bennet's mind was less difficult to develop.

She was a woman of mean understanding, little information, and uncertain temper. When she was discontented, she fancied herself nervous. Giving her the crop and the bindings had loosed a sexual creature that was tempting, biddable and entirely devoted to shared pleasure. The business of her life, on the other hand, was to get her daughters happily married so she could enjoy her husband and their frolics without interruption.

Chapter 2

Mr. Bennet was among the earliest of those who waited on Mr. Bingley in Netherfield Park. He had always intended to visit him, having fond memories of the orgies of his youth held in the lower ballrooms of the stately home. To his delight, the servants were setting up the dungeons and play areas. Perhaps in the future, Mrs. Bennet and he would be able to assuage some of the darker needs of his that his wife had yet to experience. Not wanting to arouse her curiosity, he kept his sojourn a secret. And till the evening after the visit was paid, she had no knowledge of it. Observing his second daughter employed in trimming a hat, he suddenly addressed her with:

"I hope Mr. Bingley will like it, Lizzy."

"We are not in a way to know what Mr. Bingley likes," said her mother resentfully, "since we are not to visit."

"But you forget, mamma," said Elizabeth, "that we shall meet him at the assemblies, and that Mrs. Long promised to introduce him."

"I do not believe Mrs. Long will do any such thing. She has two nieces of her own. She is a selfish, hypocritical woman, and I have no opinion of her."

7

"No more have I," said Mr. Bennet; although that was a bit untrue. He had once had the pleasure of the woman's mouth around his turgid member in the days of his misspent youth. "And I am glad to find that you do not depend on her serving you." The thought of anyone servicing his wife but him made him rather cross.

Mrs. Bennet deigned not to make any reply, but, unable to contain herself, began scolding one of her daughters in hope that they would take instruction to become proper ladies.

"Don't keep coughing so, Kitty, for Heaven's sake! Have a little compassion on my nerves. You tear them to pieces."

"Kitty has no discretion in her coughs," said her father; "she times them ill." In fact, his younger daughter had no discretion at all, which would become a problem once they were more formally introduced to polite society.

"I do not cough for my own amusement," replied Kitty fretfully. "When is your next ball to be, Lizzy?"

"To-morrow fortnight." Elizabeth said, eagerness in every line of her body.

"Aye, so it is," cried her mother, "and Mrs. Long does not come back till the day before; so it will be impossible for her to introduce him, for she will not know him herself." She glared at her husband. It would have been nice to attend. She had heard so much about Netherfield. But without Mr. Bingley's acknowledgement there would be no Netherfield. Not for her, nor for her daughters.

"Then, my dear, you may have the advantage of your friend, and introduce Mr. Bingley to her." He smiled, a devilish grin that has his wife biting her lip in anticipation—even as she was vexed with him refusing to help marry off their daughters.

"Impossible, Mr. Bennet, impossible, when I am not acquainted with him myself; how can you be so teasing?"

"I honour your circumspection. A fortnight's acquaintance is certainly very little. One cannot know what a man really is by the end of a fortnight. But if we do not venture somebody else will; and after all, Mrs. Long and her daughters must stand their chance; and, therefore, as she will think it an act of kindness, if you decline the office, I will take it on myself."

The girls stared at their father. Could it be that they would be allowed to attend the festivities at the notorious Netherfield Park?

Mrs. Bennet said only, "Nonsense, nonsense!"

"What can be the meaning of that emphatic exclamation?" cried he. "Do you consider the forms of introduction, and the stress that is laid on them, as nonsense? I cannot quite agree with you there. What say you, Mary? For you are a young lady of deep reflection, I know, and read great books and make extracts."

Mary wished to say something sensible, but knew not how. She had been fantasizing about a passage she read in a diary she had found in the library. The woman had worn a black domino mask and had men begging her to let them satisfy her. With a mask, no one would think she was plain Mary, the ugly Bennet sister.

"While Mary is adjusting her ideas," he continued, "let us return to Mr. Bingley."

Lissa Trevor

"I am sick of Mr. Bingley," cried his wife. She had been unable to coerce the man to attend an afternoon of tea. She felt like a failure.

"I am sorry to hear that; but why did not you tell me that before? If I had known as much this morning I certainly would not have called on him. It is very unlucky; but as I have actually paid the visit, we cannot escape the acquaintance now."

The astonishment of the ladies was just what he wished; that of Mrs. Bennet perhaps surpassing the rest; though, when the first tumult of joy was over, she began to declare that it was what she had expected all the while.

"How good it was in you, my dear Mr. Bennet! But I knew I should persuade you at last. I was sure you loved your girls too well to neglect such an acquaintance. Well, how pleased I am! And it is such a good joke, too, that you should have gone this morning and never said a word about it till now." She gave her husband a seductive, smoldering look and deliberate swayed out of the drawing room to head up to their bedroom.

"Now, Kitty, you may cough as much as you choose," said Mr. Bennet; and, as he spoke, he left the room, looking forward to a session of raptures with his wife.

"What an excellent father we have, girls!" said Elizabeth, when the door was shut. "I do not know how we will ever make him amends for his kindness;. At our time of life it is not so pleasant, I can tell you, to be making new acquaintances every day; but for the sake of our future, we should do anything. Lydia, my love, though you are the youngest, I dare say Mr. Bingley will dance with you at the next ball. I've heard such delicious things about what goes on at Netherfield. They say there are pleasure rooms filled with decadent and wicked things there. Let us hope that we make a good impression so he invites us to his home."

"Oh!" said Lydia stoutly, "I am not afraid; for though I am the youngest, I'm the bravest."

The rest of the evening was spent in conjecturing how soon Mr. Bingley would return Mr. Bennet's visit, and determining when they should ask him to dinner.

Chapter 3

Not all that Mrs. Bennet, however, with the assistance of her five daughters, could ask on the subject, was sufficient to draw from her husband any satisfactory description of Mr. Bingley. They attacked him in various ways—with barefaced questions, ingenious suppositions, and distant surmises. Mrs. Bennet had whipped him until she was panting and desperate, but he eluded the skill of them all, and they were at last obliged to accept the second-hand intelligence of their neighbour, Lady Lucas. Her report was highly favourable. He had a sweet disposition, but was harsh with his servants. Even Sir William had been delighted with him after spending an hour or so in Netherfield. Mr. Bingley was quite young, wonderfully handsome, extremely agreeable, and, to crown the whole, he meant to be at the next assembly with a large party. Nothing could be more delightful! To be fond of dancing was a certain step towards falling in love; and very lively hopes of Mr. Bingley's heart were entertained.

"If I can but see one of my daughters happily settled at Netherfield," said Mrs. Bennet to her husband as she knelt at his feet, her hands and feet bound together, "and all the others equally well married, I shall have nothing to wish for."

When Mr. Bennet slid his cock into her mouth, she had nothing further to say either.

In a few days Mr. Bingley returned Mr. Bennet's visit, and sat about ten minutes with him in his library. He had entertained hopes of being admitted to a sight of the young ladies, of whose beauty he had heard much and perhaps test each one as to their sensitivity and desires; but he saw only the father, who was interested in talking about arranging a threesome with a buxom maid and his lady wife. The ladies were somewhat more fortunate, for they had the advantage of ascertaining from an upper window that Mr. Bingley wore a blue coat, rode a black horse and had a firm and muscled backside.

An invitation to dinner was soon afterwards dispatched; and already had Mrs. Bennet planned the courses that were to do credit to her housekeeping and how best to show off her attributes in the blue dress, when an answer arrived which deferred it all. Mr. Bingley was obliged to be in town the following day, and, consequently, unable to accept the honour of their invitation, etc. Mrs. Bennet was quite disconcerted. She could not imagine what business he could have in town so soon after his arrival in Hertfordshire; and she began to fear that he might be always flying about from one place to another, and never settled at Netherfield as he ought to be.

Lady Lucas quieted her fears a little. A report soon followed that Mr. Bingley was to bring twelve ladies and seven gentlemen with him to the assembly.

They grieved over such a number of ladies, but

were comforted the day before the ball by hearing, that instead of twelve he brought only six with him from London—his five sisters and a cousin. And when the party entered the assembly room it consisted of only five altogether—Mr. Bingley, his two sisters, the husband of the eldest, and another young man.

Mr. Bingley was good-looking and gentlemanlike; he had a pleasant countenance, and easy, unaffected manners. His sisters were fine women, with an air of decided fashion and serene beauty. His brother-in-law, Mr. Hurst, merely looked the gentleman and was seen fondling a maid during the assembly; but his friend Mr. Darcy soon drew the attention of the room by his fine, tall person, handsome features, noble mien, and the report which was in general circulation within five minutes after his entrance, of being ridiculously wealthy. The gentlemen pronounced him to be a fine figure of a man, the ladies declared he was much handsomer than Mr. Bingley, and he was looked at with great admiration for about half the evening, till his manners gave disgust which turned the tide of his popularity. He didn't speak unless spoken too, and then only grudgingly for he was discovered to be proud; to be above his company, and above being pleased; and not all his large estate in Derbyshire could then save him from having a most forbidding, disagreeable countenance, and being unworthy to be compared with his friend.

Mr. Bingley had soon made himself acquainted with all the principal people in the room; he was lively and unreserved, danced every dance, was angry that the ball closed so early, and talked of giving one himself at Netherfield, where the food and drink would be plentiful and the music and merriments would go on until dawn. Such amiable qualities must speak for themselves. What a contrast between him and his friend! Mr. Darcy danced only once with Mrs. Long who without a care for her husband whispered to Darcy that she wanted to leave the assembly and go out on the balcony for a quick tup, and once with Miss Long, who trembled like a frightened virgin in his arms – which Mr. Darcy deduced she probably was. A part of him was intrigued by both women. He wouldn't mind debauching Mrs. Long presumably while her husband watched, and he wouldn't mind deflowering the quivering maid, again with an audience. But Mr. Darcy thought that would be too much on his first introduction to the quaint bucolic citizens of Meryton. So he declined being introduced to any other lady, and spent the rest of the evening in walking about the room, speaking occasionally to one of his own party. His character was decided. He was the proudest, most disagreeable man in the world, and everybody hoped that he would never come there again. Amongst the most violent against him was Mrs. Bennet, whose dislike of his general behaviour was sharpened into particular resentment by his having slighted one of her daughters and completely ignoring her own blue gown.

Elizabeth Bennet had been obliged, by the scarcity of gentlemen, to sit down for two dances; and during part of that time, Mr. Darcy had been standing near enough for her to hear a conversation between him and Mr. Bingley, who came from the dance for a few minutes, to press his friend to join it.

"Come, Darcy," said he, "I must have you dance. I hate to see you standing about by yourself in this stupid manner. You had much better dance or at least take Mrs. Long up on her obvious invitation."

"I certainly shall not. You know how I detest dancing, unless I am particularly acquainted with my partner. And if I take Mrs. ·Long, I would like an audience. At such an assembly as this it would be insupportable. Your sisters are engaged, and there is not another woman in the room whom it would not be a punishment to me to stand up with."

"I would not be so fastidious as you are," cried Mr. Bingley, "for a kingdom! Upon my honour, I never met with so many pleasant girls in my life as I have this evening; and there are several of them you see uncommonly pretty."

"You are dancing with the only handsome girl in the room," said Mr. Darcy, looking at the eldest Miss Bennet.

"Oh! She is the most beautiful creature I ever beheld! Her breasts are like succulent melons that I long to sample. But there is one of her sisters sitting down just behind you, who is very pretty, and I dare say very agreeable. She has a luscious mouth that makes my prick twitch. Do let me ask my partner to introduce you."

"Which do you mean?" and turning round he looked for a moment at Elizabeth, till catching her eye, he withdrew his own and coldly said: "She is tolerable, but not handsome enough to tempt me: her lips notwithstanding, I am in no humour at present to give consequence to young ladies who are slighted by other men. She looks too innocent to play games such as the ones we enjoy. I would not want to shatter her illusions. You had better return to your partner and enjoy her smiles, for you are wasting your time with me."

Mr. Bingley followed his advice. Mr. Darcy walked off; and Elizabeth remained with no very cordial feelings toward him. She was no more innocent than any of the girls here. She told the story, however, with great spirit among her friends; for she had a lively, playful disposition, which delighted in anything ridiculous.

The evening altogether passed off pleasantly to the whole family. Mrs. Bennet had seen her eldest daughter much admired by the Netherfield party. Mr. Bingley had danced with her twice, and she had been distinguished by his sisters. When the two of them stole off together for a moment alone, it wasn't scandalous, but satisfying. Jane was as much gratified by this as her mother could be, though in a quieter way. Elizabeth felt Jane's pleasure, but felt a dart of bleakness because she hadn't been coddled in the corner by an over-amorous beau.

Mary had heard herself mentioned to Miss Bingley as the most accomplished girl in the neighbourhood; and Catherine and Lydia had been fortunate enough never to be without partners, which was all that they had yet learnt to care for at a ball.

They returned, therefore, in good spirits to Longbourn, the village where they lived, and of which they were the principal inhabitants. They found Mr. Bennet still up. With a book of erotic artwork he was regardless of time; and on the present occasion he had a good deal of curiosity as to the event of an evening which had raised such splendid expectations. He had rather hoped that his wife's views on the stranger would be disappointed; but he soon found out that he had a different story to hear.

"Oh! my dear Mr. Bennet," as she entered the bedroom, "we have had a most delightful evening, a most excellent ball. I wish you had been there."

He put aside the erotic book and opened his robe to show his wife his thick erection.

"Were you well behaved?"

Mrs. Bennet blushed and shook her head.

"Tell me about the ball," he said, roughly pulling on the seams of her dress until they ripped and her breasts tumbled out of her corset. He took a small knife from his dinner tray and sliced open the seams, so the blue dress hung in tatters around her.

"Oh," she panted as her husband pinched her nipple. "Well, Jane was so admired, nothing could be like it. Everybody said how well she looked; and Mr. Bingley thought her quite beautiful, and danced with her twice! Only think of that, my dear; he actually danced with her twice! and she was the only creature in the room that he asked a second time. First of all, he asked Miss Lucas. I was so vexed to see him stand up with her!"

"You know what vexes me?" Mr. Bennet said, brooding over his wife's chest. "The love bite I gave you is fading." He stroked the reddened flesh near her nipple. She gasped when he covered it with his mouth and sucked fiercely. Mrs. Bennet squirmed as her husband used a knife to cut off her corset stays and rip the rest of her blue dress from her. He released her breast with a loud smacking sound.

"Who is your master?" Mr. Bennet said, gliding the flat edge of the knife down her quivering belly to

18

cut the ties of her undergarments.

"You are, my dear. But I'm not done telling you about Mr. Bingley. He seemed quite struck with Jane as she was going down the dance. So he inquired who she was, and got introduced, and asked her for the two next. Then the two third he danced with Miss King, and the two fourth with Maria Lucas, and the two fifth with Jane again, and the two sixth with Lizzy, and the Boulanger—"

"If he had had any compassion for me," cried her husband impatiently, stripping the rest of her clothes from her until she stood naked before him. "he would not have danced half so much! For God's sake, say no more of his partners. Oh that he had sprained his ankle in the first dance! Now, were you well behaved at the ball?"

"Oh!" she said as his fingers roughly probed between her legs. She was wet and throbbing for him.

Mr. Bennet growled and pushed her down on all fours across their bed. "Did you look at any other men?"

"There is no other man but you, my love. However, Mr. Hurst my dear, I am quite delighted with him. He is so excessively handsome! And rich. I never in my life saw anything more elegant than their dress. I dare say the lace upon Mrs. Hurst's gown—"

Here she was interrupted again. Mr. Bennet protested against any description of finery, by shoving his hard cock inside her.

"Do you like this, you little strumpet?" Mr. Bennet pulled her hips so she was nestled tight into his bucking thrusts. While he had rather a hot poker in his eye than to have gone to the assembly, he had missed dancing with his wife. Had missed the feel of her in his arms.

"Oh yes," She closed her eyes in bliss as her breasts bounced against the bedding with the wild pounding she was receiving.

"Tell me what you saw. Did you see some of what I told you happened at Netherfield.," he panted, slapping his heavy palm across her ivory buttock.

She shrieked into the mattress as he pushed her down roughly so he could penetrate her deeper.

"Oh yes, so good," she threw her head back as his ministrations became harder. His hand smacked her hard and Mrs. Bennet quivered.

"Tell me," he demanded.

"Well, I did see Mr. Hurst."

"You spied on him."

"Y-yes."

"So naughty," Mr. Bennet swatting her twice more with stinging slaps.

"He had one of the maids kneeling in front of him. Sucking on him."

"Did you like watching that?"

"Yes," she moaned.

"Did he catch you watching him?"

"Oh yes!" Mrs. Bennet came as the hard thrusts and memory of the erotic coupling brought her over the edge.

"Then what happened?" Mr. Bennet pulled out and pushed her roughly on her back. He grabbed her ankles and rested them on his shoulders. He entered her again, bending her nearly in half as he rocked into her.

"His wife."

"She caught him too?"

"Yes, but she wasn't angry. She pulled the maid into the library."

"What of her husband?"

"He was still finishing himself off. Mrs. Hurst kissed her."

Mr. Bennet felt his balls tighten and he almost spilled seed at the image. "You must have been shocked."

"Oh no, I was quite aroused. Do you think you and I could try something like that? Mrs. Lucas and I sometimes while away the hours doing that. Would you like to watch us sometime?"

That was all it took, and Mr. Bennet gave an incoherent shout and filled her with liquid heat. She was therefore obliged to seek another branch of the subject, and related, with much bitterness of spirit and some exaggeration, the shocking rudeness of Mr. Darcy.

"But I can assure you," she added, "that Lizzy does not lose much by not suiting his fancy; for he is a most disagreeable, horrid man, not at all worth pleasing."

"What?" Mr. Bennet said in a daze, marveling at his luck that not only was his wife amiable to having a woman in their bed, that she would let him watch her and her friend at play.

"So high and so conceited that there was no enduring him! He walked here, and he walked there, fancying himself so very great! Not handsome enough to dance with! I wish you had been there, my dear, to have given him one of your set-downs. I quite detest the man."

"Who?" Mr. Bennet was beyond listening as pleasure fogged his brain into a sleep filled with erotic couplings.

Chapter 4

When Jane and Elizabeth were alone, the former, who had been cautious in her praise of Mr. Bingley before, expressed to her sister just how very much she admired his ministrations.

"He is just what a young man ought to be," said Jane, "sensual, good-looking, lively; and I never felt such pleasure!—so much assurance. He had me shuddering and wet while we were fully dressed.!"

"He is also well endowed," replied Elizabeth, "which a young man ought likewise to be, if he possibly can. His technique can be practiced as long as he has the tools."

"His technique was most agreeable. I was very much flattered by his asking me to walk out on the terrace with him. I did not expect such a compliment from such a rich and powerful man."

"Did not you? I did for you. But that is one great difference between us. Compliments always take you by surprise, and me never. What could be more natural than him wanting you? He could not help seeing that you were about five times as pretty as every other woman in the room. You had him spellbound. He couldn't stop looking at your bodice. Well, he certainly

23

knows how to get what he wants and if he's that skilled with his mouth and fingers, I give you leave to like him. You have liked many a clumsier person."

"Dear Lizzy!"

"Oh! You never see a fault in anybody. All the world are good and agreeable in your eyes. I never heard you speak ill of a human being in your life. You would rather put up with some farmer's fumblings in the dark corner rather than hurt his feelings."

"I would not wish to be hasty in censuring anyone. Even the farmer could learn to love a woman, if he only had a little patience," Jane said. "But I always speak what I think. If the farmer winds up squeezing my elbow, I guide him to my breast." She smiled and winked at her sister.

"I know you do; and it is that which makes the wonder. With your good sense, to be so honestly blind to the follies and nonsense of others! Only you would see the potential good in everyone. Did you like this man's sisters, too, do you? Their manners are not equal to his."

"Certainly not—at first. But they are very pleasing women to hear others speak of it. They've been well trained in the arts of pleasure. Mrs. Hurst has a voracious appetite. I think I saw her and her husband with Mama."

"No!" Elizabeth shrieked and buried her face in the pillow.

"Miss Bingley," Jane continued. "Is to live with her brother, and keep his house; and I am much mistaken if we shall not find a very charming neighbour in her." Jane pursed her lips in a moue of pique. "Although, she doesn't seem to like to play with girls. Her eyes are solely for the men."

"Perhaps you could show her differently? Why not play with both sides?"

Jane squealed in horror. "I'd rather have only her brother."

Elizabeth listened in silence, but was not convinced that Jane would be happy without a woman as well. Her sister was at one moment giddy over a new girlfriend and then the next day bemoaning that there were no eligible bachelors The women at the assembly seemed too caught up in fripperies and nonsense rather than the art of sensual exploration. It was if they had bought into the mores of the day instead of just putting on a façade for the rest of the world to see.

; Elizabeth was very little disposed to approve of Bingley's sisters. They were in fact very fine ladies; not deficient in good humour when they were pleased, nor in the power of making themselves agreeable when they chose it, but proud and conceited. They were rather handsome, Elizabeth smiled to herself. She wouldn't mind willowing away a few hours in sweet, heated caresses. Maybe she would take Miss Bingley or Mrs. Hurst, into a darkened eave the next time. That would show Mr. Darcy she was not as innocent as he presumed.

But like Jane, Elizabeth also longed for the strong body of a man pressing against her. Here in Meryton there were not many occasions to play with a male one wasn't expected to marry soon after.

Elizabeth had high hopes for this Mr. Bingley, though.. The assembly had been just a small sampling of the pleasurable pursuits that the township could offer. He seemed intrigued enough with Jane to perhaps invite her entire family up to Netherfield Park. Elizabeth suppressed a shudder at the thought of actually stepping foot into the much gossiped about dungeons. She blew out the candle and pulled the blankets up. Reaching down between her legs, she hoped Jane fell asleep before the wetness at her core became audible when her fingers worked in earnest against her throbbing bud.

Mr. Bingley inherited property to the amount of nearly a hundred thousand pounds from his father, who had intended to purchase an estate, but did not live to do it. Mr. Bingley intended it likewise, and sometimes made choice of his county; but as he was now provided with Netherfield, it was doubtful to many of those who best knew the easiness of his temper, whether he might not spend the remainder of his days at Netherfield, and leave the next generation to purchase. Netherfield was set up as a sybarite's paradise. But its great pleasures and forbidden desires came at a great cost. Easily twenty thousand pounds a year to keep the entertainment fresh and to pay off any disgruntled fathers.

Mr. Bingley's sisters were anxious for his having an estate of his own that didn't have the notoriety of Netherfield; but, though he was now only established there , Miss Bingley was by no means unwilling to preside at his table—nor was Mrs. Hurst, who had married a man of more fashion than fortune, less disposed to consider his house as her home when it suited her. The sisters liked the distraction of deciding on which oils to have stocked or which toys to use to decorate each room. Not to mention the special time each one spent sampling the offerings.

Mr. Bingley had just come into his fortune, when he was tempted by an accidental recommendation to look at Netherfield House. He did look at it, and into it for half a day. Three eager maids and a footman enticed Mr. Bingley with everything they and the manor could offer. He was pleased with the situation, the eager, talented staff and the dungeon rooms so he took ownership immediately.

Between him and Darcy there was a very steady friendship, in spite of great opposition of character. Bingley was endeared to Darcy by the easiness, openness, and ductility of his temper, though no disposition could offer a greater contrast to his own, and though with his own he never appeared dissatisfied. Darcy was the only man Bingley would gratefully sink to his knees for – just for the pleasure of his touch and his harsh commands. On the strength of Darcy's regard, Bingley had the firmest reliance, and of his judgement the highest opinion. In understanding, Darcy was the superior, the dominant. Bingley was by no means completely submissive – especially when it came to the ladies, but Darcy was clever. He was at the same time haughty, reserved, and fastidious, and his manners, though well-bred, were not inviting.

The first time they were together, it was in the baths. Naked, Darcy just stood in front of Bingley, who had been seated on the bench. While the hot steam of the sauna obscured them a bit, Darcy grabbed the back of Bingley's head and forced his cock down his throat. Bingsley had been appalled, shocked and while he instinctively sucked, became hard as a rock. Darcy had used his mouth most roughly. When he had finished, he gave a satisfied grunt and left Bingley aching with need. Bingley had followed him out of the baths, determined to get satisfaction. But he wound up plundering a bath maid instead, who shrieked good naturedly and charged him a few pounds afterwards. Since then, the friends had experimented in different methods of control. Darcy had to always be in charge. Bingley was more easy going. In that respect his friend had greatly the advantage. Bingley was sure of being liked wherever he appeared, Darcy was continually giving offense.

The manner in which they spoke of the Meryton assembly was sufficiently characteristic. Bingley had never met with more pleasant people or prettier girls in his life. Miss Jane Bennet had captivated him into near indiscretion. If it wasn't for her lovely innocence, he would have tupped her against the wall like he had with the bath maid. She had made him hotter by dancing with him than he had been while sucking Darcy. He could not conceive of an angel more beautiful.

Darcy, on the contrary, had seen a collection of people in whom there was little beauty and no fashion, for none of whom had he felt the smallest interest, and from none received either attention or pleasure. Darcy wanted a more intense pleasure. He was saving himself for the games at Netherfield, which attracted a harsher crowd intent on their own needs. Miss Jane Bennet he acknowledged to be pretty, but she smiled too much and would no doubt trap Bingley into a dull vanilla marriage, if he wasn't careful.. Mrs. Hurst and her sister, Miss Bingley, allowed it to be so—but still they admired her and liked her, and pronounced her to be a sweet girl, and one whom they would not object to know more of. The sisters plotted as to how they would pleasure themselves with the pretty country girls before putting them back where they belonged. Unless, of course, they showed more skill than was expected. Then they could stay on at Netherfield indefinitely. Miss Bennet was therefore established as a sweet girl, and their brother felt authorized by such commendation to think of her as he chose.

Chapter 5

Within a short walk of Longbourn lived a family with whom the Bennets were particularly intimate. Sir William Lucas had been formerly in trade in Meryton, where he had made a tolerable fortune, and risen to the honour of knighthood by an address to the king during his mayoralty. He was burly and had a sexual appetite of two men. He tended to be a little lax in accepting payments. One the one hand, the taxpayer could pay in currency or on their back if they were a pretty lass – or on their hands and knees if they were a fair lad. However, after many years of accepting payment, it began to pall and he felt more of a pimp. The distinction had perhaps been felt too strongly. It had given him a disgust to his business, and to his residence in a small market town; and, in quitting them both, he had removed with his family to a house about a mile from Meryton, denominated from that period Lucas Lodge, where he could think with pleasure of his own importance, and, unshackled by business, occupy himself solely in being civil to all the world. He strove to concentrate his husbandly duties solely on his wife, but he wasn't above spying on her and her female visitors and stroking himself until he spilled his seed all over his palm. He could, of course, seek solace with another as his wife did. But no one seemed particularly forthcoming, much to his deep disappointment. For, though elated by his rank, it did not render him supercilious; on the contrary, he was all attention to everybody. By nature inoffensive, friendly, and obliging, his presentation at St. James's had made him courteous.

Lady Lucas was a very good kind of woman, not too clever to be a valuable neighbour to Mrs. Bennet. They had several children. The eldest of them, a sensible, intelligent young woman, about twenty-seven, was Elizabeth's intimate friend. They found in each other not only a confident, but also a willing adventurer in exploring their curiosity about the strange new feelings they were experiencing as they entered womanhood.

That the Miss Lucases and the Miss Bennets should meet to talk over a ball was absolutely necessary; and the morning after the assembly brought the former to Longbourn to hear and to communicate. Elizabeth and Charlotte quickly skipped off to the barns, giggling and chattering excitedly about the ball. Mr. Lucas cast a furtive glance to make sure he was alone, before heading up the stairs into his study, where he had a peephole into his wife's sitting room.

"Your Charlotte began the evening well, said Mrs. Bennet with civil self-command to her friend. "She was Mr. Bingley's first choice."

"Yes; but he seemed to like his second better," Mrs. Lucas said wryly, locking the door behind her.

"Oh! you mean Jane, I suppose, because he danced with her twice. To be sure that did seem as if he admired her—indeed I rather believe he did—I heard something about it—but I hardly know what—something about Mr. Robinson." Mrs. Bennet smiled coyly as Mrs. Lucas came in for a deep kiss. She threaded her fingers into her friend's hair, making the hair pins and netting fall on the floor. Mrs. Bennet wanted to talk about the dance, but she felt Mrs. Lucas's need in the quick way she divested both of them of their dresses.

"Perhaps you mean what I overheard between him and Mr. Robinson; did not I mention it to you? Mr. Robinson's asking him how he liked our Meryton assemblies, and whether he did not think there were a great many pretty women in the room, and which he thought the prettiest? and his answering immediately to the last question: 'Oh! the eldest Miss Bennet, beyond a doubt; there cannot be two opinions on that point.'" Mrs. Lucas said. "She takes after her mother." She cupped Mrs. Bennet's breasts in her hands bringing the turgid nipples up to her mouth to softly suck.

"Upon my word!" Mrs. Bennet sighed, throwing her head back.

Mr. Lucas watched the two disheveled women, his hand gripping himself in tight controlled strokes. He was mesmerized as his wife turned Mrs. Bennet so she was standing behind her. Mrs. Bennet now faced the peephole, and he could see the dark curls in the juncture of her quivering thighs were glistening. Fascinated, he saw his wife stroke her hands boldly down her friend's body, while her mouth was nibbling on her neck and shoulder.

"You do that so well," Mrs. Bennet breathed.

"Tell me of this mark," Mrs. Lucas said, pinching

the love bite with interest.

"It was my husband. I told him about us."

"You didn't!"

"Does that shock you?"

"It excites me. Was he angry?"

"More intrigued, I'd say. He also liked me telling him about the threesome the Hursts were engaged in."

"I missed that part of the assembly. How very fortunate, if they were pleased with our town perhaps Jane will be held at a higher worth."

"Well, that is very decided indeed—that does seem as if—but, however, it may all come to nothing, you know. Lay down, please. It's been so long since I've had my tongue inside you."

Again, Mr. Lucas saw his wife pose on the bed so he could see her pink flesh being gobbled up by the delightful Mrs. Bennet –whose white posterior was making his heart throb in time with his cock. He pumped his fist faster, watching his wife writhe under the talented tongue. His wife toyed with her breasts and damn the woman! Looked right at him. He spurted over his hand and had to take deep shallow breaths as the room tilted.

In the barn, Charlotte and Elizabeth were also naked. The two friends lay on their sides, facing each other, their chemises serving as sheets to protect them from the poking hay. They had just finished a race to see who could make the other come first just by tickling the other between the legs.

"My overhearings were more to the purpose than yours, Eliza," said Charlotte,

trying to get her breath back. As usual, Elizabeth had won the game and was licking her fingers with smug satisfaction. Charlotte wanted to wipe that smile off her face. "Mr. Darcy is not so well worth listening to as his friend, is he?—poor Eliza!—to be only just tolerable."

"I'm not vexed by his ill-treatment, for he is such a disagreeable man, that it would be quite a misfortune to be liked by him. Mrs. Long told me last night that he kissed her for half-an-hour without once opening his lips." Elizabeth leaned in and kissed Charlotte thusly.

"Are you quite sure?—is not there a little mistake?" said Charlotte, pulling away from the unsatisfying peck. "I certainly saw Mr. Darcy speaking to her."

"Aye—because she asked him at last how he liked Netherfield, and he could not help answering her; but she said he seemed quite angry at being spoken to."

"Miss Bingley told me, that he never speaks much, unless among his intimate acquaintances. With them he is remarkably agreeable."

"I do not believe a word of it, my dear Charlotte. If he had been so very agreeable, he would have tupped Mrs. Long."

Charlotte gasped at Elizabeth's crudeness, but at the same time was titillated. "Do you think so? Everyone says that he is eat up with pride, and I dare say he had heard somehow that Mrs. Long does not keep a carriage, and had come to the ball in a hack chaise."

"I do not mind his not taking Mrs. Long, but I wish he had danced with me."

"Another time, Lizzy, I would not dance with him, if I were you. I've heard he has strange appetites."

"Like what?" Elizabeth breathed, stroking the

pads of her fingers over Charlotte's nipples just to watch them harden.

Charlotte reciprocated the caress and grinned. "He likes to tie women up – men too."

"Really?" Elizabeth said and rolled on top of her friend so their nipples were squashed together.

Charlotte ran her hands down Elizabeth's back, until her hands cupped her buttocks. "Yes, then he forces them to submit to his ministrations."

Elizabeth wiggled, rubbing her body over Charlotte. "Details, please."

"I'm sure I do not know."

"I believe, Charlotte, I may safely promise you never to *dance* with him."

"You are so wicked. He is too proud, too cold, and too dangerous for the likes of us."

Elizabeth snorted.

"His pride does not offend me so much as pride often does, because there is an excuse for it. One cannot wonder that so very fine a young man, with family, fortune, everything in his favour, should think highly of himself. If I may so express it, he has a right to be proud."

"That is very true," replied Elizabeth, "and I could easily forgive his pride, if he had not mortified mine."

Chapter 6

The ladies of Longbourn soon waited on those of Netherfield. The visit was soon returned in due form. Miss Jane Bennet's pleasing manners grew on the goodwill of Mrs. Hurst and Miss Bingley as she seemed to enjoy a pleasant flirtation; and though the mother was found to be intolerable, and the younger sisters not worth speaking to, a wish of being better acquainted with them was expressed towards the two eldest. By Jane, this attention was received with the greatest pleasure. Elizabeth, however, still saw superciliousness in their treatment of everybody, hardly excepting even her sister, and could not like them, which was a disappointment as she had wanted to bring Charlotte over to them to play. Though their kindness to Jane, such as it was, had a value as arising in all probability from the influence of their brother's admiration, who had maddingly kept his distance from Jane. It was generally evident whenever they met, that he did admire her and to her it was equally evident that Jane was yielding to the preference which she had begun to entertain for him from the first, and was in a way to be very much in love; but she considered with pleasure that it was not likely to be discovered by the world in general, since Jane united, with great strength of feeling, a composure of temper and a uniform cheerfulness of manner which would guard her from the suspicions of the impertinent. Jane was very much submissive and Elizabeth suspected so was Mr. Bingley.

The thought frustrated her as she didn't know what to do. Elizabeth mentioned this to her friend Miss Lucas.

"It may perhaps be pleasant," replied Charlotte, "to be able to impose on the public in such a case; but it is sometimes a disadvantage to be so very guarded."

Charlotte, on the other hand, had decided to show Elizabeth some of the debauchery she overheard her father talk of in Netherfield Hall. Elizabeth's arms were tied to the bed with scraps of blue silk, Elizabeth had found in the rag bin. Her ankles also were bound similarly.

" If a woman conceals her affection with the same skill from the object of it, she may lose the opportunity of fixing him; and it will then be but poor consolation to believe the world equally in the dark." With that, Charlotte attached a blindfold around Elizabeth's eyes.

"Are you sure about this?" Elizabeth said feeling exposed. Even though they were in her bedroom, and she could hear her sisters bickering in the sitting room below them, the vulnerability of being stretched open and then rendered blind made her have misgivings about this.

"It's just me, silly," Charlotte said, pulling on her leather riding glove.

Elizabeth's hips came off the bed, and she gave a strangled gasp when Charlotte squeezed her breast.

Rolling Elizabeth's nipple between the butter soft material on her fingers, Charlotte watched Elizabeth's mouth open in shock. Stroking her leather clad fingers down her friend's taut stomach, Charlotte grinned as an idea occurred to her. "There is so much of gratitude or vanity in almost every attachment, that it is not safe to leave any to itself. We can all begin freely—a slight preference is natural enough; but there are very few of us who have heart enough to be really in love without encouragement."

"What do you mean?" Elizabeth said in a shaky voice that wasn't quite her own. Blind and immobile, her world had narrowed to the single caress.

Charlotte plunged two fingers inside Elizabeth, causing her to shriek.

"Hush," she said, lightly slapping the other glove across Elizabeth's lips. "Do you want your sisters in here wondering what we're doing?" She moved her fingers in quick, hard strokes – so different than their usual gentle couplings.

"Oh," Elizabeth said. "Do that again?"

"This?" Charlotte said, smacking the leather glove against Elizabeth's nipple? "Or this?"Charlotte's fingers worked fast into Elizabeth's wet slit. But before Elizabeth could answer, Charlotte removed them and jammed her drenched leather clad fingers into Elizabeth's mouth.

Elizabeth screamed again and sucked on the wet leather.

"That's a good girl," Charlotte cooed, straddling her friend's waist. "Sometimes, I wish I was a boy, so I could ride you." She sighed. "In nine cases out of ten a women had better show more affection than she feels.

For example, Bingley likes your sister undoubtedly; but he may never do more than like her, if she does not help him on. She needs to be the one tied to the bed, instead of flirting with her eyes and brushing her nipples against his arm."

Charlotte removed her fingers and Elizabeth drew deep shaky breaths. "This is the sweetest torture. Are you sure this is what they do in Netherfield?"

"Your sister will find out first," She massaged Elizabeth's breasts, tugging on the nipples. "I hear they have pincers for these." Charlotte tugged on them cruelly.

"Surely not," Elizabeth said, but she was more aroused than frightened. "Even if Jane does help him on, as much as her nature will allow, will he use her thus? Why hasn't he done this to begin with? If I can perceive her regard for him, he must be a simpleton, indeed, not to discover it too."

"Remember, Eliza, that he does not know Jane's disposition as you do," Charlotte removed the blindfold and Elizabeth blinked up at her.

"But if a woman is partial to a man, and does not endeavour to conceal it, he must find it out.."

Charlotte climbed up Elizabeth's body and knelt above her face. "If I can't ride you like a man, dearest, I will ride you like a woman." Charlotte pressed her most intimate area against Elizabeth's face. When Elizabeth did nothing but tentatively lap at her outer lips, Charlotte smacked her in the hip with the leather glove.

"Oh," Elizabeth had time to gasp before Charlotte engulfed her and began to rock. Elizabeth moaned, nearly drowning in her friend's wet heat. Her tongue probed into Charlotte's core and Charlotte squealed and rapped her harder with the glove.

"Oh Lizzie, yes. More. More. More." Each word was punctuated with another stinging slap of the glove.

Elizabeth licked her to a shuddering orgasm that had Charlotte dazed. Rattling the bedpost, Charlotte realized she was suffocating her friend and quickly jumped off. "My knees are wobbly," she grinned and kissed Elizabeth's slick face. "And you taste of me."

"Please Charlotte," Elizabeth pulled on her restraints. "It's my turn now."

"Your turn?"Charlotte said. "Not until I say so." She began with one finger pumping inside of Elizabeth.

"You think Bingley will use Jane like this?" Elizabeth said, arching her body, crying out in delight when Charlotte pushed another finger inside her.

"Perhaps he must, if he sees enough of her. But, though Bingley and Jane meet tolerably often, it is never for many hours together; and, as they always see each other in large mixed parties, it is impossible that every moment should be employed in conversing together. Jane should therefore make the most of every half-hour in which she can command his attention. She needs to bring him to the dungeons below Netherfield and let him have his way with her. If she is as responsive as you, he'll never let her go. When she is secure of him, there will be more leisure for falling in love as much as she chooses."

"Your plan is a good one," replied Elizabeth, "where nothing is in question but the desire of being well married, and if I were determined to get a rich husband, or any husband, I dare say I should adopt it.

Faster, oh please faster."

"I don't think you understand that the one tied up doesn't make the rules." Charlotte curled her fingers and hit a spot on Elizabeth that had her wailing, until Charlotte cut it off by stuffing the glove in Elizabeth's mouth. When Elizabeth's eyes rolled back to normal, Charlotte removed the glove and untied her friend. She hugged her, because Elizabeth didn't look like her normal self. Her eyes were still passion glazed, her mouth wanton.

"These are not Jane's feelings," Elizabeth said. "She is not acting by design. As yet, she cannot even be certain of the degree of her own regard nor of its reasonableness. She has known him only a fortnight. She danced four dances with him at Meryton; He fondled her breasts. She kissed him while he rubbed against her in the alcove. She saw him one morning at his own house. I think she took his cock in her mouth and has since dined with him in company four times. This is not quite enough to make her understand his character."

"Not as you represent it. Had she merely dined with him, she might only have discovered whether he had a good appetite; but you must remember that four evenings have also been spent together—and four more evenings alone at Netherfield may do a great deal. He would have her helpless and unable to stop him from doing anything he wanted to her." Charlotte rubbed Elizabeth's shoulder when she shivered.

"Yes, those four evenings have enabled them to ascertain that they both like the game Vingt-un better than Commerce; but with respect to any other leading characteristic, I do not imagine that much has been unfolded."

"Once he has Jane like I've just had you, he will marry her. I speak from experience. If I could keep you tied to bed as my personal love toy, I would."

"I would like that too," Elizabeth said.

Charlotte shook her head. "No dearest, you need someone to master you. I have just read books. You have only felt a fraction of what a master can do."

Elizabeth pressed her thighs together. "I think I need to go to Netherfield."

"For Mr. Bingley?"

"No, he's Jane's. I do wish that she will be happy with him. She likes to play with girls the way we play. Do you think there is room in Bingley's heart to allow that?"

"Well," said Charlotte, "I can't imagine a man objecting, especially if he's somehow involved in the playing. I wish Jane success with all my heart; and if she were married to him to-morrow, I should think she had as good a chance of happiness as if she were to be studying his character for a twelvemonth."

Elizabeth nodded.

"Happiness in marriage is entirely a matter of chance. If the dispositions of the parties are ever so well known to each other or ever so similar beforehand, it does not advance their felicity in the least. They always continue to grow sufficiently unlike afterwards to have their share of vexation; and it is better to know as little as possible of the defects of the person with whom you are to pass your life."

"You make me laugh, Charlotte; but it is not sound. You know it is not sound, and that you would never act in this way yourself."

Charlotte shrugged. "Watch and see. Now let's get dressed. With all your caterwauling we're pressing our luck every minute we're not dressed." She kissed Elizabeth. "I do not want any Bennet sister but you."

***

Occupied in observing Mr. Bingley's attentions to her sister, Elizabeth was far from suspecting that she was herself becoming an object of some interest in the eyes of his friend. Mr. Darcy had at first scarcely allowed her to be pretty; he had looked at her without admiration at the ball; and when they next met, he looked at her only to criticise. But no sooner had he made it clear to himself and his friends that she hardly had a good feature in her face, than he began to find it was rendered uncommonly intelligent by the beautiful expression of her dark eyes.

Darcy watched the sensuous sway of her hips. He had thought her untested and innocent, but when she lifted up her hand it bore a reddened rope mark. To this discovery succeeded some others equally mortifying. Though he had detected with a critical eye more than one failure of perfect symmetry in her form, he was forced to acknowledge her figure to be light and pleasing. Her mouth seemed made for kissing or swallowing him down; and in spite of his asserting that her manners were not those of the fashionable world, he was caught by their easy playfulness. The thought of ministering to her, teaching her to obey him made him stalk her like a jungle cat. Of this she was perfectly unaware; to her he was only the man who made himself agreeable nowhere, and who had not thought her handsome enough to dance with. Yet, she found herself wondering why he always had a riding

Lissa Trevor

quirt on him – even when he hadn't been on a horse. The memory of Charlotte's leather glove striking her flesh had Elizabeth misstep in the dance and her whole body trembled with reaction.

He began to wish to know more of her, and as a step towards conversing with her himself, attended to her conversation with others. His doing so drew her notice. It was at Sir William Lucas's, where a large party was assembled.

"What does Mr. Darcy mean," said she to Charlotte, "by listening to my conversation with Colonel Forster?"

"That is a question which Mr. Darcy only can answer. But he looks at you as if he wants to eat you up." Charlotte hid a smile behind her fan.

"But if he does it any more I shall certainly let him know that I see what he is about. He has a very satirical eye, and if I do not begin by being impertinent myself, I shall soon grow afraid of him."

"I think he'd like your fear. I think it might allow you entrance to Netherfield."

Elizabeth looked at her sharply. "Do you think?"

On his approaching them soon afterwards, though without seeming to have any intention of speaking, Miss Lucas defied her friend to mention such a subject to him; which immediately provoking Elizabeth to do it, she turned to him and said:

"Did you not think, Mr. Darcy, that I expressed myself uncommonly well just now, when I was teasing Colonel Forster to give us a ball at Meryton?"

"With great energy; but it is always a subject which makes a lady energetic."

"You are severe on us." Elizabeth licked her lips

and eyed the riding crop. "I find I've gotten a taste for . . . punishment."

Darcy's eyes narrowed on her and a cruel smile quirked.

"It will be her turn soon to be teased," said Miss Lucas. "I am going to open the instrument, Eliza, and you know what follows."

"You are a very strange creature by way of a friend!—always wanting me to play and sing before anybody and everybody! If my vanity had taken a musical turn, you would have been invaluable; but as it is, I would really rather not sit down before those who must be in the habit of hearing the very best performers."

On Miss Lucas's persevering, however, she added, "Very well, if it must be so, it must." And gravely glancing at Mr. Darcy, "There is a fine old saying, which everybody here is of course familiar with: 'Keep your breath to cool your porridge'; and I shall keep mine to swell my song."

Her performance was pleasing, though by no means capital. Mr. Darcy stood behind her for the first song, then bending as if to look at the music sheets closer, he whispered in her ear.

"If you cry out, you are ruined. If you falter in your song, I will leave you to your fate." His breath was warm, his tone menacing in her ear. It made her shiver and she felt her undergarments dampen.

Mr. Darcy, using the angle of their bodies to shield them from the onlooking crowd behind them, dipped his hand into the front of her dress. Elizabeth grew stiff, but her fingers never faltered and her voice never wavered.

45

"Good," Mr. Darcy said, rubbing his silk gloved finger over her nipples. "Taut and responsive. You follow directions. And are wanton enough to have been tied up." He slipped his hand out and rested it briefly upon her throat. She felt the vibrations in her throat as she sang and he pressed lightly on her larynx. It buzzed straight into her nether regions. Then as quickly as he came over, Mr. Darcy left.

After a song or two, and before she could reply to the entreaties of several that she would sing again, she was eagerly succeeded at the instrument by her sister Mary, who having, in consequence of being the only plain one in the family, worked hard for knowledge and accomplishments, was always impatient for display. Elizabeth retreated to the far corner of the ballroom while she regarded Mr. Darcy with equal amounts of loathing and desire. Eventually, her sisters encouraged her to join in the dancing and the rapid beat of the music made her temper flare. How dare he manhandle her and then walk away as if it hadn't shaken his world like it did hers?

Mr. Darcy stood near them in silent indignation at such a mode of passing the evening, to the exclusion of all conversation. His cock was hard, aching for the sweet ministrations of Miss Bennet, yet he could not figure out a way to draw her into his world. He was too much engrossed by his thoughts to perceive that Sir William Lucas was his neighbour, till Sir William thus began:

"What a charming amusement for young people this is, Mr. Darcy! There is nothing like dancing after all. I consider it as one of the first refinements of polished society."

"Certainly, sir; and it has the advantage also of being in vogue amongst the less polished societies of the world. Every savage can dance." Mr. Darcy's thoughts were on more savage pursuits than dancing. He was picturing Miss Bennet flat on her back beneath him.

Sir William only smiled. "Your friend performs delightfully," he continued after a pause, on seeing Bingley join the group; "and I doubt not that you are an adept in the science yourself, Mr. Darcy."

"You saw me dance at Meryton, I believe, sir."

"Yes, indeed, and received no inconsiderable pleasure from the sight. Do you often dance at St. James's?"

"Never, sir."

"Do you not think it would be a proper compliment to the place?"

"It is a compliment which I never pay to any place if I can avoid it."

"You have a house in town, I conclude?"

Mr. Darcy bowed. The house was fixed with everything needed for a night of pleasure – his pleasure, of course.

"I had once had some thought of fixing in town myself—for I am fond of superior society; but I did not feel quite certain that the air of London would agree with Lady Lucas."

He paused in hopes of an answer; but his companion was not disposed to make any. Mr. Darcy was imagining coating every inch of Miss Bennet's lithe young body in a flavoured oil.

Elizabeth at that instant was moving towards

them, and Mr. Lucas was struck with the action of doing a very gallant thing, and called out to her:

"My dear Miss Eliza, why are you not dancing? Mr. Darcy, you must allow me to present this young lady to you as a very desirable partner. You cannot refuse to dance, I am sure when so much beauty is before you." And, taking her hand, he would have given it to Mr. Darcy who, though extremely surprised, was not unwilling to receive it, when she instantly drew back, and said with some discomposure to Sir William:

"Indeed, sir, I have not the least intention of *dancing*." She slid a look of molten fury and erotic promise at Mr. Darcy. "I entreat you not to suppose that I moved this way in order to beg for a partner."

Mr. Darcy, with grave propriety, requested to be allowed the honour of her hand, but in vain. "I would not have you beg," he lied.

Elizabeth was determined; nor did Sir William at all shake her purpose by his attempt at persuasion.

"You excel so much in the dance, Miss Eliza, that it is cruel to deny me the happiness of seeing you; and though this gentleman dislikes the amusement in general, he can have no objection, I am sure, to oblige us for one half-hour."

"Mr. Darcy is all politeness," said Elizabeth, smiling.

"He is, indeed; but, considering the inducement, my dear Miss Eliza, we cannot wonder at his complaisance—for who would object to such a partner?"

Elizabeth looked archly, and turned away.

Mr. Darcy wasn't unhappy to see her go. He liked

a woman with fire. If they acquiesced too easily, where was the fun in that? He was thinking of her with some complacency, when thus accosted by Miss Bingley in the library moments later: She shut the door behind her and they were alone in the room. Miss Bingley stalked towards him like a lioness sighting her prey.

"I can guess the subject of your reverie," she said noting the bulge in his breeches.

"I should imagine not."

"You are considering how insupportable it would be to pass many evenings in this manner—in such society; and indeed I am quite of your opinion." Miss Bingley slid over to him and began unbuttoning his pants with a practiced efficiency that left Mr. Darcy a bit cold. Yet, she would offer some relief. He removed her hand and rang for a valet from Netherfield.

The man, being well trained, arrived within moments. "Yes sir?"

Mr. Darcy motioned to Miss Bingley. "I require you to punish the lady."

"Yes Master," the man bowed.

Miss Bingley simpered, her eyes hungry on the lithely muscled valet.

Mr. Darcy removed his cock and stroked it while they talked.

" I was never more annoyed! The insipidity, and yet the noise—the nothingness, and yet the self-importance of all those people! What would I give to hear your strictures on them!"

"Your conjecture is totally wrong, I assure you. Are you wearing drawers?"

"Of course not," she purred.

Mr. Darcy gestured to the valet who gripped her

in unyielding arms and backed her towards the table. "My mind was more agreeably engaged." Mr. Darcy said as the valet bent her roughly over it and lifted her skirts. "I have been meditating on the very great pleasure which a pair of fine eyes in the face of a pretty woman can bestow."

Miss Bingley looked over her shoulder and fixed her eyes on his face. For a moment, she thought he was referring to her, but he seemed to be focused inward thinking of someone else.

"You have lovely skin," the valet said, running his eyes over her rounded buttocks. "I shall enjoy marring it."

Miss Bingley shivered as he drew the riding crop out and cracked it against the table.

"O-oh," she stuttered.

"Were you expecting that on your tender backside?" he cooed, nudging her legs wide.

"Take me. Enough of these games."

He thrust into her. When she opened her mouth in pleasure, he had her bite down on the riding crop. Holding both ends, he pulled her head back as he pounded into her. She was sweet and wet, bucking back against him.

"Miss Elizabeth Bennet," Mr. Darcy grunted out, sliding his hand up and down his cock. "Would be an interesting addition to Netherfield's dungeon don't you think?"

But Miss Bingley was feeling nothing but the hard thickness of the valet's member. The riding crop was holding her in place as he used her roughly to her great satisfaction and quivering release.

Mr. Darcy watched with half lidded fascination.

"Lizzie," he groaned before releasing his seed. The valet soon followed, sheathed deep inside Miss Bingley. Mr. Darcy approached the couple. Sliding the riding crop across Miss Bingley's mouth, Mr. Darcy brought it down again near her face and she flinched.

"Miss Elizabeth Bennet!" repeated Miss Bingley as she tried to straighten up. Darcy pushed her back down. "I am all astonishment. How long has she been such a favourite?—and pray, when am I to wish you joy?"

"That is exactly the question which I expected you to ask. A lady's imagination is very rapid; it jumps from admiration to love, from love to matrimony, in a moment. I knew you would be wishing me joy. Now, it's time for him to punish you for being such a bad girl. Mr. Darcy pulled them apart and positioned them to his satisfaction.

"You sit in the chair," he told the valet.

"Yes, Master."

Her dress still bunched around her waist, Mr. Darcy positioned Miss Bingley across the valet's lap and then he settled down into an arm chair to watch.

"Nay, if you are serious about it, I shall consider the matter is absolutely settled." Miss Bingley said. "You will be having a charming mother-in-law, indeed; and, of course, she will always be at Pemberley with you."

At Mr. Darcy's command, the valet spanked her hard for that remark. He liked seeing the red pattern of his hand on her backside, so Mr. Darcy gestured for him to do it again.

"Oh," she cried. "You have a cruel hand. I only speak the truth."

Whack.

Miss Bingley whimpered, but raised herself up to meet each smack.

"You are very naughty for not wearing undergarments. What would your brother say? He's trying to get you married off after that unfortunate incident with the Count."

"It was not unfortunate," Miss Bingley sighed, then let out another cry when the valet paddled her again. "He was divine."

"Tell me of him. Of the things he taught you. I will absolve you."

"Oh please, yes."

He listened to her with perfect indifference while she chose to entertain herself in this manner; and as his composure convinced her that all was safe, her wit flowed long and in response he ordered the valet's ministrations to grow exceedingly more painful.

Chapter 7

Mr. Bennet's property consisted almost entirely in an estate of two thousand a year, which, unfortunately for his daughters, was entailed, in default of heirs male, on a distant relation; and their mother's fortune, though ample for her situation in life, could but ill supply the deficiency of his. Her father had been an attorney in Meryton, and had left her four thousand pounds.

The village of Longbourn was only one mile from Meryton; a most convenient distance for the young ladies, who were usually tempted thither three or four times a week, to pay their duty to their aunt and to a milliner's shop just over the way. She had a back room where she supplied various straps and accoutrements for more adventurous couples.

The two youngest of the family, Catherine and Lydia, were particularly frequent in these attentions; their minds were more vacant than their sisters', and when nothing better offered, a walk to Meryton was necessary to amuse their morning hours and furnish conversation for the evening; and however bare of news the country in general might be, they always contrived to learn some from their aunt, Mrs. Phillips, who was a retired dominatrix of some renown.

At present, indeed, they were well supplied both with news and happiness by the recent arrival of a militia regiment in the neighbourhood; it was to remain the whole winter, and Meryton was the headquarters.

Their visits to Mrs. Phillips were now productive of the most interesting intelligence.

To further their education, their aunt allowed them to explore one of the soldiers she had bound in her bed chamber as a slave. The soldier was kneeling nude on the floor when the sisters peeked in. He was gagged and blindfolded, but his body was perfection. Well defined muscles strained against his bonds, when the women walked in. His arms were tied behind his back with cords of leather. After their delighted shrieks subsided, Mrs. Phillips gave Catherine a feathered duster and Lydia a paddle.

"Stand up slave," Mrs. Phillips ordered.

"Can he lie down?" Lydia asked, circling around him.

"Stroke him with the feathers," her Aunt ordered.

Catherine was giggling uncontrollably, but she dusted the man, making sure that his nether regions were especially paid attention to.

"Cor, he's enormous," Lydia said, as the man's full member grew long and thick against his belly.

"Slave, get on your hands and knees," Mrs. Phillips said.

The soldier obeyed. Catherine and Lydia circled around to ogle his backside.

Lydia sighed in pleasure while Catherine tittered into the feather duster.

Mrs. Phillips sat on the man's back and pulled his

hair roughly so his neck jerked up. "He's adequate, I suppose. Lydia, hit him with that paddle."

Lydia tore her gaze from the soldier's muscled backside to look at her Aunt. "How hard?"

"As hard as you like, my dear," she said.

Lydia wound up and cracked the paddle against the man's buttocks. He groaned loudly around the gag.

"Oh, I'm so sorry," she said. "Did I hurt him?"

"Hurt him again," Mrs. Phillips purred.

She did.

"Again!"

The soldier's cries grew louder with each stroke.

Lydia was flushed and breathing heavily when her Aunt stopped her.

"There's a good girl. That's enough of that." Mrs. Phillips stood up and kicked the soldier in the side so he rolled over on his back. His organ was still swollen and all three woman looked at him fondly.

"You girls are still pure?"

They shrieked and grabbed each other, giggling.

"I mean you've obviously seen a naked man before, but you are still intact are you not."

"Of course, Auntie," Catherine said.

Lydia nodded. "I've touched one."

"Oh you have not," Catherine scolded.

"I have," Lydia said with her nose in the air. "We were dancing and my hand slipped."

"That doesn't count," Catherine scoffed.

"It does too." Lydia rounded on her sister.

"Girls, that will be enough for one day. You can come back tomorrow and perhaps we can continue your education. No man will want to marry you if you've been spoiled, but that's no reason why you can't know your way around the bedchamber."

Every day added something to their knowledge of the officers' names and connections. Their lodgings were not long a secret, and at length they began to know the officers themselves. Mr. Phillips visited them all, and this opened to his nieces a store of felicity unknown before. True to her word, their aunt let them explore the soldiers' bodies with their hands and mouths. When the time came for the officer to return the favor, he was bound to the bed and instructed exactly what to do. To Lydia's dismay, her aunt made him leave his pants on, but the magic he did with his tongue more than made up for it. Lydia and Catherine could talk of nothing but officers; and Mr. Bingley's large fortune, the mention of which gave animation to their mother, was worthless in their eyes when opposed to the regimentals of an ensign.

After listening one morning to their effusions on this subject, Mr. Bennet coolly observed:"From all that I can collect by your manner of talking, you must be two of the silliest girls in the country. I have suspected it some time, but I am now convinced."

Catherine was disconcerted, and made no answer; but Lydia, with perfect indifference, continued to express her admiration of Captain Carter, and her hope of seeing him in the course of the day, as he was going the next morning to London. Captain Carter being the one to initiate her in the delights of cunnilinguis. Lydia rubbed her thighs together just thinking about it.

"I am astonished, my dear," said Mrs. Bennet, "that you should be so ready to think your own children silly. If I wished to think slightingly of anybody's children, it should not be of my own, however."

"If my children are silly, I must hope to be always sensible of it."

"Yes—but as it happens, they are all of them very clever. As a matter of fact, my sister says they are very apt pupils."

"And just what is that old harridan teaching them anyway? This is the only point, I flatter myself, on which we do not agree. I had hoped that our sentiments coincided in every particular, but I must so far differ from you as to think our two youngest daughters uncommonly foolish."

"My dear Mr. Bennet, you must not expect such girls to have the sense of their father and mother. When they get to our age, I dare say they will not think about officers any more than we do. I remember the time when I liked a red coat myself very well—and, indeed, so I do still at my heart." Mrs. Bennet fanned herself in remembrance, not noticing the narrowing of her husband's eyes. If she saw the jealously in them, she would know that tonight she would be punished for her fantasies of another man. "And if a smart young colonel, with five or six thousand a year, should want one of my girls I shall not say nay to him; and I thought Colonel Forster looked very becoming the other night at Sir William's in his regimentals."

"Mamma," cried Lydia, "my aunt says that Colonel Forster and Captain Carter do not go so often to Miss Watson's as they did when they first came; she sees them now very often standing in Clarke's library."

"Probably buggering each other," Mr. Bennet said and went back to his book.

Mrs. Bennet was prevented replying by the

entrance of the footman with a note for Miss Jane Bennet; it came from Netherfield, and the servant waited for an answer. Mrs. Bennet's eyes sparkled with pleasure, and she was eagerly calling out, while her daughter read."Well, Jane, who is it from? What is it about? What does he say? Well, Jane, make haste and tell us; make haste, my love."

"It is from Miss Bingley," said Jane, and then read it aloud.

"MY DEAR FRIEND,—

"If you are not so compassionate as to dine to-day with Louisa and me, we shall be in danger of hating each other for the rest of our lives, for a whole day's tete-a-tete between two women can never end without a quarrel. Come as soon as you can on receipt of this. My brother and the gentlemen are to dine with the officers.—Yours ever,

"CAROLINE BINGLEY"

"With the officers!" cried Lydia. "I wonder my aunt did not tell us of that."

"Dining out," said Mrs. Bennet, "that is very unlucky."

Mr. Bennet mumbled something about brothels.

"Can I have the carriage?" said Jane.

"No, my dear, you had better go on horseback, because it seems likely to rain; and then you must stay all night."

Jane and Elizabeth exchanged secret smiles. Elizabeth knew that Jane would let Bingley have his way with her if she spent the night.

"That would be a good scheme," said Elizabeth, "if you were sure that they would not offer to send her home."

"Oh! But the gentlemen will have Mr. Bingley's chaise to go to Meryton, and the Hursts have no horses to theirs."

"I had much rather go in the coach," Jane said. She wanted to look her best and flying over the countryside on a ragged old nag wouldn't allow her to arrive looking like Mr. Bingley's future wife.

"But, my dear, your father cannot spare the horses, I am sure. They are wanted in the farm, Mr. Bennet, are they not?"

"They are wanted in the farm much oftener than I can get them."

"But if you have got them today," said Elizabeth, "my mother's purpose will be answered."

She did at last extort from her father an acknowledgment that the horses were engaged. Jane was therefore obliged to go on horseback, and her mother attended her to the door with many cheerful prognostics of a bad day. Her hopes were answered; Jane had not been gone long before it rained hard. Her sisters were uneasy for her. Would Bingley's sisters treat her ill or would Mr. Bingley come back. Her mother was delighted. The rain continued the whole evening without intermission; Jane certainly could not come back. Elizabeth found herself worrying that Jane would change her mind and dally with one of the sisters, and have Mr. Bingley walk in on the tryst.

"This was a lucky idea of mine, indeed!" said Mrs. Bennet more than once, as if the credit of making it rain were all her own. Till the next morning, however, she was not aware of all the felicity of her contrivance. Breakfast was scarcely over when a servant from Netherfield brought the following note

Lissa Trevor

for Elizabeth:

"MY DEAREST LIZZY,—

"I find myself very unwell this morning, which, I suppose, is to be imputed to my getting wet through yesterday. I'm sure you know what I mean. My kind friends will not hear of my returning till I am better. Their kind ministrations have kept up my spirits. They insist also on my seeing Mr. Jones—therefore do not be alarmed if you should hear of his having been to me—and, excepting some soreness in my throat – among other places, there is not much the matter with me.—Yours, etc."

"Well, my dear," said Mr. Bennet, when Elizabeth had read the note aloud, "if your daughter should have a dangerous fit of illness—if she should die, it would be a comfort to know that it was all in pursuit of Mr. Bingley, and under your orders."

"Oh! I am not afraid of her dying. People do not die of little trifling colds. She will be taken good care of."

Lydia and Catherine giggled into their handkerchiefs.

"As long as she stays there, it is all very well," their mother continued ignoring the interruption. "I would go and see her if I could have the carriage."

Elizabeth, feeling really anxious, was determined to go to her, though the carriage was not to be had; and as she was no horsewoman, walking was her only alternative. She declared her resolution.

"How can you be so silly," cried her mother, "as to think of such a thing, in all this dirt! You will not be fit to be seen when you get there."

"I shall be very fit to see Jane—which is all I

want." And to make sure she hasn't ruined her chances at true love by dallying with Bingley's sisters instead of with Bingley himself.

"Is this a hint to me, Lizzy," said her father, "to send for the horses?"

"No, indeed, I do not wish to avoid the walk. The distance is nothing when one has a motive; only three miles. I shall be back by dinner."

"I admire the activity of your benevolence," observed Mary, "but every impulse of feeling should be guided by reason; and, in my opinion, exertion should always be in proportion to what is required."

Elizabeth rolled her eyes at her sister. As if she knew of any exertion beyond reading her books and playing the piano badly.

"We will go as far as Meryton with you," said Catherine and Lydia. Elizabeth accepted their company, and the three young ladies set off together.

"If we make haste," said Lydia, as they walked along, "perhaps we may see something of Captain Carter before he goes."

"Maybe more than something," Catherine giggled.

In Meryton they parted; the two youngest repaired to the lodgings of one of the officers' wives, and Elizabeth continued her walk alone, crossing field after field at a quick pace, jumping over stiles and springing over puddles with impatient activity, and finding herself at last within view of the house, with weary ankles, dirty stockings, and a face glowing with the warmth of exercise.

She was shown into the breakfast-parlour, where all but Jane were assembled, and where her appearance created a great deal of surprise. That she should have walked three miles so early in the day, in such dirty weather, and by herself, was almost incredible to Mrs. Hurst and Miss Bingley; and Elizabeth was convinced that they held her in contempt for it. However, Mrs. Hurst's eyes looked hungrily at her fichu.

Elizabeth was received, however, very politely by them; and in their brother's manners there was something better than politeness; there was good humour and kindness. Mr. Darcy said very little Perhaps, he could steal a few moments alone to see if she was as willing as her sister to experience the pleasures of the flesh.

Elizabeth regarded him with a frosty look. She hadn't forgotten his bold hands and indifferent manner. Mr. Hurst said nothing at all. Mr. Darcy was divided between admiration of the brilliancy which exercise had given to her complexion, and doubt as to the occasion's justifying her coming so far alone and therefore unchaperoned. Could she be here for his pleasure? Mr. Hurst was thinking only of his breakfast.

Her inquiries after her sister were not very favourably answered. Miss Bennet had slept ill, and though up, was very feverish, and not well enough to leave her room. Elizabeth was glad to be taken to her immediately; and Jane, who had only been withheld by the fear of giving alarm or inconvenience from expressing in her note how much she longed for such a visit, was delighted at her entrance. She was not equal, however, to much conversation, and when Miss Bingley left them together, could attempt little besides expressions of gratitude for the extraordinary kindness she was treated with. Elizabeth silently attended her, noting the marks on her sister's neck.

"Jane what happened last night?"

"Oh Lizzie, wonderful things."

"Did you and Mr. Bingley . . . "

"Oh no, it's too soon for us."

"Mr. Darcy then?" Elizabeth said, feeling a searing jealousy flash through her at the thought of her beautiful, golden sister being fondled by Darcy.

"Elizabeth! Where are your thoughts? No, we were merely entertained by the staff."

"I beg your pardon?" Elizabeth's scandalized tones rang loud in the room.

"Not like that dearest. Mr. Bingley and I sat together. We kissed some. And we watched the servants put on a play – a salacious, scandalous play. We watched them coupling until I became undone. I was desperate to feel Mr. Bingley, but he demanded my mouth on him instead. Afterwards, I was feeling a bit lightheaded and I took to bed. But not before I heard the cries of pain and pleasure from the rooms down the hall."

"What was happening there?"

"I don't know," Jane said slyly, "But I think Mr. Darcy was and Bingley's two sisters were involved."

Elizabeth shrugged, "That's no concern of mine." But her breast tingled where he had groped her and her imagination wandered again.

When breakfast was over they were joined by the sisters; and Elizabeth began to like them herself, when she saw how much affection and solicitude they showed for Jane. The apothecary came, and having examined his patient, said, as might be supposed, that she had caught a violent cold, and that they must endeavour to get the better of it; advised her to return to bed, and promised her some draughts. The advice was followed readily, for the feverish symptoms increased, and her head ached acutely. Elizabeth did not quit her room for a moment; nor were the other ladies often absent; the gentlemen being out, they had, in fact, nothing to do elsewhere.

"Why don't we play a game?" Miss Bingley said.

"I'm not sure Jane is feeling up to it," Elizabeth replied, but Jane was nodding.

"Oh yes, let's do. It's dreadfully boring just to be lying here."

"And hot," Mrs. Hurst said, and started taking off her clothes.

Jane also eased out of her dressing gown.

"Why don't we give them a few moments," Miss Bingley said and clutched Elizabeth by the hand, pulling her out of the room.

"What are you doing?" Elizabeth mouthed at her sister.

But Jane was welcoming Mrs. Hurst under the covers as Miss Bingley closed the door firmly behind them.

"Come now, we're all girls here. Surely you've heard about Netherfield's notorious reputation."

Elizabeth would have balked, but she was intrigued.

"Let me take you to the forbidden room."

Elizabeth's toes curled. "Is this where Jane and your brother were yesterday? I assure you I have no desire to see a show."

Miss Bingley pushed her roughly against the wall and slanted her mouth over hers. The kiss was hard and punishing, not like the sweet caresses that she shared with Charlotte. But she found something awakening in her core at the slight pain from Miss Bingley's teeth.

Her hands clutched Miss Bingley's shoulders. Miss Bingley grabbed the front of Elizabeth's dress and ripped down the front. Stifling her cry of outrage with her mouth. Miss Bingley pinched Elizabeth's nipple until she cried out again and Elizabeth pushed her away.

Miss Bingley wiped her mouth with the back of her hand, while Elizabeth panted and tried to fix her dress.

"You've ruined it," she cried.

"I'll buy you another one twice as fine. I like seeing you in tears in your gown that put your beautiful breasts on display. You like it too, don't you?" She tweaked Elizabeth's nipple again.

"No, that hurts," Elizabeth said, but she didn't push Miss Bingley away when she cupped both of them in her hand.

"I bet you're sodding wet under that filthy dress. Take the rest of it off."

"Here?" Elizabeth said.

Miss Bingley squeezed her hands tightly. "The response is, Yes, Mistress. Are we understood?"

Elizabeth felt her quim fill with wet heat and nodded. She gasped in pain, when Miss Bingley's hands clenched around her sensitive breasts. "Yes, Mistress."

"That's good," Miss Bingley said, releasing Elizabeth. "He thought you would put up a fight. But you're not so temperamental when you're dying to be stroked like a cat."

Elizabeth was fumbling with the buttons, but Miss Bingley tore the back down with such strength that Elizabeth fell to her knees.

"Why are you being so horrid?" She asked, sliding out of the ruined dress.

"The question is," Miss Bingley said. "Why are you enjoying it so much?"

But before Elizabeth could admit or deny anything, Miss Bingley pulled her up by her hair. "He's going to be so happy with you."

"He who?"

"You are to call him Master."

Holding her hair like a leash, Miss Bingley dragged her down a set of back stairs.

"Please," Elizabeth said, trying to cover her nakedness and not trip as they made it to a cold room. Her nipples were painfully aroused and the wetness between her legs shamed her.

"Please what?" Miss Bingley said, forcing Elizabeth to her knees. She let her go as a door opened on the other side of the room.

In strode a large man, with a black executioner's mask over his face. He was naked. The muscles in his thighs flexed as he walked over to her. Elizabeth followed her gaze to his very thick and hard cock, its tip bouncing against the hard muscled planes of his stomach. He had a broad chest, equally muscled.

He approached until he was standing directly before Elizabeth. She moved her head as his cock would have brushed her lips. Suddenly, Miss Bingley was behind her forcing her head back.

"Have you sucked cock before?" The man's voice was deep, and muffled.

Elizabeth swallowed. "Not one as large as yours, Sir."

Miss Bingley laughed. "She is not as innocent as she seems."

"Do you know how to pleasure a man with your mouth?"

Elizabeth nodded, licking her lips.

"Do you want me to spill my seed inside your throat?"

Elizabeth could only stare.

"Caroline, why don't you show her how it's done."

"Yes, Master," she said and shoved Elizabeth so she went sprawling.

The big man groaned as Caroline took him all. "You are better than your brother."

Elizabeth gasped. This man had mastered both brother and sister. Had he had Jane? She mentioned none of this. She watched Miss Bingley glide her gloved hand over the man's buttock and hold on to it, while the other one cupped his sack. All the while, her head moved rhythmically up and down his shaft.

"Are you watching, Lizzie."

"Oh yes,"

"She is very talented, is she not?"

"Yes," Elizabeth breathed.

He grabbed the back of Miss Bingley's head and ruthlessly began to rock into her mouth. She clutched his backside and made a sound of distress.

"You're choking her," Elizabeth said.

"Yes," the man said unconcerned. "She must relax and take it all in. She's trying to be in control and I must let her know that she is not. Oh, her mouth is sweet. How eager she is. You must have made her very needful."

"Me?"

"Did she suck on your breasts?"

"No," Elizabeth said, feeling a bit left out.

"Good," he held Miss Bingley's head tight against him. Elizabeth saw Miss Bingley try to struggle, but it was useless. He was too strong. His backside quivered and an explosion of breath left him. Miss Bingley swallowed a few times. Then he tossed her aside. She fell limply to her side, gasping for air.

Then he turned to Elizabeth, who scurried back in fear. He was still hard, his cock glistening and twitching towards her.

"Stand up,"

Elizabeth used the wall to get up. Her knees were shaky and she couldn't understand the confusion of emotions going through her.

"We're going to take it slow with you." The man moved so their bodies were touching.

Elizabeth gasped and flinched from the heat of him against her stomach. Her nipples ached to rub across the fine hairs of his chest. "I'm afraid," she said.

"Of what? I will hurt you, but you'll find that the pain will bleed into the most intense pleasure you will have ever known. I will humiliate you, but you will find a deep satisfaction in pleasing me that will please yourself."

"I'm afraid, you will take me and there is nothing I can do to stop you."

"You are only half right. I will take you. But you can stop me at any time. Stop any of us at any time." He trailed his finger down her breast to circle her nipple. "All you have to do is cry out for your sister."

"Jane?"

The man took his hand away immediately.

"What does she have to do with this?"

"She is your salvation from me and my ministrations. Our lessons."

"What type of lessons?"

"You wanted to experience Netherfield. This is Netherfield."

Elizabeth's eyes were drawn to Miss Bingley, who had recovered and was removing her dress and chemise. His fingers went back to Elizabeth's nipples. Unlike Miss Bingley's pinching, the man's touch was as gentle as Charlotte's. But Charlotte's touch didn't light this raging need for more.

He bent his head and sucked one turgid tip. Elizabeth's knees gave out at the intensity of pleasure that hit her deep within from the tugging. He grazed his teeth over them, each pin prick more pleasure.

Releasing her nipple, he scooped her up as if she was a child and carried her over to a large bed. Miss Bingley was there with leather cuffed restraints.

"What are you doing?"

Miss Bingley hissed and twisted the nipple that had just been inside the man's mouth. "Mistress. You are to call me Mistress."

"Oh," Elizabeth said. "I'm sorry, Mistress. What are you doing?'

The man spread Elizabeth's legs and knelt between them while, Miss Bingley secured Elizabeth's arms to the bedposts.

"You've done this before," the man said, running a finger up her wet slit.

Elizabeth's legs spread wider and she tried to ease into the caress, but her arms pulled taught and the man chuckled.

"Just playing with ribbons," Elizabeth said.

"With a eunuch?" The man wondered, dipping a finger inside her.

She clenched her muscles down on it. "With my friend, Charlotte."

He slipped another finger inside her and then grunted in satisfaction, when her hips rose up to meet his questing digits.

"You'll do," he said, smoothing the curls over her mound. "Miss Bingley is going to make you come for being such an honest girl."

"Miss Bingley?" Elizabeth said in dismay, and then flinched as a flail of silk ribbons with beads on the ends slapped her bare stomach.

"If I have to tell you to call me Mistress one more time, I'm going to shove this up your bum." Miss Bingley showed her the handle of the flail.

Elizabeth's eyes grew wide.

The man chuckled. "Not for her first time, Carolyn." He moved away. "I want her drenched and screaming."

Miss Bingley climbed on the bed, like a stalking cat. She pressed her body up against him, kissing his neck. He grabbed her hair and guided her face into the juncture of Elizabeth's thighs.

Elizabeth sighed in pleasure when Miss Bingley's tongue started lapping at her. The man moved behind Miss Bingley.

"You're not unfamiliar with a woman between your legs?"

"No sir, I quite enjoy it," Elizabeth arched her back.

The man nestled in behind Miss Bingley and pushed her head deeper.

"Oh that's ever so nice." Elizabeth tugged on the restraints.

"Do you like being helpless to my whims."

"Yes, sir."

Elizabeth watched him guide his thick cock inside Miss Bingley. She felt her moan vibrated through her quim. As the man rocked into Miss Bingley, her face was pushed farther into to Elizabeth. The man leveraged his hand on Miss Bingley's shoulder and began to rock faster.

Elizabeth could hear the grunts Miss Bingley moaned into her core, while her tongue snaked up inside her. It was sweeter than fingers: with each thrust she felt a little of her control eaten away.

"I'm going to take you like this," the man vowed, staring his dark eyes into Elizabeth.

"I need to be a virgin when I marry," Elizabeth cried out the only thing she could think of that was stopping her from begging him to let her take Miss Bingley's place. Miss Bingley choked on laughter and doubled on her efforts.

The man also laughed and increased his pace.

Elizabeth was shouting in joy, in pleasure and in a screaming need to be pleasured. Miss Bingley reached up and pulled her nipples until she went wild underneath them.

Throwing her head back in exultation, Miss Bingley crowed her own pleasure. Her bell like breasts swaying against Elizabeth's leg.

"Elizabeth!" The man shouted and pulled out to spill his seed over the backside of Miss Bingley.

There was a moment of quiet when the only sound was their mingled breathing.

"That was a nice beginning," the man said. Then he got out of bed. "Clean yourselves up. I have no more use of you tonight."

When he left, Miss Bingley laid down next to Elizabeth. She pressed a kiss to her cheek. "Isn't it fortunate, then, that I'm not quite finished." Then she bent her head to thoroughly ravage Elizabeth's breasts.

When the clock struck three, Elizabeth felt that she must go, and very unwillingly said so. Miss Bingley offered her the carriage, and she only wanted a little pressing to accept it, when Jane testified such concern in parting with her, that Miss Bingley was obliged to convert the offer of the chaise to an invitation to remain at Netherfield for the present. Elizabeth most thankfully consented, and a servant was dispatched to Longbourn to acquaint the family with her stay and bring back a supply of clothes.

Of course, she wouldn't need them right away.

Chapter 8

At five o'clock the two ladies retired to dress, and at half-past six Elizabeth was summoned to dinner. To the civil inquiries which then poured in, and amongst which she had the pleasure of distinguishing the much superior solicitude of Mr. Bingley's, she could not make a very favourable answer.

Jane was by no means better, although Elizabeth wondered how much of her sister's fever was brought on my Mrs. Hurst. Elizabeth's world felt like it had been knocked on its axis. If Mrs. Hurst used Jane with even half the exuberance of Miss Bingley, it was a wonder Jane couldn't walk. Even after a brisk wash and a new dress, she could still feel Miss Bingley's mouth on her, and the hard stare of the man as he had pummeled into Miss Bingley. The sisters, on hearing Jane was still ill, repeated three or four times how much they were grieved, how shocking it was to have a bad cold, and how excessively they disliked being ill themselves; and then thought no more of the matter: and their indifference towards Jane when not immediately before them restored Elizabeth to the enjoyment of all her former dislike. At least Miss Bingley didn't insist on being called Mistress outside of the little dungeon room.

Their brother, indeed, was the only one of the party whom she could regard with any complacency. His anxiety for Jane was evident, and his attentions to herself most pleasing, although very platonic in nature. Which was a relief because she kept looking in his eyes and his bearing and she was positive he wasn't the man behind the mask. Could it have been a servant then? .

She had very little notice from any but him. Miss Bingley was engrossed by Mr. Darcy, her sister scarcely less so; and as for Mr. Hurst, by whom Elizabeth sat, he was an indolent man, who lived only to eat, drink, and play at cards; who, when he found her to prefer a plain dish to a ragout, had nothing to say to her. It was definitely not Mr. Hurst in the black mask.

When dinner was over, Elizabeth returned directly to Jane, and Miss Bingley began abusing her as soon as she was out of the room. Her manners were pronounced to be very bad indeed, a mixture of pride and impertinence; she had no conversation, no style, no beauty. Although she seemed eager enough for sex play, there wasn't enough to intrigue Miss Bingley beyond a few more trysts. Mrs. Hurst thought the same, and added:

"She has nothing, in short, to recommend her, but being an excellent walker. I shall never forget her appearance this morning. She really looked almost wild."

"She did, indeed, Louisa. I could hardly keep my countenance. I thought she would be equally wild in the dungeon. But it wasn't to be. She just lay there moaning. Very nonsensical to come at all! Why must she be scampering about the country, because her sister had a cold? Her hair, so untidy, so blowsy!"

"Yes, and her petticoat; I hope you saw her petticoat, six inches deep in mud, I am absolutely certain; and the gown which had been let down to hide it not doing its office."

"I ripped it off her, it offended me so much."

"Your picture may be very exact, Louisa," said Bingley; "but this was all lost upon me. I thought Miss Elizabeth Bennet looked remarkably well when she came into the room this morning. Her dirty petticoat quite escaped my notice."

"You observed it, Mr. Darcy, I am sure," said Miss Bingley; "and I am inclined to think that you would not wish to see your sister make such an exhibition."

"Certainly not."

"To walk three miles, or four miles, or five miles, or whatever it is, above her ankles in dirt, and alone, quite alone! What could she mean by it? It seems to me to show an abominable sort of conceited independence, a most country-town indifference to decorum. Mark my words; she'll be no one's submissive."

"It shows affection for her sister that is very pleasing," said Bingley. "Besides, you found amusement in her, although she seemed quite unwilling to look you in the eye tonight."

"I am afraid, Mr. Darcy," observed Miss Bingley in a half whisper, "that this adventure has rather affected your admiration of her fine eyes."

"Not at all," he replied; "they were brightened by the exercise." A short pause followed this speech, and

75

Mrs. Hurst began again:

"I have an excessive regard for Miss Jane Bennet, she is really a very sweet girl."

Miss Bingley made a humph sound and looked at her nails. "I'm sure I don't know about that. I got the one who likes to walk."

"Whatever do you mean by that, Caroline? Louisa have you been frolicking with Jane?" Mr. Bingley asked.

Louisa hit her sister with a napkin. "I wish with all my heart Jane was well settled. But with such a father and mother, and such low connections, I am afraid there is no chance of it. They may find that they're best chance of marriage is to hook someone here at Netherfield in the dungeons."

"Those women are not sensual creatures," cried Bingley, "They are meant to be wives not playthings. If they were penniless it would not make them one jot less agreeable."

"But it must very materially lessen their chance of marrying men of any consideration in the world," replied Darcy. He was somewhat pleased by that thought. It would be less competition for Elizabeth.

To this speech Bingley made no answer; but his sisters gave it their hearty assent, and indulged their mirth for some time at the expense of their dear friend's vulgar relations.

With a renewal of tenderness, however, they returned to Jane's room on leaving the dining-parlour, and sat with her till being summoned to coffee. She was still very poorly, and Elizabeth would not quit her at all, till late in the evening, when she had the comfort of seeing her sleep, and when it seemed to her rather right than pleasant that she should go downstairs herself.

On entering the drawing-room she found the whole party at loo, but what was most shocking was there were naked servants on their hands and knees serving as end tables. Elizabeth was immediately invited to join them; but not knowing if they meant at the card table or kneeling next to Miss Bingley she declined it. Making her sister the excuse, said she would amuse herself for the short time she could stay below, with a book. Mr. Hurst looked at her with astonishment.

"Do you prefer reading to cards?" said he; "that is rather singular." He ran a hand over his maid's back. Elizabeth noticed that a large gem was plugged into the woman's posterior. It twinkled in the dim light and for a moment, she was mesmerized by it.

"Miss Eliza Bennet," said Miss Bingley, "despises cards. She is a great reader, and has no pleasure in anything else."

"I deserve neither such praise nor such censure," cried Elizabeth; "I am not a great reader, and I have pleasure in many things." She gave Miss Bingley a pointed look.

"In nursing your sister I am sure you have pleasure," said Bingley; "and I hope it will be soon increased by seeing her quite well."

Elizabeth thanked him from her heart, and then walked towards the human male table where a few books were lying. He was well muscled and out of his backside was something that looked like a horse's tail. Images of riding him naked, had Elizabeth trembling and she knocked his books on the floor. Mr. Bingley immediately offered to fetch her others—all that his library afforded.

"And I wish my collection were larger for your benefit and my own credit; but I am an idle fellow, and though I have not many, I have more than I ever looked into."

Elizabeth assured him that she could suit herself perfectly with those in the room. She bent down to pick up the books she knocked over and found herself kneeling by Mr. Darcy. He looked down at her with a dark and enigmatic look. Her heart started knocking in her chest. Surely, he wasn't the man in the black mask.

"I am astonished," said Miss Bingley.

Elizabeth started away from Mr. Darcy and with shaky knees sat back down on the couch.

"That my father should have left so small a collection of books. What a delightful library you have at Pemberley, Mr. Darcy!"

"It ought to be good," he replied, "it has been the work of many generations." He couldn't take his eyes off Elizabeth who sat primly, leafing through a book called The Dictionary of the Vulgar Tongue. Darcy was sure she wasn't even aware of the words on the paper. What he wouldn't give to know what she had been thinking when she knelt at his feet just now. His prick twitched.

"And then you have added so much to it yourself, you are always buying books."

"I cannot comprehend the neglect of a family library in such days as these," Darcy nodded towards the other books of frank sexuality around the room

"Neglect! I am sure you neglect nothing that can add to the beauties of that noble place. Charles, when you build your house, I wish it may be half as delightful as Pemberley."

"I wish it may," he said with a wicked grin at Darcy. He had fond memories of being wildly fucked there. Some of it by Darcy, himself.

"But I would really advise you to make your purchase in that neighbourhood, and take Pemberley for a kind of model. There is not a finer county in England than Derbyshire."

"With all my heart; I will buy Pemberley itself if Darcy will sell it."

"I am talking of possibilities, Charles."

"Upon my word, Caroline, I should think it more possible to get Pemberley by purchase than by imitation."

Elizabeth was so much caught with what passed, as to leave her very little attention for her book; and soon laying it wholly aside, she drew near the card-table, and stationed herself between Mr. Bingley and his eldest sister, to observe the game.

"Why don't you sit down," Mr. Bingley said, offering the back of one of the male servants.

"Oh, I couldn't," she said, but found herself sinking down on the wide muscled expanse. It was all she could do not to gasp when the man clenched his muscles against her. How she wished her skirts weren't in the way.

"Is Miss Darcy much grown since the spring?" said Miss Bingley; "will she be as tall as I am?"

"I think she will. She is now about Miss Elizabeth Bennet's height, or rather taller." Mr. Darcy speared her with a dark look that caused flutters in her stomach. Absently, Elizabeth stroked the servant's backside and was thrilled to see Mr. Darcy's eyes narrow in anger.

"How I long to see her again! I never met with anybody who delighted me so much. Such a countenance, such manners! And so extremely accomplished for her age! Her performance on the pianoforte is exquisite."

Elizabeth wondered sourly what else Miss Bingley was delighted with about Mr. Darcy's sister.

"It is amazing to me," said Bingley, "how young ladies can have patience to be so very accomplished as they all are."

The women stared at Mr. Bingley aghast. Surely he didn't mean about pleasures of the flesh.

"All young ladies accomplished! My dear Charles, what do you mean?"

"Yes, all of them, I think. They all paint tables, cover screens, and net purses. I scarcely know anyone who cannot do all this, and I am sure I never heard a young lady spoken of for the first time, without being informed that she was very accomplished."

The three women breathed out a sigh of relief until Mr. Darcy spoke.

"Your list of the common extent of accomplishments," said Darcy, "has too much truth. The word is applied to many a woman who deserves it no otherwise than by netting a purse or covering a screen. But I am very far from agreeing with you in your estimation of ladies in general. I cannot boast of knowing more than half-a-dozen, in the whole range of my acquaintance, that are really . . . *accomplished.*"
He emphasized the last word with a dark look at Carolyn.

"Nor I, I am sure," said Miss Bingley.

And then he turned his smoldering gaze on Elizabeth.

"Then," observed Elizabeth, "you must comprehend a great deal in your idea of an accomplished woman."

"Yes, I do comprehend a great deal in it." Darcy flashed teeth and Elizabeth was reminded of a wolf.

"Oh! certainly," cried his faithful assistant, "no one can be really esteemed accomplished who does not greatly surpass what is usually met with. A woman must have a thorough knowledge of music, singing, drawing, dancing, and the modern languages, to deserve the word; and besides all this, she must possess a certain something in her air and manner of walking, the tone of her voice, her address and expressions, or the word will be but half-deserved."

"All this she must possess," added Darcy, "and to all this she must yet add something more substantial, in the improvement of her mind by extensive reading. Of experiencing life without endangering her virtue."

"I am no longer surprised at your knowing only six accomplished women. I rather wonder now at your knowing any," Elizabeth said, tossing her head. She pulled the servant's hair in vexation, before she realized what she was doing. Soothing her hand down his glossy, black hair, she took her eyes off Darcy for a moment. That was her first mistake.

"Are you so severe upon your own sex as to doubt the possibility of all this?"

"I never saw such a woman. I never saw such capacity, and taste, and application, and elegance, as you describe united." She stood up when she realized that Mr. Darcy was stalking towards her.

Mrs. Hurst and Miss Bingley both cried out against the injustice of her implied doubt, and were both protesting that they knew many women who answered this description, when Mr. Hurst called them to order, with bitter complaints of their inattention to what was going forward. He had come to play cards not argue about women. As all conversation was thereby at an end, Elizabeth quickly made her escape before Mr. Darcy made good on the promise in his eyes.

"Elizabeth Bennet," said Miss Bingley, when the door was closed on her, "is one of those young ladies who seek to recommend themselves to the other sex by undervaluing their own; and with many men, I dare say, it succeeds. But, in my opinion, it is a paltry device, a very mean art."

"Undoubtedly," replied Darcy, to whom this remark was chiefly addressed, "there is a meanness in all the arts which ladies sometimes condescend to employ for captivation. Whatever bears affinity to cunning is despicable." He stared at the closed door and plotted how he would get Miss Bennet into his bed. He would not stand idly by and watch her stroke another man. She would be taught a lesson in propriety.

Miss Bingley was not so entirely satisfied with this reply as to continue the subject.

Elizabeth joined them again, much to Darcy's surprise, only it was to say that her sister was worse, and that she could not leave her. Bingley urged Mr. Jones being sent for immediately; while his sisters, convinced that no country advice could be of any service, recommended an express to town for one of the most eminent physicians. This Elizabeth would not hear of; but she was not so unwilling to comply with their brother's proposal; and it was settled that Mr. Jones should be sent for early in the morning, if Miss Bennet were not decidedly better. Mr. Darcy adjourned to his rooms. Bingley was quite uncomfortable; his sisters declared that they were miserable. They solaced their wretchedness, however, by duets after supper, while he could find no better relief to his feelings than by giving his housekeeper directions that every attention might be paid to the sick lady and her sister.

Chapter 9

Elizabeth passed the chief of the night in her sister's room, in a state of arousal and frustration, thinking of Mr. Darcy and picturing him wielding the beaded flail on her naked back as she rode the servant with the horse's tail in his backside. In the morning, she had the pleasure of being able to send a tolerable answer to the inquiries which she very early received from Mr. Bingley by a housemaid, and some time afterwards from the two elegant ladies who waited on his sisters. She recognized one of them as the girl who had served as a table from last night.

"Excuse me?" Elizabeth said, bringing the lady away from Jane who was still feverish and restless, as not to disturb her further.

"Yes?" The woman had ice blond hair that was now tied back into a severe bun. It had been flowing over her shoulders the night before.

"Pray tell me, what was in your," Elizabeth blushed. " .. . it sparkled so. I had never seen anything like it."

"Ah," the woman's face split into a seductive smile. "If you hang around here long enough you might. That, my pretty girl, was a shaped plug that gets inserted up there."

"Doesn't it hurt?" Elizabeth asked fascinated.

"At first, but not if your Master is gentle like mine is. He makes sure the instrument is warm and well oiled. Then he eases it in. It feels like . . . possession." The maid gave an elegant shudder.

Elizabeth could only stare.

She leaned in and kissed Elizabeth. "Maybe we'll play together at some point. There are great pleasures to be had here."

In spite of this amendment, however, Elizabeth requested to have a note sent to Longbourn, desiring her mother to visit Jane, and form her own judgment of her situation. She touched her lips that still tingled from the maid's kiss. The note was immediately dispatched, and its contents as quickly complied with. Mrs. Bennet, accompanied by her two youngest girls, reached Netherfield soon after the family breakfast.

Had she found Jane in any apparent danger, Mrs. Bennet would have been very miserable; but being satisfied on seeing her that her illness was not alarming, she had no wish of her recovering immediately, as her restoration to health would probably remove her from Netherfield. She would not listen, therefore, to her daughter's proposal of being carried home; neither did the apothecary, who arrived about the same time, think it at all advisable. Elizabeth was surprised at the relief she felt to spend a few more days at Netherfield. She longed to meet the man in the black mask again. Maybe to ride her male pony and play love games with the blond maid.

After sitting a little while with Jane, on Miss Bingley's appearance and invitation, the mother and three daughters all attended her into the breakfast parlour. Bingley met them with hopes that Mrs. Bennet had not found Miss Bennet worse than she expected.

"Indeed I have, sir," was her answer. "She is a great deal too ill to be moved. Mr. Jones says we must not think of moving her. We must trespass a little longer on your kindness."

Mr. Bingley looked relieved, which caused Elizabeth to wonder what had been going on in her sister's bed."Removed!" cried Bingley. "It must not be thought of. My sister, I am sure, will not hear of her removal."

"You may depend upon it, Madam," said Miss Bingley, with cold civility, "that Miss Bennet will receive every possible attention while she remains with us."

Mrs. Bennet was profuse in her acknowledgments.

"I am sure," she added, "if it was not for such good friends I do not know what would become of her, for she is very ill indeed, and suffers a vast deal, though with the greatest patience in the world, which is always the way with her, for she has, without exception, the sweetest temper I have ever met with. I often tell my other girls they are nothing to her. You have a sweet room here, Mr. Bingley, and a charming prospect over the gravel walk. I do not know a place in the country that is equal to Netherfield. You will not think of quitting it in a hurry. The people of the village are most eager to see it returned to its former glory."

"Whatever I do is done in a hurry," replied he; "and therefore if I should resolve to quit Netherfield, I should probably be off in five minutes. At present, however, I consider myself as quite fixed here."

"That is exactly what I should have supposed of you," said Elizabeth, surprised that her mother knew of the Netherfield wild parties.

"You begin to comprehend me, do you?" cried he, turning towards her.

"Oh! yes—I understand you perfectly." She smiled at him. Her sister had chosen well. If only she could be sure that his feelings for Jane went beyond a pleasant groping and heated caresses.

"I wish I might take this for a compliment; but to be so easily seen through I am afraid is pitiful."

"That is as it happens. It does not follow that a deep, intricate character is more or less estimable than such a one as yours."

He bowed to her with a wicked gleam in his eyes that made her clap a hand over her mouth so she would giggle like her two idiot sisters were doing.

"Lizzy," cried her mother, "remember where you are, and do not run on in the wild manner that you are suffered to do at home."

"I did not know before," continued Bingley immediately, "that you were a studier of character. It must be an amusing study."

"Yes, but intimate characters are the most amusing. They have at least that advantage."

"The country," said Darcy interrupting their flirting with a scowl at Bingley, "can in general supply but a few subjects for such a study. In a country neighbourhood you move in a very confined and unvarying society."

"But people themselves alter so much, that there is something new to be observed in them forever."

Elizabeth turned the full power of her smile to him and Darcy stood transfixed as he realized he would have to have her tonight. Her virtue be damned.

"Yes, indeed," cried Mrs. Bennet, offended by his manner of mentioning a country neighbourhood. "I assure you there is quite as much of that going on in the country as in town."

Everybody was surprised, and Darcy, after looking at her for a moment, turned silently away lest the old harridan thought he was flirting with her. Mrs. Bennet, who fancied she had gained a complete victory over him, continued her triumph.

"I cannot see that London has any great advantage over the country, for my part, except the shops and public places. The country is a vast deal pleasanter, is it not, Mr. Bingley?"

"When I am in the country," he replied, "I never wish to leave it; and when I am in town it is pretty much the same. They have each their advantages, and I can be equally happy in either." Bingley spoke to soothe the tensions he saw rising. Darcy was wound tight as a top and Elizabeth seemed determined to start something.

"Aye—that is because you have the right disposition. But that gentleman," Mrs. Bennet said, looking at Darcy, "seemed to think the country was nothing at all."

"Indeed, Mamma, you are mistaken," said Elizabeth, blushing for her mother. "You quite mistook Mr. Darcy. He only meant that there was not such a variety of people to be met with in the country as in the town, which you must acknowledge to be true."

Nothing but concern for Elizabeth could enable

Bingley to keep his countenance. His sister was less delicate, and directed her eyes towards Mr. Darcy with a very expressive smile. Elizabeth, for the sake of saying something that might turn her mother's thoughts, now asked her if Charlotte Lucas had been at Longbourn since her coming away.

"Yes, she called yesterday with her father. What an agreeable man Sir William is, Mr. Bingley, is not he? So much the man of fashion! So genteel and easy! He has always something to say to everybody. That is my idea of good breeding; and those persons who fancy themselves very important, and never open their mouths, quite mistake the matter."

"Did Charlotte dine with you?" Elizabeth said, wishing she could tell her friend all about Netherfield and its pleasures.

"No, she would go home. I fancy she was wanted about the mince-pies. For my part, Mr. Bingley, I always keep servants that can do their own work; my daughters are brought up very differently. But everybody is to judge for themselves, and the Lucases are a very good sort of girls, I assure you. It is a pity they are not handsome! Not that I think Charlotte so very plain—but then she is our particular friend."

"She seems a very pleasant young woman." Mr. Bingley looked at his tea cup and wished it was filled with something more bracing, but it was just past breakfast.

"Oh! dear, yes; but you must own she is very plain. Lady Lucas herself has often said so, and envied me Jane's beauty. I do not like to boast of my own child, but to be sure, Jane—one does not often see anybody better looking."

89

Bingley couldn't disagree. His mind wandered over to sweet Jane lying abed. He had removed her night dress and touched her body while she smiled encouragingly at him. Part of him felt like a cur, she was obviously too weakened by her fever to be an active companion, but she didn't turn him away. In fact, she spread her legs for his questing fingers and mewled her pleasure as he explored every inch of her. It was a pity she had fallen asleep soon after.

" It is what everybody says. I do not trust my own partiality," Mrs. Bennet was still talking. Bingley blinked at her and tried to pay attention. " When she was only fifteen, there was a man at my brother Gardiner's in town so much in love with her that my sister-in-law was sure he would make her an offer before we came away. But, however, he did not. Perhaps he thought her too young. However, he wrote some verses on her, and very pretty they were."

"And so ended his affection," said Elizabeth impatiently, staring at the way Miss Bingley was copulating with her eyes at Mr. Darcy. There was no doubt in her mind it had been the two of them that had debauched her. And if she'd rather not have any more of Miss Bingley's ministrations, her loins tingled for more of the man with the black mask. "There has been many a one, I fancy, overcome in the same way. I wonder who first discovered the efficacy of poetry in driving away love!"

"I have been used to consider poetry as the food of love," said Darcy.

"Of a fine, stout, healthy love it may. Everything nourishes what is strong already. But if it be only a slight, thin sort of inclination, I am convinced that one good sonnet will starve it entirely away."

Darcy only smiled; and the general pause which ensued made Elizabeth tremble lest her mother should be exposing herself again. She longed to speak, but could think of nothing to say; and after a short silence Mrs. Bennet began repeating her thanks to Mr. Bingley for his kindness to Jane, with an apology for troubling him also with Lizzy. Mr. Bingley was unaffectedly civil in his answer, and forced his younger sister to be civil also, and say what the occasion required. She performed her part indeed without much graciousness, but Mrs. Bennet was satisfied, and soon afterwards ordered her carriage.

Elizabeth breathed a sigh of relief, glad that her mother would soon be gone.

However, her youngest sister put herself forward. Lydia and Kitty had been whispering to each other during the whole visit, and the result of it was, that the youngest should tax Mr. Bingley with having promised on his first coming into the country to give a ball at Netherfield.

Lydia was a stout, well-grown girl of fifteen, with a fine complexion and good-humoured countenance. She had high animal spirits, and a sort of natural self-consequence. She was very equal, therefore, to address Mr. Bingley on the subject of the ball, and abruptly reminded him of his promise; adding, that it would be the most shameful thing in the world if he did not keep it. His answer to this sudden attack was delightful to their mother's ear:

"I am perfectly ready, I assure you, to keep my engagement; and when your sister is recovered, you shall, if you please, name the very day of the ball. But you would not wish to be dancing when she is ill."

Elizabeth nearly swooned. There would be a full ball at Netherfield. If this was only a sampling of what went on, what pleasures would she find at the gala event?

Lydia declared herself satisfied. "Oh! yes—it would be much better to wait till Jane was well, and by that time most likely Captain Carter would be at Meryton again. And when you have given your ball," she added, "I shall insist on their giving one also. I shall tell Colonel Forster it will be quite a shame if he does not."

Mrs. Bennet and her daughters then departed, and Elizabeth returned instantly to Jane to tell her the news, leaving her own and her relations' behaviour to the remarks of the two ladies and Mr. Darcy; the latter of whom, however, could not be prevailed on to join in their censure of her, in spite of all Miss Bingley's witticisms on fine eyes. He had plans to make.

Chapter 10

The day passed much as the day before had done. Mrs. Hurst and Miss Bingley had spent some hours of the morning with the invalid, who continued, though slowly, to mend; and in the evening Elizabeth joined their party in the drawing-room. The loo-table and the servants, however, did not appear.

Mr. Darcy was writing, and Miss Bingley, seated near him, was watching the progress of his letter and repeatedly calling off his attention by messages to his sister. Mr. Hurst and Mr. Bingley were at piquet, and Mrs. Hurst was observing their game.

Elizabeth took up some needlework, and was sufficiently amused in attending to what passed between Darcy and his companion. The perpetual commendations of the lady, either on his handwriting, or on the evenness of his lines, or on the length of his letter, with the perfect unconcern with which her praises were received, formed a curious dialogue, and was exactly in union with her opinion of each. Miss Bingley needled the poor man so much, Elizabeth was getting a headache on his behalf. She excused herself and once out of the drawing-room felt that she could breathe again.

With a thoughtful look at the door behind her, Elizabeth marched straight for the back staircase. The one that Miss Bingley had so roughly moved her down the other day. No one seemed to be stirring and for a moment, Elizabeth wondered if she was dreamt the whole erotic affair.

When she opened the door at the bottom of the stairs, it wasn't into the servants' quarters, but into the room of delights that she had been in. Shutting the door behind her, Elizabeth began to take off her clothes. This was not a room for such things. When she was gloriously naked, she whirled around in a circle, her arms reaching out for freedom. Oh how she wished Charlotte was here. They could play with the restraints and the beaded flail.

Elizabeth looked around the room and found the flail in a vase by the enormous bed. She picked it up and ran a finger down the studded leather shaft. Her thoughts wandered on where Miss Bingley had threatened to put it.

When the door opened up on the far side, Elizabeth was rooted in place in fear. It was one thing to be here naked on her own, it was another to be caught in this place. If this was during one of the Netherfield balls, she would be thought of part of the entertainment and forced to participate in debauchery. The thought made her ache with need instead of flush with shame.

Her mouth grew dry when the servant crawled in. He was the same man she had sat on. Only in addition to having a pony's tail, his mouth was fitted with a bridal. With the flail in her hand, this was so much like her dream that she began to shake. Then she noticed who was holding his reins. It was the man with the black mask and he was as naked as she.

"It couldn't be Mr. Darcy then," she thought. "He was still upstairs writing a letter to his sister while Miss Bingley prattled on, intent on interrupting him.

"I'm so glad to see you Elizabeth," the man in the black mask said.

And though she strained to catch a familiar cadence of his voice, she could not place him. Yet his eyes were as dark and riveting as Mr. Darcy's.

"What do I call you?'

"I told you. You are to call me Master. I brought you a present. Since you didn't have a horse to ride, I have provided one for you."

"You would get rid of me, Master?" Elizabeth said, trying out the strange word. It immediately bound her to him, by a force she was unsure of, but powerful enough she could not deny it.

"If you want to ride him home, you may. Get astride him. It's the closest you're going to come to his cock."

Elizabeth inched towards the servant on his hands and knees. Did she dare?

"Throw your leg over him. Let him feel the wetness between your thighs on his bare back."

His words were pure seduction and unable to refuse, Elizabeth sat astride him.

"That's right," the man growled. "Now rock against him."

"M-master?' she stuttered.

He knelt beside them. "Like this." He put his big hands on her hips and forced her to grind against the man's back."

"Oh," Elizabeth breathed, feeling the friction against her bud.

"He's a nice horse, isn't he."

"Oh yes," Elizabeth moaned, placing her hands on the servant's shoulders.

The man tugged on the hanging tail and the servant arched, almost knocking her over.

"Careful," he said. "I wouldn't want to injure your rider. Elizabeth, why don't you use that flail on your pony when he's naughty?"

Elizabeth lightly danced it across his back. "Like this?"

"No," the man wrenched it from her grasp and snapped it against her breasts.

She cried out in shock rather than pain.

"Like this." He hit the beads against the tips of her breasts over and over.

Elizabeth bounced on the man, throwing her shoulders back. Each strike was like a dozen probing fingers plucking at her most sensual area. She felt the hot kiss of the leather reddening her breasts and it was working her to a frenzy.

"So responsive," the man groaned and leaned in to take a hot throbbing nipple into his mouth.

Elizabeth screamed then as the wet suction pushed her over the edge. She slickened the servant's back with her come and it made the friction against her core maddening.

The man's hand stroked down the silky curve of her spine to rest at the base of her back. Here, slide up on him a bit." He moved her up towards the man's shoulders. Her legs were stretched wide. It was hard to keep her balance.

The man's member was as thick and hard as she remembered. She watched in awe when he removed the servant's bit and plunged in his cock before the servant could move.

"Oh, Elizabeth, are you watching?"

"Yes," she could barely look away.

"Grab his hair again."

She reached in to delve her fingers into the silky blond mass.

"Guide his head on my cock."

Elizabeth did pushing the servant's head forward and then tugging it roughly back.

The man surprised her by reaching his fingers to plunder at her throbbing clitoris.

"Have you let another man touch you thus?" he asked.

She shook her head. "Just Charlotte."

"What have you done?"

Elizabeth could only shake her head and grip the servant's head in place while the man rolled his hips into the servant's mouth.

"Have you sucked cock?"

She nodded.

"Did you like it?"

She nodded. "I wanted more. I wound up nearly attacking Charlotte afterwards."

The man groaned. Elizabeth saw his buttocks clenching and the man's hands covered hers on the servant's head.

"Has another man taken your breasts in his mouth?"

She shook her head. "Only Charlotte."

"I should like to see the two of you together."

"I fear it will no longer be enough," Elizabeth whispered.

"What?" The man said, his entire body grew still.

"I need more."

With a grunt and a shudder, the man's hands tightened over hers. The servant made eager noises and swallowed.

"Miss Bennet, you do surprise me." He got to his feet with the lithe moves of a dancer and then helped her off of the servant. "I shall give you more."

Elizabeth shook her head. "To have more would mean I am no longer a virgin and no man would marry me then. You men have the freedom to indulge all of your desires without consequence. It is a woman's lot to deny herself the pleasure until marriage."

"Tell me, my sweet, do you ever wish you were a man?"

Elizabeth shook her head. "No, but my friend Charlotte mentioned it once."

"I see I'm going to be in competition from your friend Charlotte."

Elizabeth looked at his half flaccid member, glistening with mettle and spit. Her fingers twitched to touch it.

"You may stroke me if you like."

"I've done that before," she said and gripped him eagerly.

"Some farmer's boy, no doubt."

"Charlotte's brother," Elizabeth admitted, feeling him harden against her palm and fingers. "He wasn't as big as you."

The man laughed. "I like hearing you tell me how big I am. It shall be the same when I am nestled inside you."

Her hand faltered. "As I said, I would like to be a virgin for my husband. He would expect it of me and I will not start my marriage off with a lie."

"Virginity is over rated. I bet your husband would want you wanton and panting for him instead."

"Can't I do both?" Elizabeth wrapped her arms around his hips, nestling his member between her breasts.

He rubbed against her. "You have excellent instincts for a virgin. But I will let you decide if you wish to experience the pleasure of mating with me. First, you must see what it's like for a man." He broke away from her hold to walk to a cabinet.

Pulling out a jar of oil, he poured some down the servant's back, who hissed and arched his back.

"Thank you, Master," he spoke his first words. His voice was thick and low.

Elizabeth watched as the man pulled the pony tail completely out and poured more oil down the man's back so it dripped into his puckered hole. She was fascinated.

"Crawl closer, dear Miss Bennet," the man said, then picked up the flail and laid it across her buttocks. "The correct answer is yes, Master."

"Yes, Master," Elizabeth said.

"Hold out your hands." His fingers tightened on the flail.

"Yes Master," she said quickly and held them out. He poured oil on them until they were fully coated.

"Rub it on my cock."

"Yes, Master." Elizabeth did, coating it with the oil. He slipped in and out of her hands. She loved the slippery feel of him, so strong and warm.

"Now watch, for I will take you this way very soon, so you will still be a virgin for your husband."

Elizabeth watched the man ease into the servant. His hole expanding to take in the man's girth. The servant's face was one of concentration and intensity. The man pushed in to the hilt and just stayed in one place.

"Get back on him," the man ordered. "Face me."

Elizabeth did.

"Hold on tight with your thighs," he said. "Rub your hands over those luscious breasts while I fuck him."

She should have been affronted by his language, but she found herself bouncing on the servant and oiling her breasts indolently while watching the man pump in and out.

He was breathing heavily, but he wouldn't take his eyes off her. "This is what a man does. What a man feels. There are no consequences for our act of penetration. We go to the bridal bed with the expectation of experience. You come to it in fear. Not knowing the pleasure."

"I know there's pleasure . . . Master," Elizabeth caught herself.

"I will be in you."

She had no words. She worked her fingers over her nipples as the man pummeled the servant who was crying out. For the second time that night, the man's body tightened. Elizabeth saw his member jerk and twitch and as he slid out of the servant, the man was coated in his own mettle.

"How do you feel, Elizabeth?" He pushed her off

the servant. She lay on her back, waiting for him to cover his body with hers.

""Daring, dangerous. My ideas flow so rapidly that I have not time to express them."

The man slapped the servant on the rump."You have my leave to walk out of here."

"Thank you Master," he said.

"Send down the maid," he said.

"Yes, Master."

The man walked over to a pitcher and poured it into a basin. He cleaned himself thoroughly. But in the time he took, Elizabeth's ardor cooled and she closed her legs, feeling awkward and unsure. She inched towards her clothes.

Just as Elizabeth was about to grab her dress, he was upon her. She felt his wet member against her backside. He was hot and slick and she involuntarily rubbed up against him before she realized what she was doing and gasped.

"Nothing is more deceitful," he said, "than the appearance of humility. It is often only carelessness of opinion, and sometimes an indirect boast."

"And which of the two do you call my little recent piece of modesty?" She asked archly, trying to get away from him.

" The power of doing anything with quickness is always prized much by the possessor, and often without any attention to the imperfection of the performance. I have spent myself twice, yet feeling you underneath me has me hardening again. Your lessons aren't over this quickly Miss Bennet. You came to me of your own free will. I have not decided to let you go."

"Nay," cried Elizabeth, "this is too much."

"I have not it in me at the moment to make love to you like you deserve."

"I have not asked you to."

"You will," he said.

They both turned towards the woman who had appeared in the room. She was also naked, clips attached to her nipples and a chain hung between them. She was completely shaved between her legs. Elizabeth's mouth opened in shock. Her fingers itched to touch the smooth flesh. This was no masked stranger, it was the ladies maid who had kissed her.

"Inga," the man said, pulling himself and Elizabeth to their feet. "Miss Bennet has been lacking in orgasms tonight. Kiss her until she is clawing at you. I have something to attend."

Inga held out her hand and guided Elizabeth to the bed. "I'm so glad we get to play."

"Do those hurt?" Elizabeth said, kneeling on the bed across from her.

"Tug on the chain," Inga said.

Elizabeth did and watched the nipples stretch.

"Oh, you have a gentle touch," Inga said. "It feels like this."

She cried out when Inga pinched and stretched both of Elizabeth's nipples, pulling them so she fell into her. Inga wasted no time covering the girl'sElizabeth's her mouth and bearing her down to the bed. Their legs entangled. The chain and clips dug into Elizabeth's sensitive skin. Inga's hands roamed over Elizabeth's heated body, knowing where to touch. Elizabeth followed suit, pressing her hands to Inga's bottom to wiggle the jeweled plug. Moaning into her mouth, Inga swiped her tongue against Elizabeth's. They played like that, writhing against each other. Elizabeth was flipped on top and as Inga kissed her, she felt the man sliding a leather belt around her waist.

She knelt up to find that there was a penis dangling from the belt. Elizabeth held it in her hand, too shocked at first to realize it was being cinched around her waist. It wasn't real;, it was wooden, but it dangled off the belt he had put on her like a real phallus.

Elizabeth felt dizzy and out of sorts. Inga leaned back on the bed, raising her knees to her chest.

"Take her," the man encouraged, pushing her down on Inga. "Take her like a man."

Elizabeth was clumsy, but the man helped guide the wooden phallus inside Inga. His hands were pressed on her backsizde, as she tried to rememberdecide what to do. In the end, it was Inga locking her legs around Elizabeth's hips that joined them together intimately.

The man lay next to them. "Yes, make love to her like you secretly wish to be ravaged."

Elizabeth began to tremble, then her hips spasmed into a frenzy. She pushed herself forward into Inga's eager, receiving body. Pleasure and satisfaction warred within her as she gazed into Inga's rapturous face.

"This is what I will look like when my husband takes me," Elizabeth thought, and felt power tingle through her as she thrust harder, deeper.

Inga bounced along happily, making guttural sounds of pleasurerapture.

"You two look lovely together," the man slid his hand down Elizabeth's thrusting buttocks and began to probe her corespank her soundly.

"Yes," Elizabeth gritted out in a deep, voice she barely recognized as hers. The hot slap branded her and she became rougher in her thrusts against Inga.

Inga hips thrust frantically up. "More," she cried. "More."

, to remember at night all the foolish things that were said in the morning. And yet, upon my honour, I believe what I said of myself to be true, and I believe it at this moment. At least, therefore, I did not assume the character of needless precipitance merely to show off before the ladies."

"I dare say you believed it; but I am by no means convinced that you would be gone with such celerity. Your conduct would be quite as dependent on chance as that of any man I know; and if, as you were mounting your horse, a friend were to say, 'Bingley, you had better stay till next week,' you would probably do it, you would probably not go—and at another word, might stay a month."

"You have only proved by this," cried Elizabeth, "that Mr. Bingley did not do justice to his own disposition. You have shown him off now much more than he did himself."

"I am exceedingly gratified to watch you peak," said Bingleythe man, as Elizabeth felt like she was going to be shook apart when he slipped his hands between her thighs. by the The sensations of his fingers were doing to herpulsing inside her core, mimicked what the wooden phallus was doing to as she was pleasuring Inga."by your converting what my friend says into a compliment on the sweetness of my temper. But I am afraid you are giving it a turn which that gentleman did by no means intend; for he would certainly think better of me, if under such a circumstance I were to give a flat denial, and ride off as fast as I could."

"Would Mr. Darcy then consider the rashness of your original intentions as atoned for by your obstinacy in adhering to it?"

"Upon my word, I cannot exactly explain the matter; Darcy must speak for himself."

"Will you have me take you thus, Miss Bennet?"

"You expect me to account for opinions which you choose to call mine, but which I have never acknowledged. Allowing the case, however, to stand according to your representation, you must remember, Miss Bennet, that the friend who is supposed to desire his return to the house, and the delay of his plan, has merely desired it, asked it without offering one argument in favour of its propriety."

"To yield readily—easily—to the persuasion of a friend is no merit with you." ," Elizabeth gasped.

"To yield without conviction is no compliment to the understanding of either."

Inga shouted her completion much to Elizabeth's relief and unlocked her knees so she was free. The man helped her out of the apparatus. Inga lay limp and sighing on the bed.

"You appear to me, Mr. DarcyMaster, to allow nothing for the influence of friendship and affection."

"I'm speaking of bed sport, not an alliance."

" A regard for the requester would often make one readily yield to a request, without waiting for arguments to reason one into it. I am not particularly speaking of such a case as you have supposed about

Mr. Bingley. We may as well wait, perhaps, till the circumstance occurs before we discuss the discretion of his behaviour thereupon. But in general and ordinary cases between friend and friend, where one of them is desired by the other to change a resolution of no very great moment, should you think ill of that person for complying with the desire, without waiting to be argued into it?" there is often a declaration of something more than the physical."

"You may leave us Inga." The man jerked his head, indicating the door.

"Yes, Master."

Inga rose from the bed. Elizabeth watched the jeweled plug sway until Inga climbed the stairs. She lay back against the bed to try and get her breath.

"Will it not be advisable, before we proceed on this subject, to arrange with rather more precision the degree of importance which is to appertain to this request, as well as the degree of intimacy subsisting between the parties?"

"By all means," Elizabeth sighed, feeling her eyelids droop.," cried Bingley; "let us hear all the particulars, not forgetting their comparative height and size; for that will have more weight in the argument, Miss Bennet, than you may be aware of. I assure you, that if Darcy were not such a great tall fellow, in comparison with myself, I should not pay him half so much deference. I declare I do not know a more awful object than Darcy, on particular occasions, and in particular places; at his own house especially, and of a Sunday evening, when he has nothing to do."

"I am a man of great wealth. You are a woman of no inheritance. I desire you and you desire me."

Mr. Darcy smiled; but Elizabeth thought she could perceive that he was rather offended, and therefore checked her laugh. Miss Bingley warmly resented the indignity he had received, in an expostulation with her brother for talking such nonsense.

"I see your design, Bingley," said his friend. "You dislike an argument, and want to silence this."

"Perhaps I do. Arguments are too much like disputes. If you and Miss Bennet will defer yours till I am out of the room, I shall be very thankful; and then you may say whatever you like of me." Elizabeth admitted, reaching up a hand to caress his cheek, hidden by the silken mask.

"I want to possess you, but I am not willing to marry you."

"Because I am not wealthy?" Elizabeth felt cold all of a sudden. Was that shame that was crawling up her spine.?

"You would be exquisite here at Netherfield. There would be many men who would offer for you."

"What you ask," said Elizabeth, "is a no great sacrifice on my side; and Mr. Darcy had much better finish his letter."

"Is it? Wouldn't you rather find a husband in the depths of passion than being arranged by your mother of all people?"

Mr. Darcy took her advice, and did finish his letter. "I must think on this. I had thought for a thrilling dalliance, no more. What you're offering is a bit beyond my expectations.
"

"I understand," he said, stroking her arm. "I will be here if you need me."

Elizabeth got dressed, watching him laze in naked splendor. Would another man every be enough for her? "Tell me, Master?"

He looked up at her from deep in thought.

"If I were titled. Would you have made the same offer?"

He turned his head away, dismissing her without an answer. She waited for a moment and left the room.

When that business was over, the man in the black mask hurried up the opposite staircase and rushed into his clothes. He ripped off the mask and with a quick look in the glass, smoothed his hair back in place. He listened at the door of the drawing room where Bingley he applied to Miss Bingley Caroline and Elizabeth for an indulgence of some music. Miss Bingley moved with some alacrity to the pianoforte; and, after a polite request that Elizabeth would lead the way which the other as politely and more earnestly negatived, she seated herself..

He walked into the room and slid unnoticed into his usual desk. The letter he was writing his sister was still unfinished. He sank into the chair and fumbled for his pen, trying to even his ragged breathing and still his throbbing heart and cock.

Mrs. Hurst sang with her sister, and while they were thus employed, Elizabeth could not help observingslipped into the room, looking only slightly disheveled. A, as she turned over some music-books that lay on the instrument, she noticed how frequently Mr. Darcy's eyes were fixed on her. She hardly knew how to suppose that she could be an object of admiration to so great a man; and yet that he should look at her because he disliked her, was still more strange. He had to be the man behind the black mask. His brooding gaze was too similar to the man who had just given her a lesson in pleasure.

She could only imagine, however, at last that she drew his notice because there was something more wrong and reprehensible, according to his ideas of right, than in any other person present. The supposition did not pain her. She liked him too little to care for his approbation. He cared only for wealth and status. There was no room in him for love or affection.

After playing some Italian songs, Miss Bingley varied the charm with by a lively Scotch air; and soon afterwards Mr. Darcy, drawing near Elizabeth, said to her:

"Do not you feel a great inclination, Miss Bennet, to seize such an opportunity of dancing a reel?"

She smiled, but made no answer. Did he think to mollify her with a dance? Or was he planning on inflaming her in front of Bingley and his sisters? He repeated the question, with some surprise at her silence.

"Oh!" said she, "I heard you before, but I could not immediately determine what to say in reply. You wanted me." She gave a significant pause and looked him in the eye. It was then she saw the realization that his charade was up in his dark eyes. ", I know, to say 'Yes,' that you might have the pleasure of despising my taste; but I always delight in overthrowing those kind of schemes, and cheating a person of their premeditated contempt. I have, therefore, made up my mind to tell you, that I do not want to dance a reel at all or anything else—and now despise me if you dare."

"Indeed I do not dare."

Elizabeth, having rather expected to affront him, was amazed at his gallantry; but there was a mixture of sweetness and archness in her manner which made it difficult for her to affront anybody; and Darcy had never been so bewitched by any woman as he was by her. He really believed that were it not for the inferiority of her connections, he should be in some danger. They stared at each other a bit too long as each remembered the slide of their bodies against each other.

Miss Bingley saw, or suspected enough to be jealous; and her great anxiety for the recovery of her dear friend Jane received some assistance from her desire of getting rid of Elizabeth. Darcy no longer wanted her in the dungeon. He had stopped his punishments of her behavior with the Count once Miss Bennet stumbled upon the dungeon.

She often tried to provoke Darcy into disliking her guest, by talking of their supposed marriage, and planning his happiness in such an alliance. She knew he'd rather marry a cow than marry beneath him.

"I hope," said she, as they were walking together in the shrubbery the next day, you will give your mother-in-law a few hints, when this desirable event takes place, as to the advantage of holding her tongue; and if you can compass it, do cure the younger girls of running after officers. And, if I may mention so delicate a subject, endeavour to check that little something, bordering on conceit and impertinence, which your lady possesses."

"Have you anything else to propose for my

domestic felicity? I have another use for your mouth."

Oh! yes." Miss Bingley said. "But later. Do let the portraits of your uncle and aunt Phillips be placed in the gallery at Pemberley. Put them next to your great-uncle the judge. They are in the same profession, you know, only in different lines. As for your Elizabeth's picture, you must not have it taken, for what painter could do justice to those beautiful eyes?"

"It would not be easy, indeed, to catch their expression, but their colour and shape, and the eyelashes, so remarkably fine, might be copied."

Miss Bingley gaped up at him and at that moment they were met from another walk by Mrs. Hurst and Elizabeth herself.

"I did not know that you intended to walk," said Miss Bingley, in some confusion, lest they had been overheard.

"You used us abominably ill," answered Mrs. Hurst, "running away without telling us that you were coming out."

Then taking the disengaged arm of Mr. Darcy, she left Elizabeth to walk by herself. The path just admitted three. Mr. Darcy felt their rudeness, and immediately said:

"This walk is not wide enough for our party. We had better go into the avenue."

But Elizabeth, who had not the least inclination to remain with them, laughingly answered: "No, no; stay where you are. You are charmingly grouped, and appear to uncommon advantage. The picturesque would be spoilt by admitting a fourth. Good-bye. Have fun," she said with vicious good cheer.

She then ran gaily off, rejoicing as she rambled

about, in the hope of being at home again in a day or two. Jane was already so much recovered as to intend leaving her room for a couple of hours that evening.

Chapter 11

When the ladies removed after dinner, Elizabeth ran up to her sister, and seeing her well guarded from cold, attended her into the drawing-room.

"I should be glad to finally get out of this bed," Jane said. "Although, I can't complain. Both Bingley and his sisters were very generous with their attentions."

"I hope you know that Bingley must never know about you and his sisters," Elizabeth worried.

Jane waved a careless hand and stopped as a fit of coughing shook her.

"Maybe we should go back upstairs?" Elizabeth said.

"Nonsense, I'm fine."

In the drawing room, Jane , where she was welcomed by her two friends with

many professions of pleasure, and Elizabeth had never seen them so agreeable as they were during the hour which passed before the gentlemen appeared. Their powers of conversation were considerable. They could describe an entertainment with accuracy, relate an anecdote with humour, and laugh at their acquaintance with spirit. They seemed truly happy together, and Elizabeth felt a bit like an outsider. She longed to return downstairs for more lessons with the Master of the black mask.

But whenWhen the gentlemen entered, Jane was no longer the first object; Miss Bingley's eyes were instantly turned toward Darcy, and she had something to say to him before he had advanced many steps. He addressed himself to Jane, with a polite congratulation; Mr. Hurst also made her a slight bow, and said he was "very glad;" but diffuseness and warmth remained for Bingley's salutation. He was full of joy and attention. The world seemed to narrow to just the two of them. The first half-hour was spent in piling up the fire, lest she should suffer from the change of room; and she removed at his desire to the other side of the fireplace, that she might be further from the door. He then sat down by her, and talked scarcely to anyone else. Elizabeth, at work in the opposite corner, saw it all with great delight. Bingley was smitten. She saw it in the loving caress of his hands when he thought no one was looking.

When tea was over, Mr. Hurst reminded his sister-in-law of the card-table—but in vain. She had obtained private intelligence that Mr. Darcy did not wish for cards; and Mr. Hurst soon found even his open petition rejected. She assured him that no one intended to play, and the silence of the whole party on the subject seemed to justify her. Mr. Hurst had therefore nothing to do, but to stretch himself on one of the sofas and go to sleep. Darcy took up a book; Miss Bingley did the same; and Mrs. Hurst, principally occupied in playing with her bracelets and rings, joined now and then in her brother's conversation with Jane. Elizabeth was plotting how to leave the room unnoticed and slip downstairs.

Miss Bingley's attention was quite as much engaged in watching Mr. Darcy's progress through his book, as in reading her own; and she was perpetually either making some inquiry, or looking at his page. Miss Bingley tried to catch his attention by lowering her neckline and clearing her throat, encouraging him to look. She could not win him, however, to any conversation; he merely answered her question and read on. At length, quite exhausted by the attempt to be amused with her own book, which she had only chosen because it was the second volume of his, she gave a great yawn and said, "How pleasant it is to spend an evening in this way! I declare after all there is no enjoyment like reading! How much sooner one tires of anything than of a book! When I have a house of my own, I shall be miserable if I have not an excellent library." And a parlour downstairs that I can express my deepest desires in, she thought.

No one made any reply. She then yawned again, threw aside her book, and cast her eyes round the room in quest for some amusement; She eyed Miss Elizabeth Bennet who was inching towards the door. Wetting her lips, Miss Bingley smiled and would have intercepted the chit when Mr. Darcy's hand shot out and grabbed her wrist. Without taking his eyes off his book. He shook his head once. No. Exasperated that she wouldn't be allowed to play with the newest Netherfield plaything, when hearing her brother mentioning a ball to Jane, she turned suddenly towards him and said:

"By the bye, Charles, are you really serious in

meditating a dance at Netherfield? I would advise you, before you determine on it, to consult the wishes of the present party; I am much mistaken if there are not some among us to whom a ball would be rather a punishment than a pleasure."

"There are some that take pleasure in punishment," Elizabeth said, softly. Mr. Darcy rose from his chair and would have gone to her, but Bingley's laughter brought him back to his seat.

"If you mean Darcy," cried Bingley, "he may go to bed, if he chooses, before it begins, or during for all I care—but as for the ball, it is quite a settled thing; and as soon as Nicholls has made white soup enough, I shall send round my cards."

"I thought you were a great fan of balls, Miss Bingley," Mr. Darcy said with a hint of dryness in his voice.

"I should like balls infinitely better," she replied, "if they were carried on in a different manner." She eyed him boldly, moving in to block Elizabeth from his sight. "But there is something insufferably tedious in the usual process of such a meeting. It would surely be much more rational if conversation instead of dancing were made the order of the day."

"Much more rational, my dear Caroline, I dare say, but it would not be near so much like a ball."

Miss Bingley made no answer, and soon afterwards she got up and walked about the room. Her figure was elegant, and she walked well; but Darcy, at whom it was all aimed, was still inflexibly studious. In the desperation of her feelings, she resolved on one effort more, and, turning to Elizabeth, said:

"Miss Eliza Bennet, let me persuade you to follow

my example, and take a turn about the room. I assure you it is very refreshing after sitting so long in one attitude."

Mr. Darcy arched her a warning look, but let Miss Bingley slide an arm through Elizabeth's without comment. Bingley took the distraction to kiss Jane on the neck, licking slightly at the delicate white skin. Jane, in turn, placed her blanket as to hide her hand rubbing his trousers.

Elizabeth was surprised, but agreed to it immediately. She brushed her breast into Miss Bingley's arm. While she didn't like her Mistress personally, Elizabeth longed to be touched again. Mr. Darcy looked up. He was as much awake to the novelty of attention in that quarter as Elizabeth herself could be, and unconsciously he closed his book. He was directly invited to join their party, but he declined it, observing that he could imagine but two motives for their choosing to walk up and down the room together, with either of which motives his joining them would interfere.

"What could he mean? Miss Bingley asked. Was it possible he would allow the three of them to play together? She asked Elizabeth whether she could at all understand him.

"Not at all," was her answer; "but depend upon it, he means to be severe on us, and our surest way of disappointing him will be to ask nothing about it." Elizabeth smiled triumphantly at Mr. Darcy.

Miss Bingley, however, was incapable of disappointing Mr. Darcy in anything, and persevered therefore in requiring an explanation of his two motives.

"I have not the smallest objection to explaining them," said he, as soon as she allowed him to speak. "You either choose this method of passing the evening because you are in each other's confidence, and have secret affairs to discuss, or because you are conscious that your figures appear to the greatest advantage in walking; if the first, I would be completely in your way, and if the second, I can admire you much better as I sit by the fire."

"Oh! shocking!" cried Miss Bingley. "I never heard anything so abominable. How shall we punish him for such a speech?"

"Nothing so easy, if you have but the inclination," said Elizabeth. "We can all plague and punish one another. Tease him—laugh at him. Intimate as you are, you must know how it is to be done." Riding crops and leather gloves came to mind.

"But upon my honour, I do not. I do assure you that my intimacy has not yet taught me that."

Elizabeth caught her disbelieving snort behind a cough.

"I hope you are not taken ill as well," Mr. Darcy said. "But if we are, you are welcome to recover in the upper bedrooms as your sister has."

Jane jumped a bit at hearing herself mentioned. Bingley was breathing through

his teeth, and she looked a little disheveled. But no one paid them any mind.

"Tease calmness of manner and presence of mind!" Miss Bingley continued. "No, no; I feel he may defy us there. And as to laughter, we will not expose ourselves, if you please, by attempting to laugh without a subject. Mr. Darcy may hug himself."

Elizabeth's stomach was quivering. She would very much like to expose herself and hug Mr. Darcy – if it was indeed him in the black mask.

"Mr. Darcy is not to be laughed at!" cried Elizabeth. "That is an uncommon advantage, and uncommon I hope it will continue, for it would be a great loss to me to have many such acquaintances. I dearly love a laugh."

"Miss Bingley," said he, "has given me more credit than can be."

Miss Bingley curtsied at him mockingly.

" The wisest and the best of men—nay, the wisest and best of their actions—may be rendered ridiculous by a person whose first object in life is a joke," he said.

"Certainly," replied Elizabeth—"there are such people, but I hope I am not one of them. I hope I never ridicule what is wise and good. Follies and nonsense, whims and inconsistencies, do divert me, I own, and I laugh at them whenever I can. But these, I suppose, are precisely what you are without."

"Perhaps that is not possible for anyone," Darcy replied, deftly removing her arm from Miss Bingley's. He started to walk with her towards the drawing room door." But it has been the study of my life to avoid those weaknesses which often expose a strong understanding to ridicule."

"Such as vanity and pride," Elizabeth said, her heart beating loud in her ears.

"Yes, vanity is a weakness indeed. But pride— where there is a real superiority of mind, pride will be always under good regulation."

Elizabeth turned away to hide a smile.

"Your examination of Mr. Darcy is over, I

presume," said Miss Bingley; "and pray what is the result?" She followed them, almost on their heels.

"I am perfectly convinced by it that Mr. Darcy has no defect. He owns it himself without disguise," Elizabeth said, and turned so his arm brushed across her hardened nipples.

"No," said Darcy, "I have made no such pretension. I have faults enough, but they are not, I hope, of understanding. My temper I dare not vouch for. It is, I believe, too little yielding—certainly too little for the convenience of the world. I cannot forget the follies and vices of others so soon as I ought, nor their offenses against myself. My feelings are not puffed about with every attempt to move them. My temper would perhaps be called resentful. My good opinion once lost, is lost forever." He pulled Elizabeth along and left the drawing room, closing the door firmly on Miss Bingley when she would follow.

"That is a failing indeed!" cried Elizabeth. "Implacable resentment is a shade in a character. But you have chosen your fault well. I really cannot laugh at it. You are safe from me."

"Let us have no more games. I will take you downstairs for your next lesson. There is, I believe, in every disposition a tendency to some particular evil—a natural defect, which not even the best education can overcome."

"And your defect is to hate everybody."

"And yours," he replied with a smile, "is willfully to misunderstand them."

He began to feel the danger of paying Elizabeth too much attention.

They were in her favorite room downstairs when

he ordered her to remove her garments.

"I cannot do that," she protested.

"Very well," he said and went to leave.

"Wait," she said, unsure.

"I can strip you of your clothes."

"Yes, Master," she breathed in relief and then her eyes widened when he took a large carving knife from one of tables.

He advanced on her. She held her ground. He grabbed a fist full of her bodice and pulled her into him. His mouth was bruising on her lips, grinding into her teeth til she tasted blood. Elizabeth tried to struggle away, but the ripping sound the knife made when it pierced her dress forced her to remain stock still lest she be cut with the sawing motions. Darcy finished the punishing kiss and dragged the ruined dress to her waist.

"That hurt," she said, touching her mouth.

"You defied me. Now remove the rest of your clothes or I will punish you more."

He tossed the knife on the table and stripped his own clothes off with quick, efficient movements. He went to the wall and pulled down a long reed, with a small paddle attached to it.

Elizabeth's were more awkward and she was blushing when she removed the last of her undergarments.

"Yes," Darcy breathed, putting the reed in her mouth so he could run both his hands over her body. "So beautiful. So fine. Why are you suddenly shy, my wanton darling?" He removed the reed and cracked it against his palm. She flinched.

"The mask, it covered you before. I could pretend

it was all a fantasy. Seeing your face," Elizabeth's hands touched the bobbing head of his thick member. "And touching you thus, has made this reality."

"Get on your knees," Mr. Darcy said gently. "And show me what your mouth can do aside from argue with me and spout nonsense."

Elizabeth sank to her knees. Tentatively, she licked his member from bottom to top.

He snapped the reed down on her bare bottom and she yelped.

"Take me in your mouth."

"Yes, Master," she said and stretched her mouth wide over his throbbing phallus.

"Good," he crooned and clutched a handful of her hair. He forced himself deeper. "Open up your throat. Take me all in. That's a slut."

Elizabeth nearly choked at the length of him, but his movements were swift and she allowed him to manipulate her head up and down on him. How different he was from Charlotte's brother, who squirted in a second and ran away in embarrassment. Mr. Darcy was hard and strong. She was thrilled by the way his big body trembled as his large member slid around her mouth. Tightening her mouth around him, she sucked hard, feeling the hard kiss of the tip of him pushing between her lips.

"Elizabeth, ah, Elizabeth what you do to me."

Mr. Darcy kept her on her knees until she made him spill his seed twice more. When she dared ask for some relief for herself, he forced her on all fours.

"Am I to be a horse?" she wondered.

"I'm going to start with my fingers here." He glided his fingers over her wet heat to dance around

122

the puckered circle at the top of her bottom.

"Will I wear a diamond plug?" Elizabeth breathed.

"No, you are not owned yet. Should you come to Netherfield permanently, I will fit you with one myself."

"I haven't decided," she said. One moment she was restless to leave this place and her own darker desires, and, yet, she kept coming back.

"Then let me convince you." He poured warmed oil over her backside. He pushed some inside her with a gentle finger.

Elizabeth cried out.

"You are no stranger to questing fingers," he said.

"Not there," she sighed. "Only in the other passage."

"Hmmm," Darcy said and there was a note in his tone she couldn't decipher.

"Oh," she gasped when his finger slipped inside her.

"Gently now," he soothed her as if she was a wild horse. Her hair hung in sweaty ringlets around her face and her fine eyes were dazed with passion. Her lips taut with the effort she had spent, yet she quivered under his touch. "You are stunning. Are you sure I can't have you as a man has a woman?"

"I must remain a virgin," she cried as he stretched her ever so gently with one more finger.

He moved closer, so an oiled hand slicked over her breast and he massaged it with his palm as his fingers pumped inside her.

"But my sweet Elizabeth, you are no longer a virgin."

"What?" Her head snapped up. Those fine eyes no longer languid.

"The sex play you and Charlotte did? When her fingers entered your other passage," Darcy slid his hand down from her breast to her wet bud, probing as she reacted as if lightning had struck her. "When she did this. . ." He pushed three fingers into her passage.

Elizabeth clamped her muscles around his fingers. He filled her front and back and she shook from need.

"She broke your wall of virginity. Although you have known no man's member here." He pumped his hand faster. "You have been compromised."

"Oh." Despair and ecstasy fought each other. In the end, the driving need for release had her give up to his ministrations, and she flooded his hand on a sigh that suspiciously sounded like a sob.

He kissed down her spine. She felt his hardness rubbing against thigh.

"You have a lot to think about, my dear. Think about becoming my submissive at Netherfield. I will teach you joy and pain. You will learn true power and control. I guarantee you that you will bewitch yourself a husband who will not care about your youthful exploits."

He covered his body over hers, kneeing apart her thighs; she felt his thickness so close to her core that she ached for him inside her. She knew one thrust of her hips and he would impale her. Darcy kissed her sweetly, lovingly. "There will be no other for me or for you while I train you. You have captivated me so."

Elizabeth's head was reeling. Her body demanding his. It was too soon. She was not ready to devote herself to the proclivities of Netherfield. He trailed kisses down to her neck and when his teeth grazed her collarbone, she knew she would submit if she didn't stop him.

"But you must come to me of your own volition. There cannot be any hesitation on your part. I will be your lord and master. You will obey me or you will be punished."

He took her breast into his mouth and swirled her nipple around his tongue.

"Oh," Elizabeth held on tightly to his broad shoulders. She had no sense when it came to him. She was rapidly losing herself in the pulling sensations as he sucked the tips of her breasts with hard tugs.

"You will stay here at Netherfield to be trained, like Inga."

She would be on her hands and knees during card games. Elizabeth wasn't sure she was ready for that. She wanted his kisses and his hands all over her. She wanted the new experiences, but she wasn't prepared to pay his cost. A part of her started to hate him then.

She ran her fingers through his wavy black hair as he kissed her insensible again. She pulled his head from hers.

"Jane," she breathed, calling out for her sister to signal him to stop.

He tensed and for a horrifying moment, Elizabeth thought he wouldn't stop. It frightened and thrilled her to have the decision taken from her. Her legs parted and she was raising her hips to meet his hardness when he launched himself off her.

He left the room without another word. Elizabeth could only lay there, still tasting him in her mouth, feeling the rough push of him in the back of her neck.

She still felt his fingers in her most intimate places, but before long the temperature cooled her, and she was forced to find her bed. Alone.

Chapter 12

In consequence of an agreement between the sisters, Elizabeth wrote the next morning to their mother, to beg that the carriage might be sent for them in the course of the day. But Mrs. Bennet, who had calculated on her daughters remaining at Netherfield till the following Tuesday, which would exactly finish Jane's week, could not bring herself to receive them with pleasure before. But Elizabeth had enough of pleasure and of Darcy's mocking words. She desired to be more than a Netherfield slave, but her dowry was too small for him to see her as anything serious. It pained her to stay.

Her mother's answer, therefore, was not propitious, at least not to Elizabeth's wishes, for she was impatient to get home. Mrs. Bennet sent them word that they could not possibly have the carriage before Tuesday; and in her postscript it was added, that if Mr. Bingley and his sister pressed them to stay longer, she could spare them very well.

Of that Elizabeth had no doubt. When she finally found the energy to mount the stairs to the bedroom she shared with Jane, she had to hide herself as Bingley snuck out. He had been buttoning up his trousers. Jane was fast asleep, so Elizabeth couldn't question her on what happened.

Against staying longer, however, Elizabeth was positively resolved—nor did she much expect it would be asked; and fearful, on the contrary, as being considered as intruding themselves needlessly long, she urged Jane to borrow Mr. Bingley's carriage immediately, and at length it was settled that their original design of leaving Netherfield that morning should be mentioned, and the request made.

The communication excited many professions of concern; and enough was said of wishing them to stay at least till the following day to work on Jane; and till the morrow their going was deferred. Miss Bingley was then sorry that she had proposed the delay, for her jealousy and dislike of one sister much exceeded her affection for the other. She would miss Jane's sweet tongue.

The master of the house heard with real sorrow that they were to go so soon, and repeatedly tried to persuade Miss Jane Bennet that it would not be safe for her—that she was not enough recovered; but Jane was firm where she felt herself to be right. They had stayed too long and risked becoming as comfortable as the servants who became tables during card games.

To Mr. Darcy it was welcome intelligence— Elizabeth had been at Netherfield long enough. She attracted him more than he liked—and Miss Bingley was uncivil to her, and more teasing than usual to himself. Elizabeth had to come to him willingly. He knew he could force her, ravage her and take advantage of her innocence. He wisely resolved to be particularly careful that no sign of admiration should now escape him, nothing that could elevate her with the hope of influencing his felicity; sensible that if such an idea had been suggested, his behaviour during the last day must have material weight in confirming or crushing it. Marriage between them was preposterous. She would be an excellent slave or submissive, maybe even his long term. But she seemed to want more. Wanted to rise above her station and he couldn't give her the hope that she would achieve that with him. Steady to his purpose, he scarcely spoke ten words to her through the whole of Saturday, and though they were at one time left by themselves for half-an-hour, he adhered most conscientiously to his book, and would not even look at her. Not even when her eyes clung to him as sweetly as her mouth had.

On Sunday, after morning service, the separation, so agreeable to almost all, took place. Miss Bingley's civility to Elizabeth increased at last very rapidly, as well as her affection for Jane; and when they parted, after assuring the latter of the pleasure it would always give her to see her either at Longbourn or Netherfield, and embracing her most tenderly, she even shook hands with the former. Elizabeth took leave of the whole party in the liveliest of spirits. It would be good to get home: to break the haze of sensuality she had wrapped herself in. Normalcy would shake some sense into her. Mr. Darcy had to be mistaken about her virginity. She had known no man. So what if a flimsy barrier no longer existed?

They were not welcomed home very cordially by their mother. Mrs. Bennet wondered at their coming, and thought them very wrong to give so much trouble, and was sure Jane would have caught cold again. But their father, though very laconic in his expressions of pleasure, was really glad to see them; he had felt their importance in the family circle. The evening conversation, when they were all assembled, had lost much of its animation, and almost all its sense by the absence of Jane and Elizabeth.

They found Mary, as usual, deep in the study of thorough-bass and human nature; and had some extracts to admire, and some new observations of threadbare morality to listen to.

Catherine and Lydia had information for them of a different sort. Much had been done and much had been said in the regiment since the preceding Wednesday; several of the officers had dined lately with their uncle, a private had been flogged, and it had actually been hinted that Colonel Forster was going to be married. Elizabeth's ears perked up at the flogging, and she wiggled in her seat as she remembered the quick blows of the paddle on her posterior as she held Mr. Darcy deep in her throat.

Chapter 13

"I hope, my dear," said Mr. Bennet to his wife, as they were at breakfast the next morning, "that you have ordered a good dinner to-day, because I have reason to expect an addition to our family party."

"Who do you mean, my dear? I know of nobody that is coming, I am sure, unless Charlotte Lucas should happen to call in—and I hope my dinners are good enough for her. I do not believe she often sees such at home."

Elizabeth hoped Charlotte would call. She couldn't wait to tell her friend all about Netherfield and see what she thought about the submissive proposition.

"The person of whom I speak is a gentleman, and a stranger."

Mrs. Bennet's eyes sparkled. "A gentleman and a stranger! It is Mr. Bingley, I am sure! Well, I am sure I shall be extremely glad to see Mr. Bingley. But—good Lord! how unlucky! There is not a bit of fish to be got to-day. Lydia, my love, ring the bell—I must speak to Hill this moment."

Jane smiled down at her breakfast plate, heart thumping in tune to the heated buzz between her legs.

The passion she and Mr. Bingley shared the night she left was forefront in her mind; she could barely concentrate on her breakfast. His hands were so sure, his lips so tender.

"It is not Mr. Bingley," said her husband; "it is a person whom I never saw in the whole course of my life."

This roused a general astonishment; and he had the pleasure of being eagerly questioned by his wife and his five daughters at once.

Catherine and Lydia whispered to each other which officer they thought would visit them. Would it be the one who liked to wear women's undergarments? Or the one who liked to be led around the room with a collar and leash?

After amusing himself some time with their curiosity, Mr. Bennet thus explained: "About a month ago I received this letter; and about a fortnight ago I answered it, for I thought it a case of some delicacy, and requiring early attention. It is from my cousin, Mr. Collins, who, when I am dead, may turn you all out of this house as soon as he pleases."

Mary thought it would be nice to be turned out of this house. Perhaps, she could truly find freedom away from her oppressive mother and sisters who were either above reproach or cackling shrews. She sniffed and went back to her eggs.

"Oh! my dear," cried his wife, "I cannot bear to hear that mentioned. Pray do not talk of that odious man. I do think it is the hardest thing in the world, that your estate should be entailed away from your own children; and I am sure, if I had been you, I should have tried long ago to do something or other about it."

Jane and Elizabeth tried to explain to her the nature of an entail. They had often attempted to do it before, but it was a subject on which Mrs. Bennet was beyond the reach of reason, and she continued to rail bitterly against the cruelty of settling an estate away from a family of five daughters, in favour of a man whom nobody cared anything about.

"It certainly is a most iniquitous affair," said Mr. Bennet, "and nothing can clear Mr. Collins from the guilt of inheriting Longbourn. "

" I think it is very impertinent of him to write to you at all, and very hypocritical. I hate such false friends. Why could he not keep on quarreling with you, as his father did before him?"

Mr. Bennet read the letter to his family, pointing out that Mr. Collins had been so fortunate as to be distinguished by the patronage of the Right Honourable Lady Catherine de Bourgh, widow of Sir Lewis de Bourgh, whose bounty and beneficence was well known, as was her ministrations as the Domme of the ton before she retired. It was rumoured that she took an apprentice on once per year. However, Mr. Collins was merely a clergyman.

"At four o'clock, therefore, we may expect this peace-making gentleman," said Mr. Bennet, as he folded up the letter. "He seems to be a most conscientious and polite young man, upon my word, and I doubt not will prove a valuable acquaintance, especially if Lady Catherine should be so indulgent as to let him come to us again."

"If he is disposed to make amends, I shall not be the person to discourage him."

133

"Though it is difficult," said Jane, "to guess in what way he can mean to make us the atonement he thinks our due, the wish is certainly to his credit."

Elizabeth was chiefly struck by his extraordinary deference for Lady Catherine. Had he been at one time her submissive? Perhaps he still was. If she was only a man, she would be able to ask him. Maybe her father knew and would let some clue slip out in his conversation.

"He must be an oddity, I think," said she. "I cannot make him out.—There is something very pompous in his style.—And what can he mean by apologising for being next in the entail?—We cannot suppose he would help it if he could.—Could he be a sub—I mean sensible man, sir?"

"No, my dear, I think not. I have great hopes of finding him quite the reverse. There is a mixture of servility and self-importance in his letter, which promises well. I am impatient to see him."

"In point of composition," said Mary, "the letter does not seem defective. The idea of the olive-branch perhaps is not wholly new, yet I think it is well expressed."

To Catherine and Lydia, neither the letter nor its writer were in any degree interesting. It was next to impossible that their cousin should come in a scarlet coat, and it was now some weeks since they had received pleasure from a man in any other colour. As for their mother, Mr. Collins's letter had done away much of her ill-will, and she was preparing to see him with a degree of composure which astonished her husband and daughters.

Mrs. Bennet had figured there was only one way

to make sure she and her girls were not tossed out into the mud, should the unthinkable happen and her dear Mr. Bennet should pass first.

Mr. Collins was punctual to his time, and was received with great politeness by the whole family. Mr. Bennet indeed said little; but the ladies were ready enough to talk, and Mr. Collins seemed neither in need of encouragement, nor inclined to be silent himself.

He was a tall, heavy-looking young man of five-and-twenty. His air was grave and stately, and his manners were very formal. He had not been long seated before he complimented Mrs. Bennet on having so fine a family of daughters; said he had heard much of their beauty, but that in this instance fame had fallen short of the truth; and added, that he did not doubt her seeing them all in due time disposed of in marriage.

This gallantry was not much to the taste of some of his hearers; but Mrs. Bennet, who quarreled with no compliments, answered most readily, mentally rolling her sleeves up as if she were about to work with bread dough."You are very kind, I am sure; and I wish with all my heart it may prove so, for else they will be destitute enough. Things are settled so oddly."

"You allude, perhaps, to the entail of this estate."

"Ah! sir, I do indeed. It is a grievous affair to my poor lovely girls, you must confess. Not that I mean to find fault with you, for such things I know are all chance in this world. There is no knowing how estates will go when once they come to be entailed." Mrs. Bennet peered at him under her eyelashes.

"I am very sensible, madam, of the hardship to my fair cousins, and could say much on the subject, but that I am cautious of appearing forward and

135

precipitate. But I can assure the young ladies that I come prepared to admire them. At present I will not say more; but, perhaps, when we are better acquainted—"

He was interrupted by a summons to dinner; and the girls smiled on each other. They were not the only objects of Mr. Collins's admiration. The hall, the dining-room, and all its furniture, were examined and praised; and his commendation of everything would have touched Mrs. Bennet's heart, but for the mortifying supposition of his viewing it all as his own future property. The dinner too in its turn was highly admired; and he begged to know to which of his fair cousins the excellency of its cooking was owing. But he was set right there by Mrs. Bennet, who assured him with some asperity that they were very well able to keep a good cook, and that her daughters had nothing to do in the kitchen. He begged pardon for having displeased her. In a softened tone she declared herself not at all offended; but he continued to apologise for about a quarter of an hour.

Elizabeth cocked her head. At one point, she would have sworn he almost called her mother, Mistress.

Chapter 14

During dinner, Mr. Bennet scarcely spoke at all; but when the servants were withdrawn, he thought it time to have some conversation with his guest, and therefore started a subject in which he expected him to shine, by observing that he seemed very fortunate in his patroness.

Lady Catherine de Bourgh's attention to his wishes, and consideration for his comfort, appeared very remarkable. Mr. Bennet could not have chosen better. Mr. Collins was eloquent in her praise. The subject elevated him to more than usual solemnity of manner, and with a most important aspect he protested that "he had never in his life witnessed such behaviour in a person of rank—such affability and condescension, as he had himself experienced from Lady Catherine. She had been graciously pleased to approve of both of the discourses which he had already had the honour of preaching before her. She had also asked him twice to dine at Rosings, and had sent for him only the Saturday before, to make up her pool of quadrille in the evening.

Elizabeth wondered if Rosings had a dungeon like Netherfield and if their quadrille was done fully clothed. If Lady Catherine's reputation was as debauched as Netherfield was, she could only imagine what was expected of Mr. Collins,

Lady Catherine was reckoned proud by many people he knew, but he had never seen anything but affability in her. She had always spoken to him as she would to any other gentleman; she made not the smallest objection to his joining in the society of the neighbourhood nor to his leaving the parish occasionally for a week or two, to visit his relations. She had even condescended to advise him to marry as soon as he could, provided he chose with discretion; and had once paid him a visit in his humble parsonage, where she had perfectly approved all the alterations he had been making, and had even vouchsafed to suggest some herself—some shelves in the closet up stairs."

Elizabeth would have liked to have been a bird in a tree during those visits. She shared a smile with Jane.

"That is all very proper and civil, I am sure," said Mrs. Bennet, "and I dare say she is a very agreeable woman, albeit notorious in some manners. It is a pity that great ladies in general are not more like her with their condescending airs. Does she live near you, sir?"

"The garden in which stands my humble abode is separated only by a lane from Rosings Park, her ladyship's residence."

"I think you said she was a widow, sir? Has she any family?"

"She has only one daughter, the heiress of Rosings, and of very extensive property."

"Ah!" said Mrs. Bennet, shaking her head, "then she is better off than many girls. And what sort of young lady is she? Is she handsome?"

"She is a most charming young lady indeed. She is unfortunately of a sickly constitution, which has prevented her from making that progress in many accomplishments which she could not have otherwise failed of, as I am informed by the lady who superintended her education, and who still resides with them. But she is perfectly amiable, and often condescends to drive by my humble abode in her little phaeton and ponies."

"Has she been presented? I do not remember her name among the ladies at court."

"Her indifferent state of health unhappily prevents her being in town; and by that means, as I told Lady Catherine one day, has deprived the British court of its brightest ornament. Her ladyship seemed pleased with the idea; and you may imagine that I am happy on every occasion to offer those little delicate compliments which are always acceptable to ladies."

Elizabeth restrained a giggle at the eye roll that Jane sent her and determined herself not to look at her sister again lest she'd be snickering like Lydia and Catherine in front of their guest.

" I have more than once observed to Lady Catherine, that her charming daughter seemed born to be a duchess," Mr. Collins continued. "And that the most elevated rank, instead of giving her consequence, would be adorned by her. These are the kind of little things which please her ladyship, and it is a sort of attention which I conceive myself peculiarly bound to pay."

"You judge very properly," said Mr. Bennet, "and it is happy for you that you possess the talent of flattering with delicacy. May I ask whether these pleasing attentions proceed from the impulse of the moment, or are the result of previous study?"

"They arise chiefly from what is passing at the time, and though I sometimes amuse myself with suggesting and arranging such little elegant compliments as may be adapted to ordinary occasions, I always wish to give them as unstudied an air as possible."

Mr. Bennet's expectations were fully answered. His cousin was as absurd as he had hoped, and he listened to him with the keenest enjoyment, maintaining at the same time the most resolute composure of countenance, and, except in an occasional glance at Elizabeth, who was equally amused.

Chapter 15

Mr. Collins was not a sensible man, and the deficiency of nature had been but little assisted by education or society; the greatest part of his life having been spent under the guidance of an illiterate and miserly father; and though he belonged to one of the universities, he had merely kept the necessary terms, without forming at it any useful acquaintance.

The subjection in which his father had brought him up had given him originally great humility of manner; but it was now a good deal counteracted by the self-conceit of a weak head, living in retirement, and the consequential feelings of early and unexpected prosperity. A fortunate chance had recommended him to Lady Catherine de Bourgh when the living of Hunsford was vacant; and the respect which he felt for her high rank, and his veneration for her as his patroness, mingling with a very good opinion of himself, of his authority as a clergyman, and his right as a rector, made him altogether a mixture of pride and obsequiousness, self-importance and humility.

The former Domme of the ton, took him in and made his father's rearings seem almost nurturing in comparison. But Mr. Collins was very comfortable being fitted with a leash and walking on all fours in the

141

nude across marble ballrooms. Especially, when he was rewarded by being allowed to lick his Mistress' shiny black boots. Lady Catherine rewarded him most handsomely for his subservience, most of which was all his pleasure. He lived for her mean words and quick punishments with a lash.

Having now a good house and a very sufficient income, Mr. Collins intended to marry; and in seeking a reconciliation he meant to choose one of the Bennet daughters, if he found them as handsome and amiable as they were represented by common report. This was his plan of amends—of atonement—for inheriting their father's estate; and he thought it an excellent one, full of eligibility and suitableness, and excessively generous and disinterested on his own part.

His plan did not vary on seeing them. Miss Jane Bennet's lovely face confirmed his views, and established all his strictest notions of what was due to seniority; and for the first evening she was his settled choice. The next morning, however, made an alteration; for in a quarter of an hour's tete-a-tete with Mrs. Bennet before breakfast, she cautioned him against the very one he had fixed on.

"As to my younger daughters, I could not take upon it to say—I could not positively answer—but I do not know of any prepossession; my eldest daughter, I must just mention—I felt it incumbent to hint, was likely to be very soon engaged." Mrs. Bennet said, trying to be as implicit as possible without causing offense.

Mr. Collins had only to change from Jane to Elizabeth—and it was soon done—done while Mrs. Bennet was stirring the fire. Elizabeth, equally next to

Jane in birth and beauty, succeeded her of course.

Mrs. Bennet treasured up the hint, and trusted that she might soon have two daughters married; and the man whom she could not bear to speak of the day before was now high in her good graces.

Lydia spoke an intention of walking to Meryton .Every sister except Mary agreed to go with her; and Mr. Collins was to attend them, at the request of Mr. Bennet, who was most anxious to get rid of him, and have his library to himself. In his library he had been always sure of leisure and tranquility; and though prepared, as he told Elizabeth, to meet with folly and conceit in every other room of the house, he was used to be free from them there; his civility, therefore, was most prompt in inviting Mr. Collins to join his daughters in their walk; and Mr. Collins, being in fact much better fitted for a walker than a reader, was extremely pleased to close his large book, and go.

In pompous nothings on his side, and civil assents on that of his cousins, their time passed till they entered Meryton. The attention of the younger ones was then no longer to be gained by him. Lydia's and Catherine's eyes were immediately wandering up in the street in quest of the officers, and nothing less than a very smart bonnet indeed, or a really new muslin in a shop window, could recall them.

But the attention of every lady was soon caught by a young man, whom they had never seen before, of most gentlemanlike appearance, walking with another officer on the other side of the way. The officer bowed as they passed. All were struck with the stranger's air, all wondered who he could be; and Kitty and Lydia, determined if possible to find out, led the way across the street, under pretense of wanting something in an opposite shop, and fortunately had just gained the pavement when the two gentlemen, turning back, had reached the same spot.

Mr. Denny addressed them directly, and entreated permission to introduce his friend, Mr. Wickham, who had returned with him the day before from town, and he was happy to say had accepted a commission in their corps. This was exactly as it should be; for the young man wanted only regimentals to make him completely charming.

His appearance was greatly in his favour; he had all the best part of beauty, a fine countenance, a good figure, and very pleasing address. The introduction was followed up on his side by a happy readiness of conversation—a readiness at the same time perfectly correct and unassuming; and the whole party were still standing and talking together very agreeably, when the sound of horses drew their notice, and Darcy and Bingley were seen riding down the street.

Elizabeth felt his stare, and it took everything in her not to go to him, kneel down in front of his horse and ask him to please, Master, please teach me.

On distinguishing the ladies of the group, the two gentlemen came directly towards them, and began the usual civilities. Bingley was the principal spokesman, and Miss Jane Bennet the principal object. He was then, he said, on his way to Longbourn on purpose to inquire after her.

Jane was equally entranced with Mr. Bingley. She gave him her sweetest smiles and dabbed the top of her lips with her tongue. Mr. Bingley stuttered over his greetings, and they stared longingly at each other, constrained by society. If only she was in his guest room again, feeling his soft touch undressing her.

Mr. Darcy was beginning to determine not to fix his eyes on Elizabeth, when they were suddenly arrested by the sight of the stranger, and Elizabeth happening to see the countenance of both as they looked at each other, was all astonishment at the effect of the meeting. Both changed colour, one looked white, the other red. Mr. Wickham, after a few moments, touched his hat—a salutation which Mr. Darcy just deigned to return. What could be the meaning of it? It was impossible to imagine; it was impossible not to long to know. Could Mr. Wickham have been in the dungeon of Netherfield under Mr. Darcy's tutelage? Elizabeth pressed her hands to her suddenly hot cheeks. She was seeing submissives and dominants everywhere.

In another minute, Mr. Bingley, but without seeming to have noticed what passed, took leave and rode on with his friend.

Jane took a step forward, as if she would follow.

Mr. Denny and Mr. Wickham walked with the young ladies to the door of Mr. Phillip's house, and then made their bows, in spite of Miss Lydia's pressing entreaties that they should come in, and even in spite of Mrs. Phillips's throwing up the parlour window and loudly seconding the invitation.

"Denny, bring up your new friend. Let's see what he can offer."

"Perhaps later, Mistress Phillips," Denny said and bowed.

She narrowed her eyes at him, her expression showing that he would feel her displeasure at a later

145

date. It appeared that Denny was eager for that.

Mrs. Phillips was always glad to see her nieces; and the two eldest, from their recent absence, were particularly welcome, and she was eagerly expressing her surprise at their sudden return home, which, as their own carriage had not fetched them, when her civility was claimed towards Mr. Collins by Jane's introduction of him.

She received him with her very best politeness, which he returned with as much more, apologising for his intrusion, without any previous acquaintance with her, which he could not help flattering himself, however, might be justified by his relationship to the young ladies who introduced him to her notice. Mrs. Phillips was quite awed by such an excess of good breeding of such a submissive young man, but her contemplation of one stranger was soon put to an end by exclamations and inquiries about the dashing Mr. Wickham; of whom, however, she could only tell her nieces what they already knew, that Mr. Denny had brought him from London, and that he was to have a lieutenant's commission.

She had been watching him the last hour, she said, as he walked up and down the street, and had Mr. Wickham appeared, Kitty and Lydia would certainly have continued the occupation, but unluckily no one passed windows now except a few of the officers, who, in comparison with the stranger, were become "stupid, disagreeable fellows."

Some of them were to dine with the Phillipses the next day, and their aunt promised to make her husband call on Mr. Wickham, and give him an invitation also, if the family from Longbourn would come in the evening. Kitty and Lydia were ecstatic at the chance to fondle the new lieutenant. This was agreed to, and Mrs. Phillips protested that they would have a nice comfortable noisy game of lottery tickets, and a little bit of hot supper afterwards. The prospect of such delights was very cheering, and they parted in mutual good spirits. Mr. Collins repeated his apologies in quitting the room, and was assured with unwearying civility that they were perfectly needless. Mrs. Phillips took him aside.

"Give us a moment, dears," she said and left Jane and Elizabeth to ride herd on their younger sisters' quest to follow officers up and down the street.

"Madame?" Mr. Collins inquired.

Mrs. Phillips whipped her glove across his cheek. "Mistress, as you well know."

Mr. Collins flushed with pleasure and gratitude and sank to his knees to grovel at her feet. "Forgive me, Mistress."

"You apologize so sweetly. I'm a bit disappointed we have only a short time before my nieces miss your presence."

"I am so sorry, Mistress. I am unworthy of such attention."

"Yes, you are. But you may kiss my shoes."

"Oh thank you, sweet, kind Mistress," he said, lavishing affectionate kisses on her shoes and ankles.

"You are an ardent one aren't you," Mrs. Phillips whispered. "What I would do to you with a crop and pinchers."

Mr. Collins visibly shuddered in pleasure.

"Stand up," she ordered.

"Yes, Mistress."

147

"If you kiss my lips as feverishly as you did my shoes, I will punish you with a sweet lashing tomorrow."

Mr. Collins took her into his arms and kissed her until they were both breathless.

"I will have you naked under my whip," Mrs. Phillips promised with a rough grope to his nether regions.

"I am yours, utterly," he vowed, leaning into the caress.

"Now, rejoin my nieces and see them safely back home." She slapped him again, turning his head with the force of the blow.

Mr. Collins licked a dot of blood from the corner of his mouth.

"As my mistress commands." He bowed and went to find the Bennet sisters.

As they walked home, Elizabeth related to Jane what she had seen pass between the Mr. Darcy and Mr. Wickham, but though Jane would have defended either or both, had they appeared to be in the wrong, she could no more explain such behaviour than her sister.

Mr. Collins on his return highly gratified Mrs. Bennet by admiring Mrs. Phillips's manners and politeness. He protested that, except Lady Catherine and her daughter, he had never seen a more elegant woman; for she had not only received him with the utmost civility, but even pointedly included him in her invitation for the next evening, although utterly unknown to her before. Something, he supposed, might be attributed to his connection with them, but yet he had never met with so much attention in the whole course of his life.

Chapter 16

As no objection was made to the young people's engagement with their aunt, and all Mr. Collins's scruples of leaving Mr. and Mrs. Bennet for a single evening during his visit were most steadily resisted, the coach conveyed him and his five cousins at a suitable hour to Meryton; and the girls had the pleasure of hearing, as they entered the drawing-room, that Mr. Wickham had accepted their uncle's invitation, and was then in the house.

Kitty and Lydia could barely contain their glee at being in such close proximity to all the officers. They whirled around the room, too nervous to sit. Lydia casually listened at doors for signs of their approach. Kitty plotted the best place in the room where she could stand in the best light and be admired.

Mr. Collins was at leisure to look around him and admire, and he was so much struck with the size and furniture of the apartment, that he declared he might almost have supposed himself in the small summer breakfast parlour at Rosings; a comparison that did not at first convey much gratification; but when Mrs. Phillips understood from him what Rosings was, and who was its proprietor—when she had listened to the description of only one of Lady Catherine's drawing-rooms, and found that the chimney-piece alone had cost eight hundred pounds, she felt all the force of the compliment, and would hardly have resented a comparison with the housekeeper's room.

"Come, Mr. Collins, let me show you the rest of the house. I've heard of Lady Catherine. At one point, we moved in the same circles, but I have never met her."

"It would be my deepest pleasure to speak to you of her," he said with appropriately lowered eyes.

In describing to her all the grandeur of Lady Catherine and her mansion, with occasional digressions in praise of his own humble abode, and the improvements it was receiving, he was happily employed until the gentlemen joined them; and he found in Mrs. Phillips a very attentive listener, whose opinion of his consequence increased with what she heard, and who was resolving to retail it all among her neighbours as soon as she could.

They left the girls settled on the couches to wait for the gentlemen.

"Up these stairs," Mrs. Phillips said, with a strong hand on Mr. Collin's backside.

They entered her bedroom and Mr. Collins remarked that Lady Catherine would approve of the set up.

"Strip," she said, uncoiling the lash and cracking it against the table. He shed his clothing quickly and meekly allowed her to restrain him. She had rigged him up to a harness and pulley, his hands bound and his neck encircled with a large leather collar, black leather straps stretching across his body. By pulling at the ropes, he was aloft and spinning not far from the ceiling. "Do you often participate in these sexual tete a tetes?"

"I know little of the game at present," said he, "but I shall be glad to improve myself, for in my situation in life—" Mrs. Phillips was very glad for his compliance, but could not wait for his reason.

After securing the ropes, Mrs. Phillips spun him in circles. Mr. Collins' neck arched back and his erection was thick against his belly.

True to her words, she started the lash with hard strokes against his calves, moving up to his tightened buttocks.

"Thank you, kind Mistress. I deserve punishment."

"Yes, you horrid man," Mrs. Phillips moved in to grasp his jutting member. She stroked him fast, bringing him to the edge – just a drop of wetness on the tip, and then whipped him five more times across the back.

"Oh," he shivered. "Mistress, thank you."

"You are very well trained," Mrs. Phillips said. "I commend Lady Catherine."

She approached his penis again, this time engulfing it in her mouth and sucking it half way down her throat.

"Ah," Mr. Collins shouted. "Mistress may I come?"

Mrs. Phillips bobbed her head in quick ruthless sucks and then quickly squeezed under the head of his member until he whimpered.

"Not yet," she said. "Let's see how talented your tongue really is." She lowered the pulley so he was balanced on shaky knees. Mrs. Phillips undid her specially made skirts with three easy ties. Naked under them, she moved towards Mr. Collins who dropped to his knees. Throwing her leg over his shoulder, she pressed her core into his mouth.

Mr. Collins lapped at her with long, eager strokes.

"Faster," she commanded and rapped the lash so it hit his back and buttocks.

He moaned and leaned into her, adoring her slit with his mouth and tongue. He stroked across and then curved his tongue so it tapped against her swollen bud. Mrs. Phillips made a guttural sound in the back of her throat and whipped him in time with his tongue. He was breathing hard. His back and buttocks were fiery red from her ministrations.

Mrs. Phillips ground against his face, pushing him back on his tied hands on the floor. Mr. Collins took it and gave her pleasure until she was gasping above him. The second her release took her, Mrs. Phillips slid down and impaled herself on Mr. Collins.

"Thank you, Mistress. You taste like honey, like sunshine."

Mrs. Phillips used his hard, young body to bring herself to another quick orgasm.

"Now, you may come slave," she said and let him buck into her.

Leaning in with her gloved hand, she clasped him around the throat and tightened her hand. "You are worthless. I should choke the life out of you."

"Yes, Mistress, please. I live only for your pleasure."

Mrs. Phillips felt the stirrings of another surprise orgasm and rode him well. As her fingers tightened, the harder he bucked until she was holding on to him with both hands around his neck. He was gasping for air when he flooded his seed into her. She clamped around him with excited puffs of breath. Removing her hands before he passed out, she slid herself up and down until she completed one more time.

"Mr. Collins, you are a marvel." She offered him her mouth and showed him her pleasure by kissing him thoroughly.

To the girls, who had no such diversions and had nothing to do but to wish for an instrument, and examine their own indifferent imitations of china on the mantelpiece, the interval of waiting appeared very long. It was over at last, however.

The gentlemen did approach, and when Mr. Wickham walked into the room, Elizabeth felt that she had neither been seeing him before, nor thinking of him since, with the smallest degree of unreasonable admiration. The officers were in general a very creditable, gentlemanlike set, and the best of them were of the present party; but Mr. Wickham was as far beyond them all in person, countenance, air, and walk, as they were superior to the broad-faced, stuffy uncle Phillips, breathing port wine, who followed them into the room.

Mr. Wickham was the happy man towards whom almost every female eye was turned, and Elizabeth was the happy woman by whom he finally seated himself; and the agreeable manner in which he immediately fell into conversation, though it was only on its being a wet night, made her feel that the commonest, dullest, most threadbare topic might be rendered interesting by the skill of the speaker.

Elizabeth couldn't help but notice how different he was to Mr. Darcy. Pleasant rather than brooding with an ease of manner that made her feel flirtatious. There wasn't a coiling of dark desire and an even darker need to abase herself on her knees in front of him. She refused to acknowledge that a part of her was disappointed.

With such rivals for the notice of the fair as Mr. Wickham and the officers, Mr. Collins seemed to sink into insignificance when he returned with a slight limp; to the young ladies he certainly was nothing; but he had still at intervals a kind listener in Mrs. Phillips, and was by her watchfulness, most abundantly supplied with coffee and muffins. She would pat him like one did a beloved dog, when no one was looking. When the card-tables were placed, the guests sat down to play whist.

Mr. Wickham did not play and with ready delight was he received at the other table between Elizabeth and Lydia. At first there seemed danger of Lydia's engrossing him entirely, for she was a most determined talker; but being likewise extremely fond of lottery tickets, she soon grew too much interested in the game, too eager in making bets and exclaiming after prizes to have attention for anyone in particular.

Allowing for the common demands of the game, Mr. Wickham was therefore at leisure to talk to Elizabeth, and she was very willing to hear him, though what she chiefly wished to hear she could not hope to be told—the history of his acquaintance with Mr. Darcy. She both loathed and craved word of the man she couldn't get out of her head. She dared not even mention that gentleman. Her curiosity, however, was unexpectedly relieved. Mr. Wickham began the subject himself. He inquired how far Netherfield was from Meryton; and, after receiving her answer, asked in a hesitating manner how long Mr. Darcy had been staying there.

"About a month," said Elizabeth; and then, unwilling to let the subject drop, added, "He is a man of very large property in Derbyshire, I understand." And large other attributes as well, she thought.

"Yes," replied Mr. Wickham; "his estate there is a noble one. A clear ten thousand per annum. You could not have met with a person more capable of giving you certain information on that head than myself, for I have been connected with his family in a particular manner from my infancy."

Elizabeth could not but look surprised. "Were you intimately associated with him?" she dared to ask.

"You may well be surprised, Miss Bennet, at such an assertion, after seeing, as you probably might, the very cold manner of our meeting yesterday. Are you much acquainted with Mr. Darcy?"

"As much as I ever wish to be," cried Elizabeth very warmly. "I have spent four days in the same house with him, and I think him very disagreeable." *And desirable, and too dangerous to my virtue, such that it is.*

"I have no right to give my opinion," said Wickham, "as to his being agreeable or otherwise. I am not qualified to form one. I have known him too long and too well to be a fair judge. It is impossible for me to be impartial. But I believe your opinion of him would in general astonish—and perhaps you would not express it quite so strongly anywhere else. Here you

155

are in your own family."

"Upon my word, I say no more here than I might say in any house in the neighbourhood, except Netherfield. He is not at all liked in Hertfordshire. Everybody is disgusted with his pride. You will not find him more favourably spoken of by anyone." Darcy was feared, admired, but not liked at all. Elizabeth squelched a bit of pity that surfaced. He brought it on himself with his pride over those he considered beneath him.

"I cannot pretend to be sorry," said Wickham, after a short interruption, "that he or that any man should not be estimated beyond their deserts; but with him I believe it does not often happen. The world is blinded by his fortune and consequence, or frightened by his high and imposing manners, and sees him only as he chooses to be seen."

Elizabeth nodded emphatically. "I should take him, even on my slight

acquaintance, to be an ill-tempered man, used to having his way and always being right."

Wickham only shook his head. "I wonder," said he, at the next opportunity of speaking, "whether he is likely to be in this country much longer."

"I do not at all know; but I heard nothing of his going away when I was at Netherfield. I hope your plans will not be affected by his being in the neighbourhood."

"Oh! no—it is not for me to be driven away by Mr. Darcy. If he wishes to avoid seeing me, he must go. We are not on friendly terms, and it always gives me pain to meet him, but I have no reason for avoiding him but what I might proclaim before all the world, a sense of very great ill-usage, and most painful regrets at his being what he is."

Elizabeth breathed out. "What type of regrets?" She looked around, but no one seemed to be listening to hard to their discussion.

" His father, Miss Bennet, the late Mr. Darcy, was one of the best men that ever breathed, and the truest friend I ever had; and I can never be in company with this Mr. Darcy without being grieved to the soul by a thousand tender recollections. His behaviour to myself has been scandalous; but I verily believe I could forgive him anything and everything, rather than his disappointing the hopes and disgracing the memory of his father."

Elizabeth found the interest of the subject increase, and listened with all her heart; but the delicacy of it prevented further inquiry. If she knew what molded Mr. Darcy into the man he became would she be able to solve the puzzle of his emotions and in doing so, the strange cravings he pulled from her body.

Mr. Wickham began to speak on more general topics, Meryton, the neighbourhood, the society, appearing highly pleased with all that he had yet seen, and speaking of the latter with gentle but very intelligible gallantry.

"It was the prospect of constant society, and good society," he added, "which was my chief inducement to come here. I knew it to be a most respectable, agreeable corps, and my friend Denny tempted me further by his account of their present quarters, and the very great attentions and excellent acquaintances Meryton had procured them. Society, I own, is necessary to me. I have been a disappointed man, and my spirits will not bear solitude. I must have employment and society. A military life is not what I was intended for, but circumstances have now made it eligible. The church ought to have been my profession—I was brought up for the church, and I should at this time have been in possession of a most valuable living, had it pleased the gentleman we were speaking of just now."

"Indeed!" Elizabeth said. Did Mr. Darcy debauch a candidate of a man of the cloth? She felt flush and dizzy at the prospect. Her eyes unfocused as she pictured the two men, naked and oiled. Mr. Darcy thrusting into Mr. Wickham.

"Yes—the late Mr. Darcy bequeathed me the next presentation of the best living in his gift. He was my godfather, and excessively attached to me. I cannot do justice to his kindness. He meant to provide for me amply, and thought he had done it; but when the living fell, it was given elsewhere."

"Good heavens!" cried Elizabeth, realizing she hadn't been listening and was now wet and throbbing. She forced her mind back to the conversation and what Mr. Wickham was saying; "But how could that be? How could his will be disregarded? Why did you not seek legal redress?"

"There was just such an informality in the terms of the bequest as to give me no hope from law. A man of honour could not have doubted the intention, but Mr. Darcy chose to doubt it—or to treat it as a merely conditional recommendation, and to assert that I had forfeited all claim to it by extravagance, imprudence—in short anything or nothing. Certain it is, that the living became vacant two years ago, exactly as I was of an age to hold it, and that it was given to another man; and no less certain is it, that I cannot accuse myself of having really done anything to deserve to lose it. I have a warm, unguarded temper, and I may have spoken my opinion of him, and to him, too freely. I can recall nothing worse. But the fact is, that we are very different sort of men, and that he hates me."

"This is quite shocking! He deserves to be publicly disgraced." Was it because Mr. Wickham refused his advances? Would he try to ruin her in a similar manner if she didn't agree to become his submissive?

"Some time or other he will be—but it shall not be by me. Till I can forget his father, I can never defy or expose him."

Elizabeth honoured him for such feelings, and thought him handsomer than ever as he expressed them. For a moment, she was between him and Mr. Darcy as they moved their mouths over her naked flesh.

"But what," said she, after a pause where she had to visibly swallow. Her mouth was dry from tormenting herself with the passionate images, "can have been his motive? What can have induced him to behave so cruelly?"

"A thorough, determined dislike of me—a dislike which I cannot but attribute in some measure to jealousy. Had the late Mr. Darcy liked me less, his son might have borne with me better; but his father's uncommon attachment to me irritated him, I believe, very early in life. He had not a temper to bear the sort of competition in which we stood—the sort of preference which was often given me."

"I had not thought Mr. Darcy so bad as this—though I have never liked him. I had not thought so very ill of him. I had supposed him to be despising his fellow-creatures in general, but did not suspect him of descending to such malicious revenge, such injustice, such inhumanity as this." Elizabeth frowned. She had been seriously considering subjecting her entire future to Mr. Darcy's will. She must not let him get further under her skin if he could act like this.

After a few minutes' reflection, however, she continued, "I do remember his boasting one day, at Netherfield, of the implacability of his resentments, of his having an unforgiving temper. His disposition must be dreadful." She shivered as she wondered if Mr. Darcy would use his hands on her instead of the beaded flail. Elizabeth shifted in her seat. Where was Charlotte when she needed her? She bit her lip in discomfort and wondered if she should excuse herself to take care of the heavy pressure of desire she couldn't snap herself out of.

"I will not trust myself on the subject," replied Wickham; "I can hardly be just to him."

Elizabeth was again deep in thought, and after a time exclaimed, "To treat in such a manner the godson, the friend, the favourite of his father!" She could have added, "A young man, too, like you, whose very countenance may vouch for your being amiable"—but she contented herself with, "and one, too, who had probably been his companion from childhood, connected together, as I think you said, in the closest manner!"

I am obsessed with Mr. Darcy, she thought. Scrambling for more detail even as each new revelation damns him as a dark and devious man.

"We were born in the same parish, within the same park; the greatest part of our youth was passed together; inmates of the same house, sharing the same amusements, objects of the same parental care. My father began life in the profession which your uncle, Mr. Phillips, appears to do so much credit to—but he gave up everything to be of use to the late Mr. Darcy and devoted all his time to the care of the Pemberley property. He was most highly esteemed by Mr. Darcy, a most intimate, confidential friend. Mr. Darcy often acknowledged himself to be under the greatest obligations to my father's active superintendence, and when, immediately before my father's death, Mr. Darcy gave him a voluntary promise of providing for me, I am convinced that he felt it to be as much a debt of gratitude to him, as of his affection to myself."

"How strange!" cried Elizabeth. "How abominable! I wonder that the very pride of this Mr. Darcy has not made him just to you! If from no better motive, that he should not have been too proud to be dishonest—for dishonesty I must call it."

In the dungeon, she had thought she could see through to the real core of the man. But that was probably another mask he used to seduce her with.

"It is wonderful," replied Wickham, "for almost all his actions may be traced to pride; and pride had often been his best friend. It has connected him nearer with virtue than with any other feeling. But we are none of us consistent, and in his behaviour to me there were stronger impulses even than pride."

"Can such abominable pride as his have ever done him good?" She thought back to the moment when he almost thrust into her. Digging her nails into her palms, Elizabeth wondered why he hadn't taken her even though she called him off by speaking Jane's name. If she was truly ruined and he was such a villain, why hadn't he satisfied the buzzing lust between them?

"Yes. It has often led him to be liberal and generous, to give his money freely, to display hospitality, to assist his tenants, and relieve the poor. Family pride, and filial pride—for he is very proud of what his father was—have done this. Not to appear to disgrace his family, to degenerate from the popular qualities, or lose the influence of the Pemberley House, is a powerful motive. He has also brotherly pride, which, with some brotherly affection, makes him a very kind and careful guardian of his sister, and you will hear him generally cried up as the most attentive and best of brothers."

"What sort of girl is Miss Darcy?" Elizabeth had remembered Miss Bingley had gushed about the girl.

He shook his head. "I wish I could call her amiable. It gives me pain to speak ill of a Darcy. But she is too much like her brother—very, very proud. As a child, she was affectionate and pleasing, and extremely fond of me; and I have devoted hours and hours to her amusement. But she is nothing to me now. She is a handsome girl, about fifteen or sixteen, and, I understand, highly accomplished. Since her father's death, her home has been London, where a lady lives with her, and superintends her education."

After many pauses and many trials of other subjects, Elizabeth could not help reverting once more to the first, and saying:

"I am astonished at his intimacy with Mr.

Bingley! How can Mr. Bingley, who seems good humour itself, and is, I really believe, truly amiable, be in friendship with such a man? How can they suit each other? Do you know Mr. Bingley?" Were they lovers? Was he right now enjoying Mr. Bingley's mouth around his wonderful cock. Elizabeth licked her lips and tried to concentrate on hating him for abusing his father's will and denying the good, handsome Mr. Wickham his inheritance.

"Not at all."

"He is a sweet-tempered, amiable, charming man. He cannot know what Mr. Darcy is."

"Probably not; but Mr. Darcy can please where he chooses. He does not want abilities. He can be a conversible companion if he thinks it worth his while. Among those who are at all his equals in consequence, he is a very different man from what he is to the less prosperous. His pride never deserts him; but with the rich he is liberal-minded, just, sincere, rational, honourable, and perhaps agreeable—allowing something for fortune and figure."

Elizabeth thought of this and knew it to be true.

The whist party soon afterwards breaking up, the players gathered round the other table and Mr. Collins took his station between his cousin Elizabeth and Jane. No one noticed that he was disheveled or the deeply satisfied grin on their aunt's face. Mr. Collins did not play whist well, in fact he had lost every point; but when Mrs. Phillips began to express her concern, the usual inquiries as to his success was made by the latter. It had thereupon, he assured her with much earnest gravity that it was not of the least importance, that he considered the money as a mere trifle, and begged that she would not make herself uneasy.

"I know very well, Mistr—I mean, madam," said he, "that when persons sit down to a card-table, they must take their chances of these things, and happily I am not in such circumstances as to make five shillings any object. There are undoubtedly many who could not say the same, but thanks to Lady Catherine de Bourgh, I am removed far beyond the necessity of regarding little matters."

Mr. Wickham's attention was caught; and after observing Mr. Collins for a few moments, he asked Elizabeth in a low voice whether her relation was very intimately acquainted with the family of de Bourgh.

"Lady Catherine de Bourgh," she replied, "has very lately given him a living. I hardly know how Mr. Collins was first introduced to her notice, but he certainly has not known her long. Her reputation does precede her though. My aunt might now her better."

"You know of course that Lady Catherine de Bourgh and Lady Anne Darcy were sisters; consequently that she is aunt to the present Mr. Darcy."

Elizabeth reeled. Mr. Darcy was the nephew of one of the most Notorious Dominatrix in all of England. "No, indeed, I did not. I knew nothing at all of Lady Catherine's connections. I never heard of her existence till the day before yesterday." But it certainly made sense.

"Her daughter, Miss de Bourgh, will have a very large fortune, and it is believed that she and her cousin will unite the two estates."

This information made Elizabeth smile, as she thought of poor Miss Bingley. Vain indeed must be all her attentions, vain and useless her affection for his sister and her praise of himself, if he were already self-destined for another. It seemed that they both wouldn't be able to have him.

"Mr. Collins," said she, "speaks highly both of Lady Catherine and her daughter; but from some particulars that he has related of her ladyship, I suspect his gratitude misleads him, and that in spite of her being his patroness, she is an arrogant, conceited woman."

"I believe her to be both in a great degree," replied Wickham; "I have not seen her for many years, but I very well remember that I never liked her, and that her manners were dictatorial and insolent. She has the reputation of being remarkably sensible and clever; but I rather believe she derives part of her abilities from her rank and fortune, part from her authoritative manner, and the rest from the pride for her nephew, who chooses that everyone connected with him should have an understanding of the first class."

Elizabeth allowed that he had given a very rational account of it, and they continued talking together, with mutual satisfaction till supper put an end to cards, and gave the rest of the ladies their share of Mr. Wickham's attentions. Whatever he said, was said well; and whatever he did, done gracefully. He was a breath of fresh air and a gentleman.

Elizabeth went away with her head full of him. She could think of nothing but of Mr. Wickham, and of what he had told her, all the way home; but there was not time for her even to mention his name as they went, for neither Lydia nor Mr. Collins were once silent. Lydia talked incessantly of lottery tickets, of the fish she had lost and the fish she had won; and Mr. Collins in describing the civility of Mrs. Phillips, protesting that he did not in the least regard his losses at whist, enumerating all the dishes at supper, and repeatedly fearing that he crowded his cousins, had more to say than he could well manage before the carriage stopped at Longbourn House. Elizabeth ran up to her room without speaking to anyone and pleasured herself with fast eager strokes before her sisters could disturb her. She told herself she was thinking of the dapper Mr. Wickham, but it was the dark masked man who probed into her most intimate places that made her shake and cry out his name.

Darcy!

Chapter 17

Elizabeth related to Jane the next day what had passed between Mr. Wickham and herself. Jane listened with astonishment and concern; she knew not how to believe that Mr. Darcy could be so unworthy of Mr. Bingley's regard; and yet, it was not in her nature to question the veracity of a young man of such amiable appearance as Wickham.

She told her sister everything that had happened at Netherfield while they were there and instead of being shocked, Jane smiled knowingly.

"You are truly fortunate," she said. "I wanted to be well enough to actively participate. But the Bingleys wouldn't have me tax myself."

"What did go on between the three of you?" Elizabeth asked.

"I enjoyed them individually. I feel for Mrs. Hurst – dear Louisa—her husband is nigh useless unless there's a deck of cards. We kissed and caressed, she is most lovely and tender."

"Miss Bingley on the other hand," Elizabeth said dryly.

"She's a fiery thing," Jane agreed. "A little too rough and angry, but we enjoyed tasting each other. At the same time."

Elizabeth's eyebrows rose. "That sounds divine. Maybe Charlotte and I will try that."

Jane smiled at her knowingly. "As pleasant as the women were, it was Bingley who made my heart race."

"Did he violate you?"

"No," Jane pouted. "I asked and begged, but he was determined to keep me safe. I felt cherished and admired. And desperate for release. Thank goodness his sisters were near insatiable. I'm sorry I monopolized them for you."

"I had my hands full with Mr. Darcy."

"It wasn't just your hands that were full." Jane smiled. "He seems to have captivated you."

"But has he done so with Wickham and Bingley?" Elizabeth said. "It's those couplings I cannot get out of my mind. Is he dominating them, somehow controlling them through his force of personality and potent sexuality?"

"They have both," said she, "been deceived, I dare say, in some way or other, of which we can form no idea. Interested people have perhaps misrepresented each to the other. It is, in short, impossible for us to conjecture the causes or circumstances which may have alienated them, without actual blame on either side."

"Very true, indeed; and now, my dear Jane, what have you got to say on behalf of the interested people who have probably been concerned in the business? Do clear them too, or we shall be obliged to think ill of somebody."

"Laugh as much as you choose, but you will not laugh me out of my opinion. My dearest Lizzy, do but consider in what a disgraceful light it places Mr. Darcy, to be treating his father's favourite in such a manner, one whom his father had promised to provide for. It is impossible. No man of common humanity, no man who had any value for his character, could be capable of it. Can his most intimate friends be so excessively deceived in him? Oh! no." "He wants me. I admit it, that I want him to distraction. He won't marry me. And I only have his word, that I have been compromised from my love play with Charlotte."

"You are a bit more wanton than I am. Didn't it hurt when his fingers were in your bum?"

"A bit, but it was more a sense of being filled and fulfilled. It was over rather too quickly.

"Darling, Lizzy, you are looking for an excuse to hate him," Jane said.

"If Mr. Wickham is correct, then Mr. Darcy is a horrible person. You've seen Mr. Darcy, it all rings so true. He's so proud and harsh. How can I trust him or my feelings around him? All I have are questions! Aren't you curious about him and your Mr. Bingley?"

"I wouldn't drive myself to madness picturing the two of them together. I can much more easily believe Mr. Bingley's being imposed on, than that Mr. Wickham should invent such a history of himself as he gave me last night; names, facts, everything mentioned without ceremony. If it be not so, let Mr. Darcy contradict it. Besides, there was truth in his looks."

"It is difficult indeed—it is distressing. One does not know what to think."

"I beg your pardon; one knows exactly what to think."

But Jane could think with certainty on only one

point—that Mr. Bingley, if he had been imposed on, would have much to suffer when the affair became public.

The two young ladies were summoned from the shrubbery, where this conversation passed, by the arrival of the very persons of whom they had been speaking; Mr. Bingley and his sisters came to give their personal invitation for the long-expected ball at Netherfield, which was fixed for the following Tuesday.

The two ladies were delighted to see their dear friend again, called it an age since they had met, and repeatedly asked what she had been doing with herself since their separation. To the rest of the family they paid little attention; avoiding Mrs. Bennet as much as possible, saying not much to Elizabeth, and nothing at all to the others.

Jane kissed them both on the cheeks, lingering a bit. Elizabeth looked away as their hands brushed each other's breasts.

They were soon gone again, rising from their seats with an activity which took their brother by surprise, and hurrying off as if eager to escape from Mrs. Bennet's civilities.

The prospect of the Netherfield ball was extremely agreeable to every female of the family. Mrs. Bennet chose to consider it as given in compliment to her eldest daughter, and was particularly flattered by receiving the invitation from Mr. Bingley himself, instead of a ceremonious card.

Jane pictured to herself a happy evening in the society of her two friends, and the attentions of their brother. Now, that she was healthy, she was determine to experience the dungeons and play rooms like her sister had.

Elizabeth thought with pleasure of dancing a great deal with Mr. Wickham, and of seeing a confirmation of everything in Mr. Darcy's look and behaviour. She would not give up on her virtue to become his submissive, but that didn't mean she had to give up on pleasure.

The happiness anticipated by Catherine and Lydia depended less on any single event, or any particular person, for though they each, like Elizabeth, meant to dance half the evening with Mr. Wickham, he was by no means the only partner who could satisfy them, and a ball was, at any rate, a ball. And even Mary could assure her family that she had no disinclination for it.

"While I can have my mornings to myself," said she, "it is enough—I think it is no sacrifice to join occasionally in evening engagements. Society has claims on us all; and I profess myself one of those who consider intervals of recreation and amusement as desirable for everybody."

Elizabeth's spirits were so high on this occasion having come to the decision to embrace pleasure while still keeping a semblance of virtue, that though she did not often speak unnecessarily to Mr. Collins, she could not help asking him whether he intended to accept Mr. Bingley's invitation. And if he did, whether he would think it proper to join in the evening's amusement; and she was rather surprised to find that he entertained no scruple whatever on that head, and was very far from dreading a rebuke either from the Archbishop, or Lady Catherine de Bourgh, by venturing to dance.

"I am by no means of the opinion, I assure you,"

said he, "that a ball of this kind, given by a young man of character, to respectable people, can have any evil tendency; and I am so far from objecting to dancing myself, that I shall hope to be honoured with the hands of all my fair cousins in the course of the evening; and I take this opportunity of soliciting yours, Miss Elizabeth, for the two first dances especially, a preference which I trust my cousin Jane will attribute to the right cause, and not to any disrespect for her."

He almost sank to his knees before checking himself.

Elizabeth felt herself completely taken in. She had fully proposed being engaged by Mr. Wickham for those very dances; and to have Mr. Collins instead! her liveliness had never been worse timed. There was no help for it, however. Mr. Wickham's happiness and her own were perforce delayed a little longer, and Mr. Collins's proposal accepted with as good a grace as she could.

"Thank you, Mist--- my dear cousin."

She was not the better pleased with his gallantry from the idea it suggested of something more. It now first struck her, that she was selected from among her sisters as worthy of being mistress of Hunsford Parsonage, and of assisting to form a quadrille table at Rosings, in the absence of more eligible visitors.

The idea soon reached to conviction, as she observed his increasing civilities toward herself, and heard his frequent attempt at a compliment on her wit and vivacity; and though more astonished than gratified herself by this effect of her charms, it was not long before her mother gave her to understand that the probability of their marriage was extremely agreeable to her. While she wanted to experience mind sweeping pleasure again, she couldn't bend her mind to see Mr. Collins in that light. He was too submissive and everything she secretly feared she would become if Mr. Darcy started molding her. Elizabeth had no doubt that if she ordered Mr. Collins to cup her breasts in his hands and suck on them, he would do so without question or emotion. Just a simple, "Yes Mistress."

Elizabeth, however, did not choose to take her mother's hint, being well aware that a serious dispute must be the consequence of any reply. Mr. Collins might never make the offer, and till he did, it was useless to quarrel about him.

If there had not been a Netherfield ball to prepare for and talk of, the younger Miss Bennets would have been in a very pitiable state at this time, for from the day of the invitation, to the day of the ball, there was such a succession of rain as prevented their walking to Meryton once. No aunt, no officers, no news could be sought after—the very shoe-roses for Netherfield were got by proxy. Even Elizabeth might have found some trial of her patience in weather which totally suspended the improvement of her acquaintance with Mr. Wickham. She spent a great deal of time, with her fingers buried inside her warm, wet cleft stroking herself to ecstasy while she tried not to think about the seductive dungeons of Netherfield. She would be going for the ball. She would not slip downstairs with the crowd. She would dance and be merry with Mr. Wickham and forget about the dark devil, Mr. Darcy.

Chapter 18

Till Elizabeth entered the drawing-room at Netherfield, and looked in vain for Mr. Wickham among the cluster of red coats there assembled, a doubt of his being present had never occurred to her. It was inconceivable that the star attraction of her lurid fantasies had chosen not to appear for his opening night. The certainty of meeting him had not been checked by any of those recollections that might not unreasonably have alarmed her. She had dressed with more than usual care, and prepared in the highest spirits for the conquest of all that remained unsubdued of his heart, trusting that it was not more than might be won in the course of the evening.

But in an instant arose the dreadful suspicion of his being purposely omitted for Mr. Darcy's pleasure in the Bingleys' invitation to the officers; and though this was not exactly the case, the absolute fact of his absence was pronounced by his friend Denny, to whom Lydia eagerly applied, and who told them that Wickham had been obliged to go to town on business the day before, and was not yet returned; adding, with a significant smile, "I do not imagine his business would have called him away just now, if he had not wanted to avoid a certain gentleman here."

Elizabeth could relate as she spent time dodging the smoldering looks of Mr. Darcy.

This part of his intelligence, though unheard by Lydia, was caught by Elizabeth, and, as it assured her that Darcy was not less answerable for Wickham's absence than if her first surmise had been just, every feeling of displeasure against the former was so sharpened by immediate disappointment, that she could hardly reply with tolerable civility to the polite inquiries which he directly afterwards approached to make.

Elizabeth watched couples head for the staircases and disappear below the ballroom. She tried not to think of her own time there. Where they watching or participating? She found herself seeking out Mr. Darcy to see if he practiced below or if he was amusing himself above ground.

Attendance, forbearance, patience with Darcy, was injury to Wickham. She was resolved against any sort of conversation with him, and turned away with a degree of ill-humour which she could not wholly surmount even in speaking to Mr. Bingley, whose blind partiality provoked her.

But Elizabeth was not formed for ill-humour; and though every prospect of her own was destroyed for the evening, it could not dwell long on her spirits; and having told all her griefs to Charlotte Lucas, whom she had not seen for a week, she was soon able to make a voluntary transition to the oddities of her cousin, and to point him out to her particular notice. The first two dances, however, brought a return of distress; they were dances of mortification. Mr. Collins, awkward and solemn, apologising instead of attending, and often moving wrong without being aware of it, gave her all the shame and misery which a disagreeable partner for a couple of dances can give. The moment of her release from him was ecstasy.

When she saw Jane and Mr. Bingley walk arm and arm down the ornate staircases, she whipped her head about to see if her parents or sisters noticed. Her parents were not in sight and her sisters too involved with the soldiers to pay anyone else any mind. Elizabeth started to follow, to do what she wasn't sure. But suddenly the air in the ballroom was stifling. However before she could go more than a few feet, she was again caught up in the dancing. Over the man's shoulder, she saw her sister's golden head tip back in laughter at something Mr. Bingley had said.

Elizabeth danced next with an officer, and had the refreshment of talking of Wickham, and of hearing that he was universally liked. When those dances were over, she returned to Charlotte Lucas, and was in conversation with her, when she found herself suddenly addressed by Mr. Darcy who took her so much by surprise in his application for her hand, that, without knowing what she did, she accepted him. He walked away again immediately, and she was left to fret over her own want of presence of mind; Charlotte tried to console her:

"I dare say you will find him very agreeable."

"Heaven forbid! That would be the greatest misfortune of all! To find a man agreeable whom one is determined to hate! Do not wish me such an evil. He's merely looking to tempt me into becoming his submissive."

"And are you? Tempted that is?" Charlotte gave her an arch look when Elizabeth didn't respond.

When the dancing recommenced, however, and Darcy approached to claim her hand, Charlotte could not help cautioning her in a whisper, not to be a simpleton, and allow her fancy for Wickham to make her appear unpleasant in the eyes of a man ten times his consequence.

Elizabeth made no answer, and took her place in the set, amazed at the dignity to which she was arrived in being allowed to stand opposite to Mr. Darcy, and reading in her neighbours' looks, their equal amazement in beholding it. They stood for some time without speaking a word. His eyes were just as compelling outside of the mask as they were when he wore it. The cut of his mouth was firm, his lips sensual. She began to imagine that their silence was to last through the two dances, each lost looking their fill at the other. At first she was resolved not to break it; till suddenly fancying that it would be the greater punishment to her partner to oblige him to talk. After all, it wasn't as if they could speak freely of his odious offer. Elizabeth made some slight observation on the dance. He replied, and was again silent. After a pause of some minutes, she addressed him a second time with:—"It is your turn to say something now, Mr. Darcy. I talked about the dance, and you ought to make some sort of remark on the size of the room, or the number of couples."

He smiled, and assured her that whatever she wished him to say should be said.

Elizabeth could think of quite a few things she'd like to hear him say. Starting with, I was wrong about your virginity. Your lack of fortune doesn't matter to me. I will take you until you are screaming my name. "Ahem," she cleared her throat as she felt herself flush. "Very well. That reply will do for the present. Perhaps by and by I may observe that private balls are much pleasanter than public ones." She raised an eyebrow at him and was rewarded by seeing a faint smile cross his lips. "But now we may be silent."

"Do you talk by rule, then, while you are . . . *dancing?*" He said, giving the last word enough innuendo that she was suddenly back in that dungeon room, her arms firmly restrained.

"Sometimes. One must speak a little, you know. It would look odd to be entirely silent for half an hour together; and yet for the advantage of some, conversation ought to be so arranged, as that they may have the trouble of saying as little as possible."

"Are you consulting your own feelings in the present case, or do you imagine that you are gratifying mine?" His hand almost touched hers as they circled around each other, she felt the warmth radiating from him. How very easy it would be to submit to him.

"Both," replied Elizabeth archly; "for I have always seen a great similarity in the turn of our minds. We are each of an unsocial, taciturn disposition, unwilling to speak, unless we expect to say something that will amaze the whole room, and be handed down to posterity with all the eclat of a proverb." Dancing with him and speaking thus was more thrilling than Charlotte's kisses, which had paled to non-existence from the heated caress of his mouth on hers. She licked her lips, almost tasting him.

"This is no very striking resemblance of your own

character, I am sure," said he. "How near it may be to mine, I cannot pretend to say. You think it a faithful portrait undoubtedly." His body brushed hers as they passed in the dance. She began to feel that lightheadedness again.

"I must not decide on my own performance." Elizabeth pinched herself to regain focus. Mr. Darcy's eyes narrowed on the reddened flesh.

He made no answer, and they were again silent till they had gone down the dance, when he asked her if she and her sisters did not very often walk to Meryton. She answered in the affirmative, and, unable to resist the temptation, added, "When you met us there the other day, we had just been forming a new acquaintance."

The effect was immediate. A deeper shade of hauteur overspread his features, but he said not a word, and Elizabeth, though blaming herself for her own weakness, could not go on. She stifled a tremble and a part of her expected him to pull at riding quirt from up his sleeve and punish her. She hadn't realized how much she yearned for the sting of the crop until this moment.

At length Darcy spoke, and in a constrained manner said, "Mr. Wickham is blessed with such happy manners as may ensure his making friends— whether he may be equally capable of retaining them, is less certain."

"He has been so unlucky as to lose your friendship," replied Elizabeth with emphasis, "and in a manner which he is likely to suffer from all his life." She stared at him meaningfully. Now was his chance to tell her his side of the story. Her eyes begged him.

Say the words.

Darcy made no answer, and seemed desirous of changing the subject. At that moment, Sir William Lucas appeared close to them, meaning to pass through the set to the other side of the room; but on perceiving Mr. Darcy, he stopped with a bow of superior courtesy to compliment him on his dancing and his partner.

"I have been most highly gratified indeed, my dear sir. Such very superior dancing is not often seen. It is evident that you belong to the first circles. Allow me to say, however, that your fair partner does not disgrace you, and that I must hope to have this pleasure often repeated, especially when a certain desirable event, my dear Eliza (glancing at her sister and Bingley who had returned from downstairs) shall take place. What congratulations will then flow in! I appeal to Mr. Darcy:—but let me not interrupt you, sir. You will not thank me for detaining you from the bewitching converse of that young lady, whose bright eyes are also upbraiding me."

The latter part of this address was scarcely heard by Darcy; but Sir William's allusion to his friend seemed to strike him forcibly, and his eyes were directed with a very serious expression towards Bingley and Jane, who were dancing together. A slight sheen of sweat slicked Mr. Bingley's brow and he noticed a reddening bruise at the top of Jane's bodice.

Recovering himself, however, shortly, Mr. Darcy turned to his Elizabeth, and said, "Sir William's interruption has made me forget what we were talking of."

"I do not think we were speaking at all. Sir William could not have interrupted two people in the room who had less to say for themselves. We have tried two or three subjects already without success, and what we are to talk of next I cannot imagine."

"What think you of books?" said he, smiling.

"Books—oh! no. I am sure we never read the same, or not with the same feelings."

"We could speak of feelings," he said.

"Do you have any?"

"I have deep feelings."

"I doubt that," she said, trying to hide the bitterness she felt with a gay laugh.

"I am sorry you think so; but if that be the case, there can at least be no want of subject. We may compare our different opinions."

"No—I cannot talk of books in a ball-room; my head is always full of something else." She looked away from him and then to the stairs leading below.

"The present always occupies you in such scenes—does it?" said he, with a look of challenge. "Are you so sure of the paths you have chosen?"

"Yes, always," she replied, without knowing what she said, for her thoughts had wandered far from the subject, as soon afterwards appeared by her suddenly exclaiming, "I remember hearing you once say, Mr. Darcy, that you hardly ever forgave, that your resentment once created was unappeasable. You are very cautious, I suppose, as to its being created."

"I am," said he, with a firm voice.

"And never allow yourself to be blinded by prejudice?" She implored him, giving him the opening to speak of Mr. Wickham.

"I hope not."

"It is particularly incumbent on those who never

181

change their opinion, to be secure of judging properly at first."

"May I ask to what these questions tend?" he asked, annoyed that she couldn't just put her hand in his and walk downstairs and into her new future. He would see that she was well treated and punished only by hand. He wouldn't even share her in pleasure. Couldn't she see he was breaking all of his rules by giving her the chance to come to him?

"Merely to the illustration of your character," said she, endeavouring to shake off her gravity. "I am trying to make it out."

"And what is your success?"

She shook her head. "I do not get on at all. I hear such different accounts of you as puzzle me exceedingly."

"I can readily believe," answered he gravely, "that reports may vary greatly with respect to me; and I could wish, Miss Bennet, that you were not to sketch my character at the present moment, as there is reason to fear that the performance would reflect no credit on either. You must trust me. If there is not trust, there is no intimacy to be had."

"But if I do not take your likeness now, I may never have another opportunity."

"There are always opportunities. Shall we talk a walk downstairs and explore some of them?"

Elizabeth clamped her mouth shut before her traitorous tongue told him yes, anything as long as he made the world narrow to just the two of them again. When she felt she could speak rationally, she told him what was foremost on his mind. "I cannot find my pleasure without knowing why you have treated Mr.

Wickham so ill."

"I would by no means suspend any pleasure of yours," he coldly replied. "I do not explain myself."

She said no more, and they went down the other dance and parted in silence; and on each side dissatisfied, though not to an equal degree, for in Darcy's breast there was a tolerable powerful feeling towards her, which soon procured her pardon, and directed all his anger against another.

They had not long separated, when Miss Bingley came towards her, and with an expression of civil disdain accosted her:

"So, Miss Eliza, I hear you are quite delighted with George Wickham!" Miss Bingley tossed her head in disdain. "Your sister has been talking to me about him, and asking me a thousand questions; and I find that the young man quite forgot to tell you, among his other communication, that he was the son of old Wickham, the late Mr. Darcy's steward. Let me recommend you, however, as a friend, not to give implicit confidence to all his assertions; for as to Mr. Darcy's using him ill, it is perfectly false; for, on the contrary, he has always been remarkably kind to him, though George Wickham has treated Mr. Darcy in a most infamous manner. I do not know the particulars, but I know very well that Mr. Darcy is not in the least to blame, that he cannot bear to hear George Wickham mentioned. I pity you, Miss Eliza, for this discovery of your favorite's guilt; but really, considering his descent, one could not expect much better."

Elizabeth thought she looked rather shrill and high strung tonight. Jane wasn't giving her a second glance because she was looking at Mr. Bingley as if the moon shined out of his eyes. Mr. Darcy, in foul temper, was also not looking to spend time in Miss Bingley's presence.

"Mr. Wickham's guilt and his descent appear by your account to be the same," said Elizabeth angrily; "for I have heard you accuse him of nothing worse than of being the son of Mr. Darcy's steward, and of that, I can assure you, he informed me himself."

"I beg your pardon," replied Miss Bingley, turning away with a sneer. "Excuse my interference—it was kindly meant."

"Insolent girl!" said Elizabeth to herself. "You are much mistaken if you expect to influence me by such a paltry attack as this. I see nothing in it but your own willful ignorance and the malice of Mr. Darcy." She then sought her eldest sister, who has undertaken to make inquiries on the same subject of Bingley.

Jane met her with a smile of such sweet complacency, a glow of such happy expression, as sufficiently marked how well she was satisfied with the occurrences of the evening. Elizabeth instantly read her feelings, and at that moment solicitude for Wickham, resentment against his enemies, and everything else, gave way before the hope of Jane's being in the fairest way for happiness.

"I want to know," Elizabeth said with a countenance no less smiling than her sister's. "What you have learnt about Mr. Wickham? But perhaps you have been too pleasantly engaged to think of any third person; in which case you may be sure of my pardon."

"No," replied Jane, "I have not forgotten him; but I have nothing satisfactory to tell you. Mr. Bingley does not know the whole of his history, and is quite ignorant of the circumstances which have principally offended Mr. Darcy; but he will vouch for the good conduct, the probity, and honour of his friend, and is perfectly convinced that Mr. Wickham has deserved much less attention from Mr. Darcy than he has received; and I am sorry to say by his account as well as his sister's, Mr. Wickham is by no means a respectable young man. I am afraid he has been very imprudent, and has deserved to lose Mr. Darcy's regard."

"Mr. Bingley does not know Mr. Wickham himself?" Elizabeth pressed.

"No; he never saw him till the other morning at Meryton."

"I have not a doubt of Mr. Bingley's sincerity," said Elizabeth warmly; "but you must excuse my not being convinced by assurances only. Mr. Bingley's defense of his friend was a very able one, I dare say; but since he is unacquainted with several parts of the story, and has learnt the rest from that friend himself, I shall venture to still think of both gentlemen as I did before."

"As you wish, dearest Lizzy." Jane frowned at her. "However, are you sure you are determined to paint Mr. Darcy the villain because he has told you some hard truths about you?"

When Elizabeth bowed her head and stared as if fascinated at her fingernails, Jane

then changed the discourse to one more gratifying to each, and on which there could be no difference of sentiment. Elizabeth listened with delight to the happy, though modest hopes which Jane entertained of Mr. Bingley's regard, and said all in her power to heighten her confidence in it.

On their being joined by Mr. Bingley himself, Elizabeth withdrew to Miss Lucas; to whose inquiry after the pleasantness of her last partner she had scarcely replied, before Mr. Collins came up to them, and told her with great exultation that he had just been so fortunate as to make a most important discovery.

"I have found out," said he, "by a singular accident, that there is now in the room a near relation of my patroness. I happened to overhear the gentleman himself mentioning to the young lady who does the honours of the house the names of his cousin Miss de Bourgh, and of her mother Lady Catherine."

"You are not going to introduce yourself to Mr. Darcy!" Elizabeth cried.

"Indeed I am. I shall entreat his pardon for not having done it earlier. I believe him to be Lady Catherine's nephew. It will be in my power to assure him that her ladyship was quite well yesterday se'nnight."

Elizabeth tried hard to dissuade him from such a scheme, assuring him that Mr. Darcy would consider his addressing him without introduction as an impertinent freedom, rather than a compliment to his aunt.

But Mr. Collins would not hear a word of sense and with a low bow he left her to attack Mr. Darcy, whose reception of his advances she eagerly watched, and whose astonishment at being so addressed was very evident.

Her cousin prefaced his speech with a solemn bow and though she could not hear a word of it, she felt as if hearing it all, and saw in the motion of his lips the words "apology," "Hunsford," "Lady Catherine de Bourgh, and "Master." It vexed her to see him expose himself to such a man.

Mr. Darcy was eyeing him with unrestrained wonder, and when at last Mr. Collins allowed him time to speak, replied with an air of distant civility. Mr. Collins, however, was not discouraged from speaking again, and Mr. Darcy's contempt seemed abundantly increasing with the length of his second speech, and at the end of it he only made him a slight bow, and moved another way.

Elizabeth watched him to see if he would go down below to amuse himself with Inga or another. What would she do if he held out his hand to Miss Bingley and she came running?

"Don't clench your hands into fists," Charlotte said in her ear.

"I'm not," she said hotly, but of course she had been.

Charlotte intercepted Mr. Collins as he returned, beaming from his perceived victory at speaking with his benefactrix's nephew.

"Bless you Charlotte," Elizabeth said under her breath. She didn't think she could bear more of her cousin's pertinence.

As Elizabeth had no longer any interest of her own to pursue, she turned her attention almost entirely on her sister and Mr. Bingley; and the train of agreeable reflections which her observations gave birth to, made her perhaps almost as happy as Jane. She saw her in idea settled in that very house, in all the felicity which a marriage of true affection could bestow; and she felt capable, under such circumstances, of endeavouring even to like Bingley's two sisters.

Her mother's thoughts she plainly saw were bent the same way. She was talking to that Lady Lucas freely, openly, and of nothing else but her expectation that Jane would soon be married to Mr. Bingley.

Elizabeth attempted to quiet her mother and change the subject, but Mrs. Bennet was incapable of fatigue while enumerating the advantages of the match. Bingley was such a charming young man, and so rich, and living but three miles from them, were the first points of self-gratulation; and then it was such a comfort to think how fond the two sisters were of Jane, and to be certain that they must desire the connection as much as she could do.

To Elizabeth's utter mortification, her mother went on and on, saying it was, moreover, such a promising thing for her younger daughters, as Jane's marrying so greatly must throw them in the way of other rich men.

Elizabeth looked down the table at Kitty and Lydia who were behaving as if they wanted a turn in the dungeons themselves. Surely their father could do something about that, but he was nowhere to be seen.

At long last Mrs. Bennet concluded with many good wishes that Lady Lucas might soon be equally fortunate, though evidently and triumphantly believing there was no chance of it.

In vain did Elizabeth endeavour to check the rapidity of her mother's words, or persuade her to describe her felicity in a less audible whisper.

Nothing that she could say, however, had any influence. Her mother would talk of her views in the same intelligible tone. Elizabeth blushed and blushed again with shame and vexation. She could not help frequently glancing her eye at Mr. Darcy, though every glance convinced her of what she dreaded; for though he was not always looking at her mother, she was convinced that his attention was invariably fixed by her.

The expression of his face changed gradually from indignant contempt to a composed and steady gravity.

She wanted to explain to him that it was just the way her mother was and she was harmless in her own way, but the words stuck in her throat.

At length, however, Mrs. Bennet had no more to say And Elizabeth began to revive. But not long was the interval of tranquillity; for, when supper was over, singing was talked of, and she had the mortification of seeing Mary, after very little entreaty, preparing to oblige the company.

By many significant looks and silent entreaties, did she endeavour to prevent such a proof of complaisance, but in vain; Mary would not understand them; such an opportunity of exhibiting was delightful to her, and she began her song. Mary's powers were by no means fitted for such a display; her voice was weak, and her manner affected.

Elizabeth was in agonies. She looked at Jane, to see how she bore it; but Jane was very composedly talking to Bingley. She looked at his two sisters, and saw them making signs of derision at each other, and at Darcy, who continued, however, imperturbably grave. She looked at her father to entreat his interference, lest Mary should be singing all night. He took the hint, and when Mary had finished her second song, said aloud,

"That will do extremely well, child. You have delighted us long enough. Let the other young ladies have time to exhibit."

Mary, though pretending not to hear, was somewhat disconcerted; and Elizabeth, sorry for her, and sorry for her father's speech, was afraid her anxiety had done no good.

To Elizabeth it appeared that, had her family made an agreement to expose themselves as much as they could during the evening, it would have been impossible for them to play their parts with more spirit or finer success; and happy did she think it for Bingley and her sister that some of the exhibition had escaped his notice, and that his feelings were not of a sort to be much distressed by the folly which he must have witnessed. That his two sisters and Mr. Darcy, however, should have such an opportunity of ridiculing her relations, was bad enough, and she could not determine whether the silent contempt of the gentleman, or the insolent smiles of the ladies, were more intolerable.

At the end of her rope, Elizabeth realized that nothing would paint her family in a better light. She might as well please herself. She moved to the staircase, dodging soldiers and nodding at other guests. A hand on her arm stopped her just as she was to place a foot on the stairs. Mr. Darcy's fingers gripped her elbow that she was sure to be bruised the next morning.

"There is nothing down there for you."

"I beg to differ, sir."

"Master," he whispered. "And does this mean you are mine?"

She shook her head. "I am beyond mortification and this night is surely the worst of my life. I seek redemption of it."

Mr. Darcy cocked his head at her. "Come to the library with me," he said.

"I told you I do not wish to discuss books with you."

"And perhaps I was not clear that no man but I will touch you."

Elizabeth's breath caught in her throat. "Will you touch me?"

He cocked an eyebrow at her.

"Master," she whispered.

"Walk," he ordered and together they sauntered into the library. He all but shoved her inside and bolted the door closed.

"I will be ruined, if we were seen."

"No one pays attention to such things at Netherfield," he told her.

"I dislike you," she said.

"Good," he said indifferently. "I have a urge to make you like me less."

"I don't know how that is possible . . . Oh!" She gave a little scream as he crossed the room with the quickness of a panther. With a cruel twist of her arm, he propelled her to the reading couch and laid her across his lap.

"What are you doing?" she asked, trying to get up as he pulled her skirts over her head.

"Such virtue," he mocked, "Wearing undergarments to Netherfield." He yanked them off, ripping them. "You will leave without them."

"You're a beast," she raged, even as pleasure

191

pooled deep in her belly.

"So lovely," Mr. Darcy said in a shaking voice. "How you drive me to madness. Just when I think I cannot loathe your family more, the sound of your voice wipes them all from my mind." He slapped his big hand on the sweet white curve of her buttocks.

"Oh," she hiccupped into the red velvet of the couch.

"This," he spanked her again. "Is for your intolerable manners as we danced." Whack. "This is for mentioning that reprobate Wickham." Whack."

"Please," Elizabeth sobbed. Her posterior was burning and she was growing wet between her legs.

Whack. "Please what?"

"Please, Master, no more."

Whack. "Don't top from the bottom."

"What?" she asked.

Whack. "That is for your mother."

"Please Master, another."

"Indeed." He gave her three rapid smacks.

"Thank you, Master," she whispered. Her bottom was hot and raw from his ministrations, but she felt the shame her family caused drifting away.

Whack.

She flinched.

"That was for your sister's abysmal piano playing."

Elizabeth stifled a giggle even as tears rolled down her cheek. "Master, please." *Love me* came unbidden to her lips and she swallowed it before it erupted into the room.

Whack.

"That was for your idiot cousin who dared speak

to me so familiarly."

Whack, Whack

"That was for your two youngest sisters whose behavior is this side of appalling."

"Thank you, Master," she said.

He rubbed his hand over her burning flesh. She felt his hardness pressing against his belly.

Whack. That was the hardest of all and she shrieked in pain.

"That was for making me think of nothing else but your sweet body. Are you going to let me have you?"

"No, Master," she said, bracing for the next slap. But he merely rubbed her bottom, soothing her while inflaming her senses.

"Your mouth says no," he said and rolled her off him so she landed artlessly on the floor. Her skirts were still up around her waist. "But your body begs for me."

He lay between her thighs, touching his mouth to her sensitive folds. Elizabeth writhed, wishing she could think of Charlotte or the damnable Mr. Wickham – even Miss Bingley, but there was no one but Mr. Darcy. He licked every inch of her core, paying attention to the swollen, sensitive bud that had her bucking her hips into his face as he serviced her with his tongue and fingers.

"Darcy," she moaned, shattering into a thousand pieces. "Why can't I hate you?"

"Everyday could be like this," he said. "You are the only one stopping this."

"I . . .," she said helplessly.

"No more words," he unbuttoned his pants and

guided her head to him.

Elizabeth lunged for him, almost knocking them off balance.

"Yes," he hissed out as she took out her aggression by sucking him down her throat.

She wanted to break his calm, his control.

His fingers twisted in her hair, tangling each curl through his hands. She opened her eyes to look up at him and found him staring at her, mesmerized.

"You please me, sweet Elizabeth," he said, sounding hollow and shocked.

Elizabeth slid her mouth up and down, reveling in the feel of him in her throat. Her tongue lapped circles around him.

"I would have you naked, covered in oil."

She bobbed her head faster, loving the sound of his harsh breathing.

"Your feet tied over your head."

Her mouth was making wet, sucking sounds.

"I would penetrate you until you remember no other touch by mine," he gritted out. His body tensed. Elizabeth flung her arms around his hips, keeping him locked down her throat as he came.

"Oh sweet Elizabeth. Mine. Only mine," he roared.

Pulling her head back, he kissed her, deep, devouring. She felt as if she was drowning.

"You must leave, or surrender to me," he said.

"I cannot," she cried. "Wretched creature that I am. Wretched creature that you are."

He helped her to her feet and held her until she gained back her balance. Smoothing her skirts over her still stinging backside, he kissed her and she could still taste herself on his lips.

"Think on my offer. Your family does you no favors."

She straightened away from him. "I love my family. And I am more than the sum of their personalities."

He watched her leave the library with a thoughtful frown.

The rest of the evening brought Elizabeth little amusement She was at least free from the offense of Mr. Darcy's further notice; though often standing within a very short distance of her, quite disengaged, he never came near enough to speak.

The Longbourn party were the last of all the company to depart, and, by a manoeuvre of Mrs. Bennet, had to wait for their carriage a quarter of an hour after everybody else was gone, which gave them time to see how heartily they were wished away by some of the family.

Darcy said nothing at all. Mr. Bennet, in equal silence, was enjoying the scene. Mr. Bingley and Jane were standing together, a little detached from the rest, and talked only to each other

Chapter 19

The next day opened a new scene at Longbourn. Mr. Collins made his declaration in form. "May I hope, madam, for your interest with your fair daughter Elizabeth, when I solicit for the honour of a private audience with her in the course of this morning?"

Before Elizabeth had time for anything but a blush of surprise, Mrs. Bennet answered instantly, "Oh dear!—yes—certainly. I am sure Lizzy will be very happy—I am sure she can have no objection. Come, Kitty, I want you up stairs." And, gathering her work together, she was hastening away, when Elizabeth called out:

"Dear madam, do not go. I beg you will not go. Mr. Collins must excuse me. He can have nothing to say to me that anybody need not hear. I am going away myself."

Even if she could sit down this morning without a painful reminder of Mr. Darcy, she couldn't accept her cousin's offer.

"No, no, nonsense, Lizzy. I desire you to stay where you are." And upon Elizabeth's seeming really, with vexed and embarrassed looks, about to escape, she added: "Lizzy, I insist upon your staying and hearing Mr. Collins."

Elizabeth would not oppose such an injunction—and a moment's consideration making her also sensible that it would be wisest to get it over as soon and as quietly as possible, she sat down again. Winced at the flare of pain and the phantom caress of Mr. Darcy's hand. She tried to conceal, by incessant employment the feelings which were divided between distress and diversion. Mrs. Bennet and Kitty walked off, and as soon as they were gone, Mr. Collins began.

"Believe me, my dear Miss Elizabeth, that your modesty, so far from doing you any disservice, rather adds to your other perfections. I have your respected mother's permission for this address. You can hardly doubt the purport of my discourse, however your natural delicacy may lead you to dissemble; my attentions have been too marked to be mistaken. Almost as soon as I entered the house, I singled you out as the companion of my future life."

Elizabeth's spirits sank. Here was her offer of marriage. The chance to prove to Mr. Darcy that she could marry without being trained as his submissive. She knew that Mr. Collins would either not care or notice that the wall of her virginity had been scaled – or would that be plundered? Elizabeth's mind roamed on more pleasant thoughts before she forced herself to hear what her cousin was saying to her.

"But before I am run away with by my feelings on this subject, perhaps it would be advisable for me to state my reasons for marrying—and, moreover, for coming into Hertfordshire with the design of selecting a wife, as I certainly did."

The idea of Mr. Collins, with all his solemn

197

composure, being run away with by his feelings, made Elizabeth so near laughing, that she could not use the short pause he allowed in any attempt to stop him further, and he she daydreamed again as he spoke in loving terms about Lady de Bourgh.

Perhaps he should marry her, Elizabeth thought with a sympathetic pang. Lady de Bourgh or her daughter would never accept him, just as her nephew would not overlook her own ignoble status in society.

If she married Mr. Collins, she would be subservient not to her husband but to the grand dame of the ton herself. While the thought might have held titillation for her at one time, Elizabeth only wanted Darcy. But she wanted him proposing marriage instead of Mr. Collins. She tried to look at her cousin fondly. She tried to at least consider his request. But it was too ludicrous. He was too odd and the fact that he was more submissive than some of Netherfield's slaves left her cold inside. Theirs would never be a grand passion.

"The fact is," Mr. Collins said, breaking through Elizabeth's thoughts, "that being, as I am, to inherit this estate after the death of your honoured father (who, however, may live many years longer), I could not satisfy myself without resolving to choose a wife from among his daughters, that the loss to them might be as little as possible, when the melancholy event takes place—which, however, as I have already said, may not be for several years. This has been my motive, my fair cousin, and I flatter myself it will not sink me in your esteem. "

It was absolutely necessary to interrupt him now.

"You are too hasty, sir," she cried. "You forget that I have made no answer. Let me do it without further loss of time. Accept my thanks for the compliment you are paying me. I am very sensible of the honour of your proposals, but it is impossible for me to do otherwise than to decline them."

"I am not now to learn," replied Mr. Collins, with a formal wave of the hand, "that it is usual with young ladies to reject the addresses of the man whom they secretly mean to accept, when he first applies for their favour; and that sometimes the refusal is repeated a second, or even a third time. I am therefore by no means discouraged by what you have just said, and shall hope to lead you to the altar ere long."

Elizabeth stared at him unblinking.

"Upon my word, sir," cried Elizabeth, "your hope is a rather extraordinary one after my declaration. I do assure you that I am not one of those young ladies (if such young ladies there are) who are so daring as to risk their happiness on the chance of being asked a second time. I am perfectly serious in my refusal. You could not make me happy, and I am convinced that I am the last woman in the world who could make you so.

Indeed, Mr. Collins, all praise of me will be unnecessary. You must give me leave to judge for myself, and pay me the compliment of believing what I say. I wish you very happy and very rich, and by refusing your hand, do all in my power to prevent your being otherwise. In making me the offer, you must have satisfied the delicacy of your feelings with regard to my family, and may take possession of Longbourn estate whenever it falls, without any self-reproach. This matter may be considered, therefore, as finally settled."

And rising as she thus spoke, she would have quitted the room in desperate relief, had Mr. Collins not thus addressed her:

"When I do myself the honour of speaking to you next on the subject, I shall hope to receive a more favourable answer than you have now given me."

"Really, Mr. Collins," cried Elizabeth with some warmth, "you puzzle me exceedingly. If what I have hitherto said can appear to you in the form of encouragement, I know not how to express my refusal in such a way as to convince you of its being one."

"You must give me leave to flatter myself, my dear cousin, that your refusal of my addresses is merely words of course. You should take it into further consideration, that in spite of your manifold attractions, it is by no means certain that another offer of marriage may ever be made you."

Elizabeth reeled as if struck. If this was the nature of bridegrooms she would die happily an old maid.

" Your portion is unhappily so small that it will in all likelihood undo the effects of your loveliness and amiable qualifications. "

His words, so close to Mr. Darcy's was like a red flag waved in front of a bull.

"I do assure you, sir," she said, her voice shaking with suppressed rage. "That I have no pretensions whatever to that kind of elegance which consists in tormenting a respectable man. Unless it's with a riding crop."

It was Mr. Collins turn to flinch. The heated look in his eyes surprised her and she back tracked. "I would rather be paid the compliment of being believed sincere. I thank you again and again for the honour you have done me in your proposals, but to accept them is absolutely impossible. My feelings in every respect forbid it. Can I speak plainer? Do not consider me now as an elegant female, intending to plague you, but as a rational creature, speaking the truth from her heart."

"You are uniformly charming!" cried he, with an air of awkward gallantry; "and I am persuaded that when sanctioned by the express authority of both your excellent parents, my proposals will not fail of being acceptable."

To such perseverance in wilful self-deception Elizabeth would make no reply, and immediately and in silence withdrew; determined, if he persisted in considering her repeated refusals as flattering encouragement, to apply to her father, whose negative might be uttered in such a manner as to be decisive, and whose behaviour at least could not be mistaken for the affectation and coquetry of an elegant female.

Elizabeth left the room as fast as her throbbing posterior allowed her. Each flash of pain felt as if Mr. Darcy was mocking her.

Chapter 20

Mr. Collins was not left long to the silent contemplation of his successful love; for Mrs. Bennet, having dawdled about in the vestibule to watch for the end of the conference, no sooner saw Elizabeth open the door and with quick step pass her towards the staircase, than she entered the breakfast-room, and congratulated both him and herself in warm terms on the happy prospect or their nearer connection.

"I feel as if I have gained a son," she gushed.

Mr. Collins received and returned these felicitations with equal pleasure, and then proceeded to relate the particulars of their interview, with the result of which he trusted he had every reason to be satisfied, since the refusal which his cousin had steadfastly given him would naturally flow from her bashful modesty and the genuine delicacy of her character.

Although belying that delicacy, Mr. Collins was intrigued by the fire he saw in Elizabeth's eyes when she spoke of the riding crop. It was one thing to dally with dominant women – surely he loved nothing more. But to spend one's life with one, it would be exhausting. Of course, before the pall set it, in would be rather exciting.

His information, however, startled Mrs. Bennet; she would have been glad to be equally satisfied that her daughter had meant to encourage him by protesting against his proposals, but she dared not believe it, and could not help saying so.

"But, depend upon it, Mr. Collins," she added, "that Lizzy shall be brought to reason. I will speak to her about it directly. She is a very headstrong, foolish girl, and does not know her own interest but I will make her know it."

"Pardon me for interrupting you, madam," cried Mr. Collins; "but if she is really headstrong and foolish, I know not whether she would altogether be a very desirable wife to a man in my situation, who naturally looks for happiness in the marriage state. If therefore she actually persists in rejecting my suit, perhaps it were better not to force her into accepting me, because if liable to such defects of temper, she could not contribute much to my felicity."

Elizabeth was lovely, but he wanted a modicum of peace in his house. He was not only having second thoughts about his proposal, but already his mind was pursuing another bride. One that wasn't so . . .spirited.

"Sir, you quite misunderstand me," said Mrs. Bennet, alarmed. "Lizzy is only headstrong in such matters as these. In everything else she is as good-natured a girl as ever lived. I will go directly to Mr. Bennet, and we shall very soon settle it with her, I am sure."

She would not give him time to reply, but hurrying instantly to her husband, called out as she entered the library, "Oh! Mr. Bennet, you are wanted immediately; we are all in an uproar. You must come and make Lizzy marry Mr. Collins, for she vows she will not have him, and if you do not make haste he will change his mind and not have her."

Mr. Bennet raised his eyes from his book as she entered, and fixed them on her face with a calm unconcern which was not in the least altered by her communication. They had spent most of last night frolicking with enthusiasm they hadn't shared in many years. The ball at Netherfield had awoken a passion in him for experimentation. He set aside his book, which was a catalog of toys to be used in sexual play. They would have time to peruse this together when this current kerfuffle was over.

"I have not the pleasure of understanding you," said he, when she had finished her speech. "Of what are you talking?" In truth, he had been watching her lovely bosom rise and fall in agitation.

"Of Mr. Collins and Lizzy. Lizzy declares she will not have Mr. Collins, and Mr. Collins begins to say that he will not have Lizzy."

"And what am I to do on the occasion? It seems an hopeless business." He went to pick up his book again, but his dear wife was not finished.

"Speak to Lizzy about it yourself. Tell her that you insist upon her marrying him."

He sighed. There would be no peace until this was resolved. "Let her be called down. She shall hear my opinion."

Mrs. Bennet rang the bell, and Miss Elizabeth was summoned to the library.

"Come here, child," cried her father as she appeared. "I have sent for you on an affair of importance. I understand that Mr. Collins has made you an offer of marriage. Is it true?" Elizabeth replied that it was. "Very well—and this offer of marriage you have refused?"

"I have, sir." She blinked back tears, trying to find the words to sway her dear father. She could not tell him of the dark feelings for Mr. Darcy. Or how shamed Mr. Collins made her feel when he mentioned that she should not expect any other man to offer for her. What was the good of her virginity if it was prized far lower than her dowry?

"Very well. We now come to the point. Your mother insists upon your accepting it. Is it not so, Mrs. Bennet?"

"Yes, or I will never see her again." Mrs. Bennet crossed her arms in front of her ample bosom, but Mr. Bennet was not to be sidetracked.

"An unhappy alternative is before you, Elizabeth. From this day you must be a stranger to one of your parents. Your mother will never see you again if you do not marry Mr. Collins, and I will never see you again if you do."

Elizabeth could not but smile at such a conclusion of such a beginning, but Mrs. Bennet, who had persuaded herself that her husband regarded the affair as she wished, was excessively disappointed.

"Thank you, father," she said and skipped gaily out of his library.

"What do you mean, Mr. Bennet, in talking this way? You promised me to insist upon her marrying him."

"My dear," replied her husband, "I have two small favours to request. First, that you will allow me the free use of my understanding on the present occasion; and secondly, of my room. I shall be glad to have the library to myself as soon as may be."

"This is no jest. Who will take us in if Mr. Collins puts us out upon your demise?"

"You must hope then, my dear, that mortal event will not happen for a long time hence."

"I must hope for something that quells my nerves," Mrs. Bennet said.

A wicked gleam appeared in her husband's eyes and she immediately began shaking her head. "No. Absolutely not. In fact, not ever again."

He got up and went to a special wooden armoire. He removed the ornate key from his pocket. Mrs. Bennet raised a hand to her quivering lips.

"No," she said again, this time with less resolution in her voice. "You should have forced Elizabeth to marry Mr. Collins."

Opening the door, Mr. Bennet pulled out leather restraints. He slipped them over his wife's wrists and tightened them behind her back.

"I will not stand for this," she said.

He pulled her over to the armoire. "Then kneel," he said. "I have something for your nerves." With a firm push, Mrs. Bennet was on her knees before her husband, her hands trapped behind her back.

"Mr. Bennet," she said in a breathy, excited voice. And then she couldn't speak as her husband angled his cock into her mouth.

He held her head tight against his hips, letting her accept all of him to the back of her throat. "That's it, my dear. Take it all. You just suck while I put together a little surprise for you."

He guided her head up and down on him. "Just like that my love. Just like that."

Mrs. Bennet took out her frustrations on her husband's thick phallus. She sucked hard and long down the tempting length of him. His firm hand on the back of her head drove all thoughts of the horrid Mr. Collins from her mind. She concentrated on tasting him, enjoying the soothing motions of pleasuring him.

"Ah my darling, I'm ready for you. I do not want to spend myself down your throat." He eased out of her. Mrs. Bennet felt oddly bereft until he bent her over his desk and hauled up her skirts.

Kicking her feet wider, Mr. Bennet smoothed the layers of cloth over his wife's bound arms.

"Aren't you pretty down there," he said, fingering her wetness. "Like a pink flower."

He ran his palms over her exposed backside. "Are you wondering what delights I have for you madam?"

Mrs. Bennet tried to hang on to her righteous indignation. "I am not the least bit . . . Oh!" she ended with when Mr. Bennet drizzled warmed oil into her backside. She felt a warm slick, solid probe against her posterior.

"What are you doing?" she asked.

Mr. Bennet eased the slim, rosewood phallus inside his wife's anus. "How does that feel?" he asked.

"Tight," she breathed.

He positioned himself to slip into her other opening that eagerly clenched around him.

"Full," she giggled. "And oh so wonderful."

"Let me ease your nerves, my dear." He hauled her back against him and drummed her body into the desk.

Mrs. Bennet writhed, feeling stretched and completely filled. Her husband's rhythmic thrusts pushed the wooden one as well so it was as if she was enjoying two men inside her at once. The thought was so thrilling, so delicious that she began to move her hips to allow him deeper access. Her hands were bound tight otherwise she'd be rubbing herself as well.

"How are your nerves now, my dear?" He asked, picking up speed so her breasts mashed against his desk. "I fear I cannot keep up this pace."

She looked over her shoulder. He clamped a hand on it to drive himself deeper.

"Yes," she groaned out, deep and satisfied.

He slapped her plump butt cheek and pistoned inside her.

"Yes," she shrieked and wildly pushed back as need and desire clashed with the desperate building sensation. She felt herself at the precipice and her vision darkened with the force of her orgasm. Mr. Bennet followed shortly with a harsh shout and another smack on her exposed buttocks.

Pulling out, he fixed himself and left her recovering face down on the desk. She felt boneless as he lifted one leg, slid a leather loop around it and then did the same for the other.

"What?" she muttered, drunk on the aftermath of bliss.

Leather rolled up her legs, tightening on her thighs. The wooden phallus in her backside dipped inside her and pleasure cascaded again. She heard the tightening of a restraint, but couldn't fathom what it was until a second phallus entered her quim. She cried out, and Mr. Bennet hauled her back to her feet by her bound arms.

Her chemise and dress fell correctly, but the phalluses inside her stayed.

Mr. Bennet grasped the back of her head, kissing her startled face. His free hand swatted her rump making her tighten around the wooden rods.

"There now, keep those in until tonight. It should do wonders for your nerves."

Mrs. Bennet could only nod in a dazed manner, until a sharp pinch on her nipples drew her eyes up to her husband's. He pinched the other one, tugging them both until he had her full attention. "If they're not in place when I come to bed tonight, you'll feel the full force of my disproval. Do you understand?"

Voiceless, she nodded.

"That's my wife." He kissed her again and with another swat on her rump, sent her away.

Mr. Collins, meanwhile, was meditating in solitude on what had passed. He thought too well of himself to comprehend on what motives his cousin could refuse him; and though his pride was hurt, he suffered in no other way. His regard for her was quite imaginary; and the possibility of her deserving her mother's reproach prevented his feeling any regret.

While the family were in this confusion, Charlotte Lucas came to spend the day with them. She was met in the vestibule by Lydia, who, flying to her, cried in a half whisper, "I am glad you are come, for there is such fun here! What do you think has happened this morning? Mr. Collins has made an offer to Lizzy, and she will not have him."

Charlotte hardly had time to answer, before they

were joined by Kitty, who came to tell the same news.Charlotte's reply was spared by the entrance of Jane and Elizabeth.

They were joined by Mr. Collins, who entered the room with an air more stately than usual, and on perceiving whom, Mrs. Bennet said to the girls, "Now, I do insist upon it, that you, all of you, hold your tongues, and let me and Mr. Collins have a little conversation together."

Elizabeth passed quietly out of the room, Jane and Kitty followed, but Lydia stood her ground, determined to hear all she could; and Charlotte, detained first by the civility of Mr. Collins, whose inquiries after herself and all her family were very minute, and then by a little curiosity, satisfied herself with walking to the window and pretending not to hear. She looked at Mr. Collins out of the side of her eyes.

In a doleful voice Mrs. Bennet began the projected conversation: "Oh! Mr. Collins!"

"My dear madam," replied he, "let us be for ever silent on this point. Far be it from me," he presently continued, in a voice that marked his displeasure, "to resent the behaviour of your daughter."

Charlotte nearly snorted. Lizzie had hurt his pride all right.

"You will not, I hope, consider me as showing any disrespect to your family, my dear madam, by thus withdrawing my pretensions to your daughter's favour, without having paid yourself and Mr. Bennet the compliment of requesting you to interpose your authority in my behalf. My conduct may, I fear, be objectionable in having accepted my dismission from your daughter's lips instead of your own. But we are all liable to error. I have certainly meant well through the whole affair. My object has been to secure an amiable companion for myself, with due consideration for the advantage of all your family, and if my manner has been at all reprehensible, I here beg leave to apologise."

Charlotte straightened away from the window and demurely cast her eyes down. If Elizabeth was throwing husbands away, surely she wouldn't mind if Charlotte cast her net in the same sea.

Chapter 21

The discussion of Mr. Collins's offer was now nearly at an end, and Elizabeth had only to suffer from the uncomfortable feelings necessarily attending it, and occasionally from some peevish allusions of her mother. As for the gentleman himself, his feelings were chiefly expressed, not by embarrassment or dejection, or by trying to avoid her, but by stiffness of manner and resentful silence. He scarcely ever spoke to her, and the assiduous attentions which he had been so sensible of himself were transferred for the rest of the day to Miss Lucas, whose civility in listening to him was a seasonable relief to them all, and especially to her friend.

A few days later, a letter was delivered to Miss Jane Bennet. It came from Netherfield. The envelope contained a sheet of elegant, little, hot-pressed paper, well covered with a lady's fair, flowing hand; and Elizabeth saw her sister's countenance change as she read it, and saw her dwelling intently on some particular passages. With a glance, Jane invited her to follow her up stairs. When they had gained their own room, Jane, taking out the letter, said:

"This is from Caroline Bingley; what it contains

has surprised me a good deal. The whole party has left Netherfield by this time, and are on their way to town—and without any intention of coming back again. "

"Well," Elizabeth said. "Did she say why the family is leaving or when they'll be back? The suddenness of their removal surprised her, but she saw nothing in it really to lament; it was not to be supposed that their absence from Netherfield would prevent Mr. Bingley's being there; and as to the loss of their society, she was persuaded that Jane must cease to regard it, in the enjoyment of his. If she were to be Bingley's wife, she should not further dally with his sisters, no matter how delightful the intercourse was.

"Mr. Darcy is impatient to see his sister." Jane read.

Elizabeth flinched at hearing his name. She was used to calling out for him in her head, and rethinking his offer time and time again.

Jane continued reading Miss Bingley's letter, not noticing her sister's visceral reaction to the mention of Mr. Darcy.

"To confess the truth, we are scarcely less eager to meet her again. I really do not think Georgiana Darcy has her equal for beauty, elegance, and accomplishments; and the affection she inspires in Louisa and myself is heightened into something still more interesting, from the hope we dare entertain of her being hereafter our sister. My brother admires her greatly already; he will have frequent opportunity now of seeing her on the most intimate footing; her relations all wish the connection as much as his own; and a sister's partiality is not misleading me, I think,

213

when I call Charles most capable of engaging any woman's heart. With all these circumstances to favour an attachment, and nothing to prevent it, am I wrong, my dearest Jane, in indulging the hope of an event which will secure the happiness of so many?"

"No one who has ever seen you together can doubt his affection," Elizabeth said, snatching the letter up and shaking her head at the prim penmanship. "Miss Bingley, I am sure, cannot. She is not such a simpleton. Could she have seen half as much love in Mr. Darcy for herself, she would have ordered her wedding clothes. But the case is this: We are not rich enough or grand enough for them," Elizabeth said bitterly. Mr. Darcy had said as much to her. "Miss Bingley is the more anxious to get Miss Darcy for her brother, from the notion that when there has been one intermarriage, she may have less trouble in achieving a second; in which there is certainly some ingenuity, and I dare say it would succeed, if Miss de Bourgh were out of the way. But, my dearest Jane, you cannot seriously imagine that because Miss Bingley tells you her brother greatly admires Miss Darcy, he is in the smallest degree less sensible of your merit than when he took leave of you on Tuesday, or that it will be in her power to persuade him that, instead of being in love with you, he is very much in love with her friend."

"If we thought alike of Miss Bingley," replied Jane, "your representation of all this might make me quite easy. But I know the foundation is unjust. Caroline is incapable of wilfully deceiving anyone; and all that I can hope in this case is that she is deceiving herself."

Elizabeth rolled her eyes. Jane would never see anything but the good in people. She wouldn't fathom that Caroline Bingley was a jealous, sniping shrew. "He'll be back," Elizabeth said. "I promise you."

"What if I was too forward?" Jane whispered. "What if I chased him away with my wantonness?"

"Nonsense," Elizabeth said. "Don't give this letter a second thought. He'll be back by Christmas." Elizabeth kissed her sister on the forehead. "I mean it." She waggled her finger in warning and then went back downstairs to see if she could speak to avoid Mr. Collins long enough to get a message to Charlotte.

Jane lay down on the bed and reread the letter over and over again. Finally, she tossed it aside and closed her eyes.

"Oh Mr. Bingley," she sighed, remembering the furtive way he stole into her bedchamber.

"Miss Bennet," he had said, "Forgive my boldness but my desire to see you outweighs common sense – common decency as well."

"I would forgive you anything," she said to him, her breathing quickened when he knelt on the bed.

"Would you forgive me this, my dearest one?" Mr. Bingley had slipped her sleeping gown off her shoulders and down over her breasts.

Her nipples had puckered at being exposed to the cool night air.

At the memory, Jane reached inside her bodice and fondled while thinking of what Mr. Bingley did next.

She had let him look his fill, admiring as his fingers trembled when at last he deigned to touch them. His mouth was warm, tongue stroking across her peaks. His lips had clamped down on one nipple, sucking it deep in his mouth.

"Mr. Bingley!" Jane had cried out in delight.

"Do I go too far?" He raised his head to look at her in concern. "Here you lie sick in my house and I can do naught but take advantage of you. I assure you, my darling Miss Bennet, I am not a cad."

Jane did not tell him that his sisters gone farther and with less remorse. But he had something she wanted that his sisters couldn't provide no matter how talented their tongues were. She reached for his breeches and his eyes went wide.

"My darling," he had said as she freed his large member from his pants. "Are you sure?"

Jane had nodded and pulled him close so his hardness was nestled between her two breasts.

Remembering how he slid out of his pants so she could feel his skin against hers, Jane pulled up her skirts in her lonely bedroom and traced her fingers over the throbbing bud between her legs. Her other hand idly pinched her nipples, tugging and stretching them.

Bingley had settled himself between her breasts. His hands squeezed the sides of her pillowy mounds against his thick member and he began to move up and down. Wickedly, Jane had stretched her tongue out so the head of him hit it at each stroke. Her hands ran over his muscled buttocks, feeling them flex. With him grunting and her licking, he soon spilled his seed over her neck.

"I apologize, my dear Miss Bennet. Allow me to clean you up."

Jane shivered as her fingers rocked her to orgasm

when she recalled his tongue licking her dry.

"I would have you in my mouth, Mr. Bingley," she said when he was finished.

"I would not tax you further lest your illness worsen," he said and kissed her until she was nearly stripping the clothes off him in desperation.

"Mr. Bingley," she begged, grasping his hardness.

"I could lose myself inside of you," he said, pushing up her skirts to play with the wet folds between her legs.

"Take me, Mr. Bingley. Make me your own," she cried."When you are better, Miss Bennet. Until then, find peace in my lips and fingers."

He spoke no more to her until Jane had shrieked in pleasure into her pillow.

Jane fingered herself to another delicious orgasm, picturing Mr. Bingley's fine form attended her in a most intimate manner. Elizabeth had to be right. He would be back for her in time for Christmas.

Chapter 22

The Bennets were engaged to dine with the Lucases and again during the chief of the day was Miss Lucas so kind as to listen to Mr. Collins. Elizabeth took an opportunity of thanking her.

"It keeps him in good humour," said she, "and I am more obliged to you than I can express."

"I'm sorry we haven't more time together," Elizabeth said, smiling at her.

Charlotte looked taken aback. "I could not compare to the delights of Netherfield."

Elizabeth would never tell her she was correct, but Charlotte knew from her body language and the way she would stare out the open window as if expecting someone – someone who wasn't Charlotte.

So Charlotte assured her friend of her satisfaction in being useful in regards to Mr. Collins, and that it amply repaid her for the little sacrifice of her time. This was very amiable, but Charlotte's kindness extended farther than Elizabeth had any conception of; its object was nothing else than to secure her from any return of Mr. Collins's addresses, by engaging them towards herself. Such was Miss Lucas's scheme; and appearances were so favourable, that when they parted at night, she would have felt almost secure of success if he had not been to leave Hertfordshire so very soon.

But here she did injustice to the fire and independence of his character, for it led him to escape out of Longbourn House the next morning with admirable slyness, and hasten to Lucas Lodge to throw himself at her feet

His reception, however, was of the most flattering kind. Miss Lucas perceived him from an upper window as he walked towards the house, and instantly set out to meet him accidentally in the lane. But little had she dared to hope that so much love and eloquence awaited her there.

"Miss Lucas," Mr. Collins began, stopping as Charlotte took off her head scarf and wrapped it around his neck.

"Follow me," she said with a sultry smile.

Dumbfounded, Mr. Collins allowed himself to be lead into the Lucas' home and they very quietly crept up the stairs to Charlotte's bedchamber.

"What I mean to say, Miss Lucas. . .," he began again.

"Silence," she ordered.

And with years of training kicking in, his mouth snapped shut.

"Sit down on the bed and remove your clothes," she told him.

When he went to open his mouth to protest, she gave him her most severe look and he obeyed without comment.

"Watch me," she said and slowly stripped off her apron.

His eyes were fever bright. When he tried to

speak again, she wrapped the scarf around his mouth to gag him.

"Untie my stays," she ordered after slipping out of her dress. Charlotte liked that his fingers made quick work of the garment and she pulled off her chemise to stand naked in front of him.

His eyes were cold and accessing and for some reason that excited her.

"Now you," she ordered. "Let's see if you have what I want."

Mr. Collins left the scarf in place and quickly undressed.

"That's very nice," Charlotte said, as he stood at attention awaiting further orders.

She smoothed her hand over his hard cock that was curving up towards his stomach. He closed his eyes in pleasure when she stroked it a few times.

Pushing him back roughly on the mattress, Charlotte tore off the scarf. But before he could say a word, she straddled his face.

"I like girls," she told him as his hands came up to clutch her hips. "I don't mind sharing, if you don't."

Mr. Collins moaned against her. Charlotte shivered at the vibration. "Push your tongue into me. Oh, that's nice. Elizabeth was better, though."

Mr. Collins moaned again and his tongue picked up a feverish paste. "I had her sweet mound in my mouth. I suckled on her pretty little melons." Charlotte squeezed her own breasts as her hips rocked on his face. "You like that?"

He moaned his assent.

"We could get a maid and share her. Or perhaps you could just watch me and her. One that resembles

Lizzie, I think. You like that?" She repeated. Mr. Collins' tongue was near dancing inside of her, his fingers tight on her plump buttocks. "I can see that you do."

Charlotte tilted her head back and pictured the scene. Her voice trembled when she shared it with him. "I would lie on my back and our lovely Lizzie maid would be on all fours, servicing me like you are now. You could take her from behind. I'll hold her hair in place against me until we both have satisfaction." Charlotte's limbs quivered and she felt herself drench his face. She moved off him and with deliberate movements impaled herself on his turgid staff.

"Yes," he groaned. "All that and more." He filled his hands with her ample bosom and bucked his hips, lifting her up off the mattress.

"Oh," she said, surprised. "I was expecting pain, but you fill me nicely." She ground into him and started to bounce. He massaged her breasts quite nicely as she levered herself up and down.

"What shall I do, Mistress?" Mr. Collins asked, eyes glazed. His fingers rolling her nipples.

Charlotte squeezed her muscles tightly around his cock, watching his reaction. It was if all air had left his lungs. "I think I'm tired of doing all the work," she said. Climbing off him, she lay on her back next to him and spread her legs.

As he entered her, Mr. Collins earnestly entreated her to name the day that was to make him the happiest of men

Miss Lucas, who accepted him solely from the pure and disinterested desire of an establishment, cared not how soon that establishment were gained. "Faster," she ordered, lifting her hips up to meet his. She wrapped her legs around his waist, hooking her ankles together. Mr. Collins was thick and she liked how he felt slipping in and out of her. She kissed him and tasted herself on his lips.

"Mmmm," she purred, sucking the juices off his mouth and tongue.

Mr. Collins, to be sure, was neither sensible nor agreeable; his society was irksome, but still he would be her husband.

The least agreeable circumstance in the business was the surprise it must occasion to Elizabeth Bennet, whose friendship Charlotte valued beyond that of any other person. She thought of Lizzie as Mr. Collins pounded into her. Lizzie who had subtlety moved away from her ever since Netherfield. It must be Mr. Darcy's ministrations. She pictured Lizzie being ridden by the dour Mr. Darcy. It was titillating.

"Harder," she told the Mr. Darcy in her head. It was Mr. Collins who obeyed, driving into her body until she started to shake.

"Yes," she said and bit his shoulder.

Mr. Collins grunted in pain, but didn't stop his pleasurable ministrations.

"Husband," Charlotte tried out the word as tremors racked her. His release soon followed with a tortured grunt that left him slightly speechless. "You'll do," she said.

Miss Lucas called on the Bennets soon after breakfast, Mr. Collins having snuck out just past midnight.. Charlotte took Lizzie's hand firmly in hers and they walked hand in hand to the barn together.

Elizabeth felt a flush of trepidation. She didn't

want to pleasure herself with Charlotte – at least not without Mr. Darcy watching. And did that thought anger her! But before she could explain to Charlotte these confusing feelings, Charlotte related the events of the day before. The possibility of Mr. Collins's fancying himself in love with her friend had once occurred to Elizabeth within the last day or two; but that Charlotte could encourage him seemed almost as far from possibility as she could encourage him herself, and her astonishment was consequently so great as to overcome at first the bounds of decorum, and she could not help crying out:

"Engaged to Mr. Collins! My dear Charlotte— impossible! He's a dreadful bore. You would be tortured to listen to him day in and day out."

The steady countenance which Miss Lucas had commanded in telling her story, gave way to a momentary confusion here on receiving so direct a reproach; though, as it was no more than she expected, she soon regained her composure, and calmly replied:

"Why should you be surprised, my dear Eliza? Do you think it incredible that Mr. Collins should be able to procure any woman's good opinion, because he was not so happy as to succeed with you? Or do you think I should be an old maid, pining away for lack of your affections?"

But Elizabeth had now recollected herself, and making a strong effort for it, was able to assure with tolerable firmness that the prospect of their relationship was highly grateful to her "I wish only that you are happy."

"I see what you are feeling," replied Charlotte. "You must be surprised, very much surprised—so lately as Mr. Collins was wishing to marry you. But when you have had time to think it over, I hope you will be satisfied with what I have done. I am not romantic, you know; I never was. I ask only a comfortable home; and considering Mr. Collins's character, connection, and situation in life, I am convinced that my chance of happiness with him is as fair as most people can boast on entering the marriage state."

Elizabeth quietly answered "Undoubtedly;" and after an awkward pause, they returned to the rest of the family. Charlotte did not stay much longer, and Elizabeth was then left to reflect on what she had heard. It was a long time before she became at all reconciled to the idea of so unsuitable a match.

Elizabeth felt persuaded that no real confidence could ever subsist between them again. Her disappointment in Charlotte made her turn with fonder regard to her sister, of whose rectitude and delicacy she was sure her opinion could never be shaken, and for whose happiness she grew daily more anxious, as Bingley had now been gone a week and nothing more was heard of his return. Of course, Mr. Darcy had gone with him so even if Elizabeth had changed her mind about becoming a Netherfield strumpet, she would have to write a letter instead of running across the countryside to be in his arms. Not that was what she was even remotely thinking about doing. At least when she was awake and in the company of other people.

Whenever Charlotte came to see them, Mrs. Bennet concluded her to be anticipating the hour of possession; and whenever she spoke in a low voice to Mr. Collins, was convinced that they were talking of the Longbourn estate, and resolving to turn herself and her daughters out of the house, as soon as Mr. Bennet were dead. She complained bitterly of all this to her husband.

"Indeed, Mr. Bennet," said she, "it is very hard to think that Charlotte Lucas should ever be mistress of this house, that I should be forced to make way for her, and live to see her take her place in it!"

"My dear, do not give way to such gloomy thoughts. Let us hope for better things. Let us flatter ourselves that I may be the survivor."

This was not very consoling to Mrs. Bennet, and therefore, instead of making any answer, she went on as before.

Chapter 23

Miss Bingley's next letter put an end to doubt. Mr. Bingley was not coming back for Christmas – if ever. Hope was over, entirely over; and when Jane could attend to the rest of the letter, she found little, except the professed affection of the writer, that could give her any comfort. Miss Darcy's praise occupied the chief of it. Her many attractions were again dwelt on, and Caroline boasted joyfully of their increasing intimacy, and ventured to predict the accomplishment of the wishes which had been unfolded in her former letter.

"I will not repine," Jane said. "It cannot last long. He will be forgot, and we shall all be as we were before."

Elizabeth could not oppose such a wish; and from this time Mr. Bingley's name was scarcely ever mentioned between them.

Mr. Bennet treated the matter differently. "So, Lizzy," said he one day, "your sister is crossed in love, I find. I congratulate her. Next to being married, a girl likes to be crossed a little in love now and then. It is something to think of, and it gives her a sort of distinction among her companions. When is your turn to come? You will hardly bear to be long outdone by Jane. Now is your time. Here are officers enough in Meryton to disappoint all the young ladies in the country. Let Wickham be your man. He is a pleasant fellow, and would jilt you creditably."

"Thank you, sir, but a less agreeable man would satisfy me. We must not all expect Jane's good fortune."

"True," said Mr. Bennet, "but it is a comfort to think that whatever of that kind may befall you, you have an affectionate mother who will make the most of it."

Elizabeth gave an unladylike snort.

Mr. Wickham's society was of material service in dispelling the gloom which the late perverse occurrences had thrown on many of the Longbourn family. They saw him often, and to his other recommendations was now added that of general unreserve.

The whole of what Elizabeth had already heard, Mr. Wickham's claims on Mr. Darcy, and all that he had suffered from him, was now openly acknowledged and publicly canvassed; and everybody was pleased to know how much they had always disliked Mr. Darcy before they had known anything of the matter. Elizabeth was resigned that while she had made the right decision, it was a rather lonely one.

Lydia, on the other hand, chose not to be lonely. She was looking out the window of her aunt's house when Mr. Wickham happened on by. Mrs. Phillips had gone out to the market so Lydia thought this was the perfect time to show her that she could handle gentlemen callers by herself – especially if it was an officer. Doubly so if it was an officer who might fancy her hoity toity sister.

"Yoo hoo, Mr. Wickham!"

He looked up. "Good day, Miss Bennet."

"Won't you stop in for some tea?"

If Mr. Wickham seemed aghast at her forward manners he did no more than look around to see if anyone else had noticed and then quickly hurried inside. Lydia stifled a delighted shriek and ran down the stairs so fast, she nearly clambered into the man.

"I have to admit, Mr. Wickham, I do not have any tea made," she said.

"I have to admit, my dear Miss Bennet, I do not want any."

Wickham was lean and broad shouldered with a mane of blond hair kept in check by a leather tie. Lydia and her sister hadn't the pleasure of trying their newly learned arts on him.

"I was wondering, Mr. Wickham, if you could help me with my studies. My aunt has been teaching me the ways of . . ." Lydia wished she had a fan to use as a prop. "Punishment and desire," she said, boldly looking him in the eyes instead.

To her great surprise, Mr. Wickham started disrobing. Lydia stifled a giggle by covering her mouth. Her eyes goggled at the finely articulated muscles on his arms and stomach. When he stepped out of his trousers, she couldn't stop staring at the thick muscle between his legs.

"You're supposed to give an order . . . Mistress," he said with a sardonic smile.

"Touch yourself," she said.

"Like this?" he asked, sliding a slow hand down his chest to his stomach and then back up again.

"Oh yes, quite like that," she breathed.

"Or would you like me to hold my cock?"

Lydia's giggle died in her mouth when he stretched the flesh and began to pump his fist up and down the hardening shaft. She had to concentrate on her breathing when his hand moved so fast it was a blur.

"Stop," she said.

He slowed down but he didn't stop.

"I like it better slow," she told him.

"I'll remember that," he said.

"You must kiss me," Lydia took a bold step towards him, angling her cheek towards him.

He took his hand away from his cock to take her face into both hands. Her squeal was lost as his mouth crashed down on hers. It was a gentle kiss that seduced, even thought she could feel the power in his hands. His tongue teased her lips open and invited her to play. All too soon, he ended it and slid his hands from her cheeks down to her bodice where he held her breasts in his hands.

Lydia's eyes were closed and she could barely open them as his thumbs teased circles over her nipples. Her legs were damp and shaking.

"Command me, Mistress," he said, but then took her mouth in another blistering kiss.

His thumbs sparked sensations down to her core, which throbbed to the beat of her rapid heart.

"Do you want me to pleasure you, Mistress?" He said, sliding his lips to her ear.

"Yes, that. Pleasure me." Lydia squeaked as he

crouched to the floor and in one swift move stood up, taking her skirts with him.

"Hold these," he said, stuffing them in her hands.

"But," she said, then gasped when he put a bold hand on her limb and entwined it around his waist.

She could feel the hot probe of him near her most intimate spot. He grabbed the other leg and she dropped her skirts to hang on to his shoulders otherwise she'd topple to the ground. Mr. Wickham's sure hands were now on her buttocks and he placed her on top of his hard shaft.

Lydia screamed at the penetration. Then screamed again when he pushed her against the wall. He was so thick and hot. He was burning her with such intense pleasure, she couldn't stop screaming.

"Yes! Yes! Wickham! Yes!"

Wincing, Mr. Wickham covered her mouth with his again – anything to silence her. She'd have half the neighborhood in here soon. She was tight and slippery wet. Eager and innocent. If only she was rich as well. Oh well, he shrugged, can't have everything.

Lydia's screams were muffled by Wickham's invading tongue. Her nails dug bloody half moons into his shoulders. Her thighs tightened against his waist, nearly cutting off his air. He wiggled his hips in a slow, pattern trying to ease her first time. But she was having none of it, bucking like a wild cat. He finally gave up and loved her hard and fast until he was screaming back into her mouth as the orgasm shook his entire body.

Unpeeling her legs from him, he put her off him. Lydia nearly slid bonelessly to the floor.

"Is that it, then?" She said, her brow furrowed.

Mr. Wickham got dressed as swiftly as he had undressed. "Whatever do you mean?"

"I was expecting the earth to move. It was nice, but . . ." Lydia drifted off in confusion.

"Little love, you didn't come?"

She shook her head.

"Come here," he said. "We have to hurry."

He sat her on his lap and she cuddled into him.

"Please kiss me," she said. "That was ever so pleasant."

Mr. Wickham parted her thighs with his hand.

She winced. "No more inside me. I'm sore."

"Of course, my Mistress." He kissed her then and she wrapped her arms around his head.

His fingers were gentle, tickling first then bolder as his knuckle grazed her engorged bud. She made a shriek again and he deepened the kiss while he massaged the bud.

"This was what she meant," Lydia thought as sparks started going off in her mind. His mouth was sweet and pliant, allowing her to explore his depths with her tongue. She ground down on her knuckle as pleasure exploded in her.

"There now," Mr. Wickham kissed her forehead. "You are going to make a formidable dominatrix."

"I am?" she said, still quivering from her release.

"Exactly so," He kissed her one last time, groping her breasts. "Perhaps next time, you'll allow me to kiss you other places."

"Other places?" Lydia breathed and wished again for her fan when he walked out.

Chapter 24

On the following Monday, Mrs. Bennet had the pleasure of receiving her brother and his wife, who came as usual to spend the Christmas at Longbourn Mrs. Gardiner took a look a poor dejected Jane and offered a change of scene – welcoming her to go back to London with them after the holiday.

Jane accepted her aunt's invitation with pleasure.

Mrs. Gardiner, however, wasn't done with her good deeds. She noticed the dashing Mr. Wickham and Elizabeth were being very amiable to each other. At the first opportunity, she pulled her niece aside and said, "You are too sensible a girl, Lizzy, to fall in love merely because you are warned against it; and, therefore, I am not afraid of speaking openly. Seriously, I would have you be on your guard. I have nothing to say against him; he is a most interesting young man; and if he had the fortune he ought to have, I should think you could not do better. But as it is, you must not let your fancy run away with you. You have sense, and we all expect you to use it. Your father would depend on your resolution and good conduct, I am sure. You must not disappoint your father."

"My dear aunt, this is being serious indeed."

"Yes, and I hope to engage you to be serious likewise."

"Well, then, you need not be under any alarm. I will take care of myself, and of Mr. Wickham too. He shall not be in love with me, if I can prevent it."

"Elizabeth, you are not serious now."

"I beg your pardon, I will try again. At present I am not in love with Mr. Wickham; no, I certainly am not. But he is, beyond all comparison, the most agreeable man I ever saw—and if he becomes really attached to me—I believe it will be better that he should not. I see the imprudence of it."

"Oh! that abominable Mr. Darcy!" Elizabeth thought. She was in love with him. And it seemed to be as impossible relationship as Mr. Bingley and dear, Jane. ."

"Perhaps it will be as well if you discourage Mr. Wickham coming here so very often. At least, you should not remind your mother of inviting him."

"As I did the other day," said Elizabeth with a conscious smile: "But Lydia whinged so loud and long that she gave in.

As it turned out, her aunt needn't have worried. Shortly after Christmas, Mr. Wickham became attached to a young heiress who stood to inherit ten thousand pounds. Coincidently, Mr. Wickham's visits were now few and very far between.

All this was acknowledged to Mrs. Gardiner; and after relating the circumstances, she thus went on: "I am now convinced, my dear aunt, that I have never been much in love; for had I really experienced that pure and elevating passion, I should at present detest his very name, and wish him all manner of evil. But my feelings are not only cordial towards him; they are even impartial towards Miss King. Kitty and Lydia take his defection much more to heart than I do. They are young in the ways of the world, and not yet open to the mortifying conviction that handsome young men must have something to live on as well as the plain."

Thursday was to be Charlotte's wedding day, and on Wednesday Miss Lucas paid her farewell visit; and when she rose to take leave, Elizabeth, ashamed of her mother's ungracious and reluctant good wishes, and sincerely affected herself, accompanied her out of the room. As they went downstairs together, Charlotte said:

"I shall depend on hearing from you very often, Eliza."

"That you certainly shall."

"And I have another favour to ask you. Will you come and see me?"

"We shall often meet, I hope, in Hertfordshire."

"I am not likely to leave Kent for some time. Promise me, therefore, to come to Hunsford."

Elizabeth could not refuse, though she foresaw little pleasure in the visit.

The wedding took place; the bride and bridegroom set off for Kent from the church door, and everybody had as much to say, or to hear, on the subject as usual. Elizabeth soon heard from her friend; and their correspondence was as regular and frequent as it had ever been; that it should be equally unreserved was impossible.

Elizabeth could never address her without feeling that all the comfort of intimacy was over, and though determined not to slacken as a correspondent; it was for the sake of what had been, rather than what was.

A few months went by and Elizabeth found that absence had increased her desire of seeing Charlotte again, and weakened her disgust of Mr. Collins. When the invitation to accompany Charlotte's family to Hunsford arrived, Elizabeth eagerly accepted. The journey would moreover give her a peep at Jane; and, in short, as the time drew near, she would have been very sorry for any delay.

Her visit with Jane was short and bittersweet. While happy to see her sister again, it was difficult to see her trying to bravely go on, nursing a broken heart.

She couldn't help but to exclaim to her aunt once Jane had sighed and excused herself to retire early to bed. " I have a very poor opinion of young men who live in Derbyshire; and their intimate friends who live in Hertfordshire are not much better. I am sick of them all. Thank Heaven! I am going to-morrow where I shall find a man who has not one agreeable quality, who has neither manner nor sense to recommend him. Stupid men are the only ones worth knowing, after all."

"Take care, Lizzy; that speech savours strongly of disappointment," her aunt said.

When they left the high road for the lane to Hunsford the next day, every eye was in search of the Parsonage, and every turning expected to bring it in view. The palings of Rosings Park was their boundary on one side. Elizabeth smiled at the recollection of all that she had heard of its inhabitants.

At length the Parsonage was discernible. The garden sloping to the road, the house standing in it, the green pales, and the laurel hedge, everything declared they were arriving. Mr. Collins and Charlotte appeared at the door, and the carriage stopped at the small gate which led by a short gravel walk to the house, amidst the nods and smiles of the whole party. In a moment they were all out of the chaise, rejoicing at the sight of each other. Mrs. Collins welcomed her friend with the liveliest pleasure, and Elizabeth was more and more satisfied with coming when she found herself so affectionately received.

When Mr. Collins said anything of which his wife might reasonably be ashamed, which certainly was not unseldom, she involuntarily turned her eye on Charlotte. Once or twice she could discern a faint blush; but in general Charlotte wisely did not hear.

Mr. Collins was pleased to inform them that the whole party was asked to dine at Rosings that evening.

When the ladies were separating for the toilette, he said to Elizabeth—

"Do not make yourself uneasy, my dear cousin, about your apparel. Lady Catherine will not think the worse of you for being simply dressed. She likes to have the distinction of rank preserved."

From what Elizabeth remembered her aunt telling her about Lady Catherine, she had most of London society either on their knees or begging to be put there. The fact that she was Mr. Darcy's aunt made her miss him. She had come to a decision. The next time, she saw Mr. Darcy she would take him up on his offer. She cared not a whit for her virginity, nor for finding a husband. She wanted him. These past months she felt only half alive. She saw herself in Jane and swore she would not wither for lack of her true love. Elizabeth would fight for him and make him want her enough to overlook her lack of fortune.

As the weather was fine, they had a pleasant walk of about half a mile across the park. From the entrance-hall, of which Mr. Collins pointed out, with a rapturous air, the fine proportion and the finished ornaments, they followed the servants through an ante-chamber, to the room where Lady Catherine, her daughter, and Mr. Darcy were sitting. Her ladyship, with great condescension, arose to receive them.

Elizabeth froze and the world stopped as the two of them looked at each other. She hadn't expected to see him, and his presence sent an otherworldly chill through her. Would his aunt notice if they slipped off together? Lady Catherine was a tall, large woman, with strongly-marked features, which might once have been handsome. Her air was not conciliating, nor was her manner of receiving them such as to make her visitors forget their inferior rank. She was not rendered formidable by silence; but whatever she said was spoken in so authoritative a tone, as marked her self-importance.

When, after examining the mother, in whose countenance and deportment she soon found some resemblance of Mr. Darcy, she turned her eyes on the daughter, she could almost have joined in Maria's astonishment at her being so thin and so small. There was neither in figure nor face any likeness between the ladies. Miss de Bourgh was pale and sickly; her features, though not plain, were insignificant; and she spoke very little, except in a low voice.

Was Darcy here courting the sickly Maria?

The dinner was exceedingly handsome, although Elizabeth tasted none of it.

When the ladies returned to the drawing-room, there was little to be done but to hear Lady Catherine talk, even though all Elizabeth wanted to do was follow Mr. Darcy. But Lady Catherine commandeered the conversation without any intermission till coffee came in, delivering her opinion on every subject in so decisive a manner, as proved that she was not used to have her judgement controverted.

" Do you play and sing, Miss Bennet?"

"A little."

"Oh! then—some time or other we shall be happy to hear you. Our instrument is a capital one, probably superior to——You shall try it some day. . Are any of your younger sisters out?"

"Yes, ma'am, all."

"All! What, all five out at once! Very odd! And you only the second. The younger ones out before the elder ones are married! Your younger sisters must be very young?"

"Yes, my youngest is not sixteen. Perhaps she is full young to be much in company. But really, ma'am, I think it would be very hard upon younger sisters, that they should not have their share of society and amusement, because the elder may not have the means or inclination to marry early. The last-born has as good a right to the pleasures of youth at the first. And to be kept back on such a motive! I think it would not be very likely to promote sisterly affection or delicacy of mind."

"Upon my word," said her ladyship, "you give your opinion very decidedly for so young a person. Pray, what is your age?"

"With three younger sisters grown up," replied

Elizabeth, smiling, "your ladyship can hardly expect me to own it."

Lady Catherine seemed quite astonished at not receiving a direct answer; and Elizabeth suspected herself to be the first creature who had ever dared to trifle with so much dignified impertinence. She could almost see the old dominatrix in her prime in the haughty look she was giving her.

"You cannot be more than twenty, I am sure, therefore you need not conceal your age."

"I am not one-and-twenty."

When the gentlemen had joined them, and tea was over, the card-tables were placed. Lady Catherine, Mr. Darcy, and Mr. and Mrs. Collins sat down to quadrille; and as Miss de Bourgh chose to play at cassino, the two girls had the honour of assisting Mrs. Jenkinson to make up her party. Their table was superlatively stupid. Scarcely a syllable was uttered that did not relate to the game.

A great deal more passed at the other table. Lady Catherine was generally speaking—stating the mistakes of the three others, or relating some anecdote of herself. Mr. Collins was employed in agreeing to everything her ladyship said, thanking her for every fish he won, and apologising if he thought he won too many.

" There are few people in England, I suppose, who have more true enjoyment of music than myself, or a better natural taste," Lady Catherine said. "If I had ever learnt, I should have been a great proficient. And so would Anne, if her health had allowed her to apply. I am confident that she would have performed delightfully. How does Georgiana get on, Darcy?"

Mr. Darcy spoke with affectionate praise of his sister's proficiency.

"I am very glad to hear such a good account of her," said Lady Catherine; "and pray tell her from me, that she cannot expect to excel if she does not practice a good deal."

"I assure you, madam," he replied, "that she does not need such advice. She practises very constantly."

"So much the better. It cannot be done too much; and when I next write to her, I shall charge her not to neglect it on any account. I often tell young ladies that no excellence in music is to be acquired without constant practice. I have told though Mrs. Collins has no instrument, she is very welcome, as I have often told her, to come to Rosings every day, and play on the pianoforte in Mrs. Jenkinson's room. She would be in nobody's way, you know, in that part of the house."

Mr. Darcy looked a little ashamed of his aunt's ill-breeding, and made no answer.

"Miss Bennet would not play at all amiss if she practised more, and could have the advantage of a London master. She has a very good notion of fingering."

The look Mr. Darcy shot Elizabeth was full of heady things: humour, desire, and the familiar traces of lust.

"Though her taste is not equal to Anne's. Anne would have been a delightful performer, had her health allowed her to learn," Lady Catherine continued, unaware of the heated glances between her nephew and Miss Bennet.

Elizabeth looked at Darcy to see how cordially he assented to his cousin's praise; but neither at that moment nor at any other could she discern any symptom of love; and from the whole of his behaviour to Miss de Bourgh she derived this comfort for Miss Bingley, that he might have been just as likely to marry her, had she been his relation.

When Lady Catherine and her daughter had played as long as they chose, the tables were broken up, the carriage was offered to Mrs. Collins, gratefully accepted and immediately ordered. The party then gathered round the fire to hear Lady Catherine determine what weather they were to have on the morrow.

There was no chance to speak a word alone to Mr. Darcy. When she tried, Lady Catherine interrupted them, changing the subject. Elizabeth wasn't comfortable airing her feelings with such a crowd and the only hint that Mr. Darcy was as eager to speak with her alone was the dark brooding looks he gave her.

As soon as they had driven from the door, Elizabeth was called on by her cousin to give her opinion of all that she had seen at Rosings, which, for Charlotte's sake, she made more favourable than it really was. But her commendation, though costing her some trouble, could by no means satisfy Mr. Collins, and he was very soon obliged to take her ladyship's praise into his own hands.

Chapter 25

.

On the following morning Mr. Darcy came to visit. He brought with him a Colonel Fitzwilliam, the younger son of his uncle

"I may thank you, Eliza, for this piece of civility. Mr. Darcy would never have come so soon to wait upon me," Mr. Collins said.

Elizabeth had scarcely time to disclaim all right to the compliment, before their approach was announced by the door-bell, and shortly afterwards the three gentlemen entered the room. Colonel Fitzwilliam, who led the way, was about thirty, not handsome, but in person and address most truly the gentleman.

Mr. Darcy looked just as he had been used to look in Hertfordshire—paid his compliments, with his usual reserve, to Mrs. Collins, and whatever might be his feelings toward her friend, met her with every appearance of composure. Elizabeth merely curtseyed to him without saying a word.

It wasn't long before the Colonel bid Mr. Collins for a tour of the estate and Charlotte, seeing the penetrating looks between her friend and Mr. Darcy, slipped out of the drawing room shortly afterward.

"You mean to frighten me, Mr. Darcy, by coming

to see me? There is a stubbornness about me that never can bear to be frightened at the will of others. My courage always rises at every attempt to intimidate me."

"I shall not say you are mistaken," he replied, "because you could not really believe me to entertain any design of alarming you; and I have had the pleasure of your acquaintance long enough to know that you find great enjoyment in occasionally professing opinions which in fact are not your own."

Elizabeth laughed heartily at this picture of herself, delight at seeing him again filling her to the point where she did not know how to begin to tell him that she was his. "I have thought of you often," said he, smilingly.

"Me?" Elizabeth said. "The girl you once said was tolerable, but not handsome enough to tempt you?" She wanted him, but she wasn't going to make it easy for him.

"Perhaps," said Darcy, "I should have judged better, had I sought an introduction; but I am ill-qualified to recommend myself to strangers."

"Why does a man of sense and education, and who has lived in the world, ill qualified to recommend himself to strangers?"

"Would you believe me shy?"

"I would believe you anything but," she said, feeling suddenly shy herself.

"I've missed you," he said.

"How very suddenly you all quitted Netherfield last November, Mr. Darcy! It must have been a most agreeable surprise to Mr. Bingley to see you all after him so soon; for, if I recollect right, he went but the

243

day before. He and his sisters were well, I hope, when you left London?"

"Perfectly so, I thank you."

She found that she was to receive no other answer, and, after a short pause added:

"I think I have understood that Mr. Bingley has not much idea of ever returning to Netherfield again?"

"I have never heard him say so; but it is probable that he may spend very little of his time there in the future. He has many friends, and is at a time of life when friends and engagements are continually increasing."

"If he means to be but little at Netherfield, it would be better for the neighbourhood that he should give up the place entirely, for then we might possibly get a settled family there. I had such great experiences there." Elizabeth licked her lips and cast her eyes down, lest he see how she burned for him. "But, perhaps, Mr. Bingley did not take the house so much for the convenience of the neighbourhood as for his own, and we must expect him to keep it or quit it on the same principle."

"I should not be surprised," said Darcy, "if he were to give it up as soon as any eligible purchaser offers."

Elizabeth made no answer. She was afraid of talking longer of his friend; and, having nothing else to say, was now determined to leave the trouble of finding a subject to him.

He took the hint, and soon began with,

"Would you like to take a walk with me?" he asked.

"Very much so," she said, accepting his hand as

she rose.

They walked as swiftly as decorum permitted, each not saying anything until they reached a gazebo overlooking a duck pond.

"Mr. Darcy," Elizabeth started to say, but he pulled her up hard against him and smothered her words with a kiss that made her world tilt. A breeze blew through the structure, stirring her dress but she was lost to the pine scent of the forest and his warm mouth stirring feelings she had thought she had imagined. His hair on the nape of his neck was silky when she stroked her fingers through them. Her other hand rested on his dear cheek.

"I must have you," he said.

"Here?" Elizabeth raised shocked eyes to his. "Anyone can walk by and see us."

"Yes," he said. "Have you reconsidered my offer?"

"If Mr. Bingley isn't returning to Netherfield, there will be no dungeon for us."

"There is one in Pemberley."

She was shocked to her core. "I will be ruined. There is no hiding our practices like we could at Netherfield. It was close to my home and Mr. Bingley had two sisters in residence."

"You could be visiting my sister, Georgiana. I will make sure there are enough chaperones to distract the most ambitious gossips"

"You tempt me. I had made up my mind if we were to play at Netherfield, but Pemberley..."

"Then it's settled. Undress. Now."

Elizabeth's hands went to her lacings. "Your voice, it compels me."

"It's because you recognize me as your Master."

"I do," she said and looked around self consciously.

"As your Master, you must not only give me your body, but your trust. I will protect your reputation. I'll allow no other to have you until you ask me to release you from training. I will keep you safe and unseen." He pulled a length of silk fabric from his pocket. "Believe it or not, this will make it easier." He wrapped it gently over his eyes and tied securely.

"I can't see," Elizabeth said, reaching a hand up to touch the blindfold.

He caught her hand. "It is not my will for you to see."

Elizabeth felt his hands on her shoulders and his body pressed against her until she had backed up against the wall.

"Undo your lacings. I have a great desire to kiss your lovely breasts."

Fingers shaking, Elizabeth did as he bade her. Mr. Darcy scooped them out of her chemise, baring her breasts to the chill air.

"So lovely," he said, tracing the sloping curves with a calloused thumb.

His mouth clamped on one pink tip, sucking hard. Elizabeth was glad for the supporting presence of the wood at her back as her knees threatened to buckle. He moved to the next one and bit gently. Her hands reached for him as he broke the luscious tugging.

"Put your hands behind your head," he said. "It will lift your breasts up."

Elizabeth did, shivering as her wet nipples caught a breeze. In the next instant, a stinging lash hit her sensitive tips and she cried out.

"Quiet," Darcy said.

Elizabeth bit her lip as she heard the swishing sound before four thick leather bands feathered over her breasts. He danced them across her soft mounds. She arched into the leather bands, not knowing when he would flick his wrists and the tingling sensations that warmed to pleasure would peak to a stinging pain instead of the heavy attention that was decadent. The air would cool her and the leather strokes would heat up into . . . snap . . . the bands pinched over them. He moved so she was always surprised when the blow slapped her breasts.

"So obedient," he breathed. She could hear the civilization leaking away from his voice. He sounded darker and dangerous. "You please me."

He kissed her breasts. "You're hot here from the lashes. Do you like that?"

"Yes, Master," she said.

"Come this way," he pulled her hands from the back of her head and let her to the center of the gazebo.

He lay her across the table. Elizabeth felt him slide his folded up jacket under her head. Mr. Darcy bent her knees up to her chest. She moaned as the chill air hit her exposed parts. He arranged her dress up around her waist.

"No begging to save your virginity for your bridegroom?"

"It matters not," she said. "Men are only interested in my dowry or lack thereof. It is as you said. If I could bring pleasure to my marriage bed, that it where the true worth is."

"I didn't say anything so cynical," Mr. Darcy

Lissa Trevor

said. "You are an intelligent, passionate woman. You would do any man proud."

"If only I was rich as well," Elizabeth said. "But it is no matter. Is it your intent to talk to me, Master? Or to initiate me into the ways of men and women?"

The leather flogger hit the backs of her thighs, hard. It was like being slapped by wet tongues. He struck her twice more and the sensation took her breath. It was not quite pain, not quite pleasure.

"If I wish it," he said.

"Of course," Elizabeth managed when the air cooled the area enough she could form words again.

"I wish to show you a great many things. But you must be silent. There are people walking near."

Elizabeth panicked, tried to get up. In that moment, Mr. Darcy shoved inside her. When her mouth opened to shout, scream, moan – Elizabeth wasn't sure, but the handle of the flogger blocked the sound to a throaty grunt.

"They aren't even looking this way," he said, holding her tight against him. "Do not give them an excuse to investigate. I would hate to cut this activity short. You, Miss Bennet are tight and wet. Do you like the feel of me inside you?"

"Mmmm," Elizabeth said.

He rocked into her. "I'm in deeper than I thought I'd get. You sheathe me well. Do you see how your virginity concerns have vanished? It's over and done. Now there is only pleasure."

Elizabeth felt complete and whole. Now, she understood what she and Charlotte came close to, but missed. This driving desire, the utter feeling of freedom, of having no responsibilities and behaving irresponsibly. Giving in to her Master. Knowing it would all be all right because he had control.

"Oh," she moaned around the leather in her mouth. His pace was steady and delicious as her body got used to the size of him. So much nicer than fingers. So much thicker and quicker.

"Miss Bennet, you are perfect. Just as I dreamed. In my every imagining since you looked at me at Netherfield. I want you to come with me deep inside you. So I'm going to stop moving."

Elizabeth bit down on the flogger and grunted in frustration. Her hips began to move against him, her muscles clamping down on him as she reached for that pinnacle.

"Yes, you know what you like. That pleases me." He rammed deep once more holding her thighs against his chest. He slid out of her halfway, so he could reach between them and rub his thumb over her tender bud.

Elizabeth's teeth clenched on the flogger and she whipped her head back and forth.

"How I've longed for you." His fingers danced along each sensitive peak and valley, until the rubbing sensations pulsed through to her very core and she felt the wonderful tension that had been building drench him in sheer pleasure as she clamped down on him, riding out her release as lights exploded under her eyelids.

"Perfect," he choked out and then with short, deep thrusts answered her measure for measure.

When he pulled out, Elizabeth was bereft. Her legs cramped, but held when he stood her up. Gently, he put her breasts back into her chemise, tied her lacings, Unwinding the blindfold from her eyes, he assured her again, "You were perfect."

Elizabeth felt that she was awakening into a brighter new world, where Mr. Darcy would be her Master and she would submit to him all that she had.. All too soon, they returned to the Collins' to pretend that their world had not altered.

Chapter 26

More than once did Elizabeth, in her rambles within the park, unexpectedly meet Mr. Darcy. Each time, he took her to the gazebo overlooking the water and taught her the pleasures of submitting to him. Elizabeth never felt so happy or so free..

She was engaged one day as she walked, in perusing Jane's last letter, and dwelling on some passages which proved that Jane had not written in spirits, when, instead of being again surprised by Mr. Darcy, she saw on looking up that Colonel Fitzwilliam was meeting her. Putting away the letter immediately and forcing a smile past her disappointment, she said:

"I did not know before that you ever walked this way."

"I have been making the tour of the park," he replied, "as I generally do every year, and intend to close it with a call at the Parsonage. Are you going much farther?"

"No, I should have turned in a moment."

And accordingly she did turn, and they walked towards the Parsonage together.

"If Darcy doesn't put it off again, we'll be sad to leave Kent on Saturday."

Elizabeth felt a pain in her heart, even though she told herself that love wouldn't—couldn't have a place in her arrangement with Mr. Darcy. He would leave and she would wait for him to summon her to Pemberley.

"I imagine your cousin brought you down with him chiefly for the sake of having someone at his disposal." She said and because her treacherous heart couldn't stop the words continued with, "I wonder he does not marry, to secure a lasting convenience of that kind. But, perhaps, his sister does as well for the present, and, as she is under his sole care, he may do what he likes with her."

"No," said Colonel Fitzwilliam, "that is an advantage which he must divide with me. I am joined with him in the guardianship of Miss Darcy."

"Are you indeed? And pray what sort of guardians do you make? Does your charge give you much trouble? Young ladies of her age are sometimes a little difficult to manage, and if she has the true Darcy spirit, she may like to have her own way."

She is a very great favourite with some ladies of my acquaintance, Mrs. Hurst and Miss Bingley. I think I have heard you say that you know them."

"I know them a little. Their brother is a pleasant gentlemanlike man—he is a great friend of Darcy's."

"Oh! yes," said Elizabeth drily; "Mr. Darcy is uncommonly kind to Mr. Bingley, and takes a prodigious deal of care of him." She remembered what her man in the black mask said about Mr. Bingley compared to his sister.

"Care of him! Yes, I really believe Darcy does

take care of him in those points where he most wants care. From something that he told me in our journey hither, I have reason to think Bingley very much indebted to him."

"What is it you mean?"

"Darcy congratulated himself on having lately saved his friend from the inconveniences of a most imprudent marriage."

"Did Mr. Darcy give you reasons for this interference?"

"I understood that there were some very strong objections against the lady."

"And what arts did he use to separate them?"

"He did not talk to me of his own arts," said Fitzwilliam, smiling. "He only told me what I have now told you."

Elizabeth made no answer, and walked on, her heart swelling with indignation. After watching her a little, Fitzwilliam asked her why she was so thoughtful.

"I am thinking of what you have been telling me," said she. "Your cousin's conduct does not suit my feelings. Why was he to be the judge?"

"You are rather disposed to call his interference officious?"

"I do not see what right Mr. Darcy had to decide on the propriety of his friend's inclination, or why, upon his own judgement alone, he was to determine and direct in what manner his friend was to be happy.."

"That is not an unnatural surmise," said Fitzwilliam, "but it is a lessening of the honour of my cousin's triumph very sadly."

She would not trust herself with an answer, and therefore, abruptly changing the conversation talked on indifferent matters until they reached the Parsonage. There, shut into her own room, as soon as their visitor left them, she could think without interruption of all that she had heard.. It was if she had just awoken from a sensual impossible dream. What had she been thinking, giving herself to a man such as Mr. Darcy? That he had been concerned in the measures taken to separate Bingley and Jane she had never doubted; but she had always attributed to Miss Bingley the principal design and arrangement of them.

If his own vanity, however, did not mislead him, he was the cause, his pride and caprice were the cause, of all that Jane had suffered, and still continued to suffer. He had ruined for a while every hope of happiness for the most affectionate, generous heart in the world; and no one could say how lasting an evil he might have inflicted.

"There were some very strong objections against the lady," were Colonel Fitzwilliam's words; and those strong objections probably were, her having one uncle who was a country attorney, and another who was in business in London.

"To Jane herself," she exclaimed, "there could be no possibility of objection; all loveliness and goodness as she is!—her understanding excellent, her mind improved, and her manners captivating."

When she thought of her mother, her confidence gave way a little; but she would not allow that any objections there had material weight with Mr. Darcy, whose pride, she was convinced, would receive a deeper wound from the want of importance in his friend's connections, than from their want of sense; and she was quite decided, at last, that he had been partly governed by this worst kind of pride, and partly by the wish of retaining Mr. Bingley for his sister.

The agitation and tears which the subject occasioned, brought on a headache; and it grew so much worse towards the evening, that, added to her unwillingness to see Mr. Darcy, it determined her not to attend her cousins to Rosings, where they were engaged to drink tea. Mrs. Collins, seeing that she was really unwell, did not press her to go and as much as possible prevented her husband from pressing her; but Mr. Collins could not conceal his apprehension of Lady Catherine's being rather displeased by her staying at home.

Elizabeth couldn't give a fig. If she had to face her Master tonight, she was sure she'd be the one attacking him– and not for pleasure either.

Lady Catherine wasted no time hoisting her daughter off on her two nephews, while she brought the Collins' into the playroom after dinner. It was too bad the Bennet girl wasn't here. Lady Catherine had been looking forward to punishing the little chit's insolence from the previous night. She would just have to take it out on Mr. Collins and his wife.

This wasn't the first time Charlotte had been down here. She felt a thrill that it was similar to what Lizzie felt in Netherfield. Although instead of Mr. Darcy wielding the whip, it was Lady Catherine. She would have preferred her daughter for aesthetic reasons, but Lady Catherine was training her how to use the whip – as long as she pleasured her.

So without prompting, the Collins' undressed the Lady as they had done countless times before. Charlotte admired the fine cloth, and folded it just as she knew her Mistress liked. Lady Catherine sat in her chair and tossed a leg over the arm. Lady Catherine affixed a stern glare at her, that had Charlotte's heart thumping with excitement. Lady Catherine brooked no impertinence, no disobeying.

"Kneel, girl."

Charlotte obediently knelt between her legs and started lapping at the woman's exposed parts. Lady Catherine grabbed her roughly by the hair and forced her deeper. Charlotte licked harder, probing with her tongue until she found the woman's pearl. She sucked on it and was rewarded when Lady Catherine rubbed the leather down her back and lightly tickled her backside with the swishing leather straps.

"Stroke yourself, Collins," she ordered. "Come on your wife's back."

Charlotte alternated licking and sucking, curving her tongue deep inside the woman.

"Your wife is very talented. She pleases me."

"Thank you, my Mistress."

"You should thank her. I was upset Miss Bennet was not here to lavish attention on my breasts. I wasn't going to let you have relief. But your wife is going to bring me soon and she can pleasure me there while you take her place."

"Thank you, Mrs. Collins," he panted.

Lady Catherine forced Charlotte's head deeper. Charlotte inserted her tongue inside the woman's passage. Lady Catherine grunted in pleasure and rocked on her face. Charlotte hummed so the vibration hit her most sensitive areas and felt her face being drenched.

"I came before you Mr. Collins," Lady Catherine

frowned.

"I'm sorry, my Mistress."

"Lick my pleasure off your wife's face."

Lady Catherine got up and watched the couple. Charlotte raised her face up and Mr. Collins lapped eagerly. She brought the whip down on his back.

"Thank you, Mistress."

Lady Catherine knelt on the floor beside them, squeezing Charlotte's breasts.

"Thank you Mistress," Charlotte breathed.

Lady Catherine pinched her nipple hard. "You will not play me, dear girl. I've been doing this when you were in small clothes. Get on your hands and knees."

Charlotte did.

"Take her hard and fast, Collins. I want to hear your bodies slamming together."

Charlotte hissed when her husband entered her roughly. The slap of their bodies was loud in the room. Lady Catherine drove Mr. Collins into a frenzy with cracks of the flogger on his feet and thighs.

Charlotte closed her eyes and reached between her legs and rubbed herself until she was enjoying the hard grunting thrusts.

"Don't think I didn't see that, naughty girl," Lady Charlotte said. "But as I said, your tongue pleases me."

"Please Mistress," Mr. Collins shouted. "I am ready to come."

"Pull out," Lady Charlotte ordered.

He obeyed.

"Turn over Mrs. Collins."

Charlotte did. Her fingers still bringing her pleasure.

"You may expend yourself on your wife's breasts."

Charlotte watched her husband pump his fist and shoot hot, white clumps over her sensitive nipples.

"Suck it all up." Lady Charlotte said.

"Thank you, Mistress," Charlotte moaned as her sensitive tips got attention and she spasmed with bliss.

Chapter 27

While the Collins were gone, Elizabeth, as if intending to exasperate herself as much as possible against Mr. Darcy, chose for her employment the examination of all the letters which Jane had written to her since her being in Kent. While simmering at the pain Mr. Darcy caused her sister, she was suddenly roused by the sound of the door-bell. To her utter amazement, she saw Mr. Darcy walk into the room.

In a hurried manner he immediately began an inquiry after her health, imputing his visit to a wish of hearing that she were better. She answered him with cold civility.

"Are you unwell?"

"Most grieviously so," she managed to get out between her clenched teeth.

He sat down for a few moments, and then getting up, walked about the room. Elizabeth was surprised, but said not a word. She would not speak to him first. His cousin must have told him of their conversation and Mr. Darcy was now here to apologize. After a silence of several minutes, he came towards her in an agitated manner, and thus began:

"In vain I have struggled. It will not do. My

feelings will not be repressed. You must allow me to tell you how ardently I admire and love you."

Elizabeth's astonishment was beyond expression. She stared, coloured, doubted, and was silent. This he considered sufficient encouragement; and the avowal of all that he felt, and had long felt for her, immediately followed.

He spoke well; but there were feelings besides those of the heart to be detailed; and he was not more eloquent on the subject of tenderness than of pride. His sense of her inferiority—of its being a degradation—of the family obstacles which had always opposed to inclination, were dwelt on with a warmth which seemed due to the consequence he was wounding, but was very unlikely to recommend his suit. And she would have thought that the hours in the gazebo with him would have made him sweeter in his wooing. She could only stare at him in shock. She was "perfect" when he was inside her and she was restrained, but here in the common room she was "inferior."

Roused to resentment by his subsequent language, Elizabeth lost all compassion in anger.

He concluded with representing to her the strength of that attachment which, in spite of all his endeavours, he had found impossible to conquer; and with expressing his hope that it would now be rewarded by her acceptance of his hand.

As he said this, she could easily see that he had no doubt of a favourable answer. He spoke of apprehension and anxiety, but his countenance expressed real security. Such a circumstance could only exasperate farther, and, when he ceased, the colour rose into her cheeks, and she said:

"No."

Mr. Darcy, who was leaning against the mantelpiece with his eyes fixed on her face, seemed to catch her answer with no less resentment than surprise. His complexion became pale with anger, and the disturbance of his mind was visible in every feature. He was struggling for the appearance of composure, and would not open his lips till he believed himself to have attained it. The pause was to Elizabeth's feelings dreadful. At length, with a voice of forced calmness, he said:

"And this is all the reply which I am to have the honour of expecting! I might, perhaps, wish to be informed why, with so little endeavour at civility, I am thus rejected. But it is of small importance. I thought this is what you wanted. You have given your virginity to your bridegroom after all." He finished with a half laugh, as if expecting she was having a lark at his expense.

"I might as well inquire," replied she, "why with so evident a desire of offending and insulting me, you chose to tell me that you liked me against your will, against your reason, and even against your character? Was not this some excuse for incivility, if I was uncivil? But I have other provocations. You know I have. Had you asked me thus at the gazebo, my answer would have been different. However, do you think that any consideration would tempt me to accept the man who has been the means of ruining, perhaps for ever, the happiness of a most beloved sister?"

As she pronounced these words, Mr. Darcy changed colour.

She paused, and saw with no slight indignation

261

that he was listening with an air which proved him wholly unmoved by any feeling of remorse. He even looked at her with a smile of affected incredulity.

"Can you deny that you have done it?" she repeated.

With assumed tranquillity he then replied: "I have no wish of denying that I did everything in my power to separate my friend from your sister, or that I rejoice in my success. Towards him I have been kinder than towards myself."

Elizabeth disdained the appearance of noticing this civil reflection, but its meaning did not escape, nor was it likely to conciliate her. She wanted to draw blood.

"But it is not merely this affair," she continued, "on which my dislike is founded. Long before it had taken place my opinion of you was decided. Your character was unfolded in the recital which I received many months ago from Mr. Wickham. On this subject, what can you have to say? In what imaginary act of friendship can you here defend yourself? or under what misrepresentation can you here impose upon others?"

"You take an eager interest in that gentleman's concerns," said Darcy, in a less tranquil tone, and with a heightened colour.

"Who that knows what his misfortunes have been, can help feeling an interest in him?"

"His misfortunes!" repeated Darcy contemptuously; "yes, his misfortunes have been great indeed."

"And of your infliction," cried Elizabeth with energy. "You have reduced him to his present state of poverty—comparative poverty. You have withheld the advantages which you must know to have been designed for him. You have deprived the best years of his life of that independence which was no less his due than his desert. You have done all this! and yet you can treat the mention of his misfortune with contempt and ridicule."

"And this," cried Darcy, as he walked with quick steps across the room, "is your opinion of me! After what we've shared? After what I've taught you?"

Elizabeth turned away. "I suppose now you will ruin me."

"This is the estimation in which you hold me? I thank you for explaining it so fully. My faults, according to this calculation, are heavy indeed! But perhaps," added he, stopping in his walk, and turning towards her, "these offenses might have been overlooked, had not your pride been hurt by my honest confession of the scruples that had long prevented my forming any serious design. These bitter accusations might have been suppressed, had I, with greater policy, concealed my struggles, and flattered you into the belief of my being impelled by unqualified, unalloyed inclination; by reason, by reflection, by everything. But disguise of every sort is my abhorrence. Nor am I ashamed of the feelings I related. They were natural and just. Could you expect me to rejoice in the inferiority of your connections?—to congratulate myself on the hope of relations, whose condition in life is so decidedly beneath my own?"

Elizabeth felt herself growing more angry every moment; yet she tried to the utmost to speak with composure when she said:

" From the very beginning—from the first

263

Lissa Trevor

moment, I may almost say—of my acquaintance with you, your manners, impressing me with the fullest belief of your arrogance, your conceit, and your selfish disdain of the feelings of others, were such as to form the groundwork of disapprobation on which succeeding events have built so immovable a dislike. I foolishly thought you could be different. But first Wickham, then my dearest Jane, and finally your disappointment in what I can offer you as a bride. I don't know what to say."

"You have said quite enough, madam. I perfectly comprehend your feelings, and have now only to be ashamed of what my own have been. Forgive me for having taken up so much of your time, and accept my best wishes for your health and happiness."

And with these words he hastily left the room, and Elizabeth heard him the next moment open the front door and quit the house.

The tumult of her mind, was now painfully great. She knew not how to support herself, and from actual weakness sat down and cried for half-an-hour. Her astonishment, as she reflected on what had passed, was increased by every review of it. That she should receive an offer of marriage from Mr. Darcy! That he should have been in love with her for so many months! So much in love as to wish to marry her in spite of all the objections which had made him prevent his friend's marrying her sister, and which must appear at least with equal force in his own case—was almost incredible!

It was gratifying to have inspired unconsciously so strong an affection. But his pride, his abominable pride—his shameless avowal of what he had done with respect to Jane—his unpardonable assurance in acknowledging, though he could not justify it, and the unfeeling manner in which he had mentioned Mr. Wickham, his cruelty towards whom he had not attempted to deny, soon overcame the pity which the consideration of his attachment had for a moment excited. She continued in very agitated reflections till the sound of Lady Catherine's carriage made her feel how unequal she was to encounter Charlotte's observation, and hurried her away to her room.

Chapter 28

Mr. Darcy and his entourage had left by the time Elizabeth forced herself downstairs the next day. Mr. Collins told her that he was devastated not to say goodbye in person, but he left her a letter.

With no expectation of pleasure, but with the strongest curiosity, Elizabeth opened the letter, and, to her still increasing wonder, perceived an envelope containing two sheets of letter-paper, written quite through, in a very close hand. The envelope itself was likewise full. It was dated from Rosings, at eight o'clock in the morning. She barely noticed Charlotte trying to unobtrusively read over her shoulder. But Elizabeth grabbed her wrap and wandered outside to walk down the lane while reading the letter.

"I had not been long in Hertfordshire, before I saw, in common with others, that Bingley preferred your elder sister to any other young woman in the country. But it was not till the evening of the dance at Netherfield that I had any apprehension of his feeling a serious attachment. I had often seen him in love before. At that ball, while I had the honour of dancing with you, I was first made acquainted, by Sir William

Lucas's accidental information, that Bingley's attentions to your sister had given rise to a general expectation of their marriage. He spoke of it as a certain event, of which the time alone could be undecided.

From that moment I observed my friend's behaviour attentively; and I could then perceive that his partiality for Miss Bennet was beyond what I had ever witnessed in him. Your sister I also watched. Her look and manners were open, cheerful, and engaging as ever, but without any symptom of peculiar regard, and I remained convinced from the evening's scrutiny, that though she received his attentions with pleasure, she did not invite them by any participation of sentiment.

If you have not been mistaken here, I must have been in error. Your superior knowledge of your sister must make the latter probable. If it be so, if I have been misled by such error to inflict pain on her, your resentment has not been unreasonable. But I shall not scruple to assert, that the serenity of your sister's countenance and air was such as might have given the most acute observer a conviction that, however amiable her temper, her heart was not likely to be easily touched. That I was desirous of believing her indifferent is certain—but I will venture to say that my investigation and decisions are not usually influenced by my hopes or fears. I did not believe her to be indifferent because I wished it; I believed it on impartial conviction, as truly as I wished it in reason.

The situation of your mother's family, though objectionable, was nothing in comparison to that total want of propriety so frequently, so almost uniformly betrayed by herself, by your three younger sisters, and occasionally even by your father.

Bingley left Netherfield for London, on the day following, as you, I am certain, remember, with the design of soon returning. The part which I acted is now to be explained. His sisters' uneasiness had been equally excited with my own; our coincidence of feeling was soon discovered, and, alike sensible that no time was to be lost in detaching their brother, we shortly resolved on joining him directly in London. We accordingly went—and there I readily engaged in the office of pointing out to my friend the certain evils of such a choice. I described, and enforced them earnestly. But, however this remonstrance might have staggered or delayed his determination, I do not suppose that it would ultimately have prevented the marriage, had it not been seconded by the assurance that I hesitated not in giving, of your sister's indifference. He had before believed her to return his affection with sincere, if not with equal regard.

But Bingley has great natural modesty, with a stronger dependence on my judgement than on his own. To convince him, therefore, that he had deceived himself, was no very difficult point. To persuade him against returning into Hertfordshire, when that conviction had been given, was scarcely the work of a moment.

If I have wounded your sister's feelings, it was unknowingly done and though the motives which governed me may to you very naturally appear insufficient, I have not yet learnt to condemn them.

With respect to that other, more weighty accusation, of having injured Mr. Wickham, I can only refute it by laying before you the whole of his connection with my family. Of what he has particularly accused me I am ignorant; but of the truth of what I shall relate, I can summon more than one witness of undoubted veracity. Mr. Wickham spent his inheritance and when I refused to finance whatever endeavor had caught his eye, he took it ill.

"I must now mention a circumstance which I would wish to forget myself, and which no obligation less than the present should induce me to unfold to any human being. Having said thus much, I feel no doubt of your secrecy. My sister, who is more than ten years my junior, was left to the guardianship of my mother's nephew, Colonel Fitzwilliam, and myself. About a year ago, she was taken from school, and an establishment formed for her in London; and thither also went Mr. Wickham, undoubtedly by design; He so far recommended himself to Georgiana, whose affectionate heart retained a strong impression of his kindness to her as a child, that she was persuaded to believe herself in love, and to consent to an elopement.

She was then but fifteen, which must be her excuse; and after stating her imprudence, I am happy to add, that I owed the knowledge of it to herself. I joined them unexpectedly a day or two before the intended elopement, and then Georgiana, unable to support the idea of grieving and offending a brother whom she almost looked up to as a father, acknowledged the whole to me. You may imagine what I felt and how I acted. Regard for my sister's credit and feelings prevented any public exposure; but I wrote to Mr. Wickham, who left the place immediately. Mr. Wickham's chief object was unquestionably my sister's

Lissa Trevor

fortune, which is thirty thousand pounds.

"You may possibly wonder why all this was not told you last night; but I was not then master enough of myself to know what could or ought to be revealed. I will only add, God bless you.

Fitzwilliam Darcy

Elizabeth did not expect the letter to contain a renewal of his offers. She had formed no expectation at all of its contents. Her feelings as she read were scarcely to be defined.

With amazement did she first understand that he believed any apology to be in his power; and steadfastly was she persuaded, that he could have no explanation to give, which a just sense of shame would not conceal.

She grew absolutely ashamed of herself when she re-read the part with Wickham. Of neither Darcy nor Wickham could she think without feeling she had been blind, partial, prejudiced, absurd.

"How despicably I have acted!" she cried; How humiliating is this discovery! I could not have been more wretchedly blind! But vanity, not love, has been my folly. Pleased with the preference of one, and offended by the neglect of the other, on the very beginning of our acquaintance, I have courted prepossession and ignorance, and driven reason away, where either were concerned. Till this moment I never knew myself."

When she came to that part of the letter in which her family were mentioned in terms of such mortifying, yet merited reproach, her sense of shame was severe. The justice of the charge struck her too forcibly for denial, and the circumstances to which he particularly alluded as having passed at the Netherfield ball, and as confirming all his first disapprobation, could not have made a stronger impression on his mind than on hers.

Her first thought was to confide in Charlotte, but Mr. Collins stared so disapprovingly at her she could only wonder what Lady Catherine had said about her absence the prior evening – especially if she suspected that Elizabeth was the reason her nephews left post haste this morning.

She heard a familiar sound of a belt being cracked and for a moment, Elizabeth had the hope that Mr. Darcy hadn't left at all. Perhaps he was here to punish her and in taking his punishment, they could resolve their harsh words.

But as she came up to the house, she happened to look in the window first before entering. To her great surprise and slight mortification, Mr. Collins was hanging from the ceiling post, held straining by his wrists, naked and erect. He had clips on his nipples and on the heavy sack between his legs. Red stripes covered his back as Charlotte, also naked, struck him with more force than Mr. Darcy had ever used on her. She hit him so hard that Elizabeth flinched with the blow.

While part of her admired seeing her friend's lovely naked body, she wished that it was Mr. Darcy wielding the leather tails. The Collins' love play was silent, almost grim, but Lizzie couldn't glance away. When Charlotte twirled Mr. Collins around and took him in her mouth, Elizabeth thought of Mr. Darcy's member in her own throat. It had been since

271

Netherfield. She vowed the first thing she would do would be to worship his thick member like Charlotte was doing to her husband. Elizabeth watched Charlotte's lovely mouth slide up and down Mr. Collins' shaft. She could see why he married her. Charlotte stopped as he began to clench his muscles. She went flogged him faster, this time across his buttocks until he sprayed a white column of pleasure against his stomach.

Elizabeth felt flushed and warm. Charlotte climbed on the table and cut him down, so he fell hard on the floor. Before he could recover, she kicked him on his back and sat on his face. Then she turned and locked eyes with Elizabeth, who gasped and almost retreated. But the sheer happiness in her friend's face, made her smile and watch the show appreciatively. Grinning harder, Charlotte cupped her breasts at her friend and offered them to her playfully. Elizabeth waggled her tongue at her and Charlotte shifted her weight faster against Mr. Collins, who had grasped her hips.

Charlotte arched, her plum-shaped breasts flattening. The muscles in her legs and stomach tightened and Elizabeth watched in envy as her friend achieved bliss. Charlotte beckoned to her, but Elizabeth shook her head. She walked to the gazebo to give her friend a chance to dress. There was also a small part of her that hoped Mr. Darcy would be there. She thought of the red welts on Mr. Collins buttocks and how excited it made her to hear the crack of the leather.

Chapter 29

The next day, while Elizabeth and Charlotte were having tea in her parlour, Mr. Collins came in with a letter from Jane with terrible news. Their sister Lydia had eloped – with none other than Wickham. But even worse, no one could find them to confirm the marriage.

"Lizzie are you all right?" Charlotte said in concern when she saw the colour drain from her face.

"I must go home immediately. My mother is ill," Elizabeth prevaricated. She couldn't bear the shame if they were to find out.

With the aid of one of Lady Catherine's carriages, Elizabeth made haste to her family and in agony they all waited for news of Lydia and Wickham. When her Uncle sent a letter saying they had been found and would be wed, it was met with mixed feelings. Mr. Bennet was sure his brother-in-law had paid a dear sum for this event to take place. But there was nothing else to do.

Their sister's wedding day arrived; and the family was assembled in the breakfast room to receive them. Smiles decked the face of Mrs. Bennet as the carriage drove up to the door; her husband looked impenetrably grave; her daughters, alarmed, anxious, uneasy.

The easy assurance of the young couple, indeed, was enough to provoke him. Elizabeth was disgusted, and even Jane was shocked. Lydia was Lydia still; untamed, unabashed, wild, noisy, and fearless. She turned from sister to sister, demanding their congratulations; and when at length they all sat down, looked eagerly round the room, took notice of some little alteration in it, and observed, with a laugh, that it was a great while since she had been there.

One morning, soon after their arrival, as she was sitting with her two elder sisters, she said to Elizabeth: "Lizzy, I never gave you an account of my wedding, I believe. You were not by, when I told mamma and the others all about it. Are not you curious to hear how it was managed?"

"No really," replied Elizabeth; "I think there cannot be too little said on the subject."

"La! You are so strange! But I must tell you how it went off. We were married, you know, at St. Clement's, because Wickham's lodgings were in that parish. I was so afraid, you know, that something would happen to put it off, and then I should have gone quite distracted.Well, and so just as the carriage came to the door, my uncle was called away upon business to that horrid man Mr. Stone. And then, you know, when once they get together, there is no end of it. Well, I was so frightened I did not know what to do, for my uncle was to give me away; and if we were beyond the hour, we could not be married all day. But, luckily, he came back again in ten minutes' time, and then we all set out. However, I recollected afterwards that if he had been prevented going, the wedding need not be put off, for Mr. Darcy might have done as well."

"Mr. Darcy!" repeated Elizabeth, in utter amazement.

"Oh, yes!—he was to come there with Wickham, you know. But gracious me! I quite forgot! I ought not to have said a word about it. I promised them so faithfully! Well, the cats out of the bag now."

"Why was he there?"

"We had the coincidence of meeting him on the road and he remained with us on the journey. I was so surprised when he deigned to speak to us. You remember how boarish and rude he was at Netherfield?"

Elizabeth flushed, but it wasn't his rudeness she remembered.

"He was so kind to Wickham and I." Lydia fluttered her eyelashes. "He gave us quite a wedding gift you know."

Elizabeth was speechless. It wasn't her Uncle that paid a great sum for Lydia's dowry, but her own dear, Master. The man who proposed and she sent away because of her pride.

Mr. Darcy had followed Lydia and Wickham purposely to town, he had taken on himself all the trouble and mortification attendant on such a research; in which supplication had been necessary to a woman whom he must abominate and despise, and where he was reduced to meet, frequently meet, reason with, persuade, and finally bribe, the man whom he always most wished to avoid, and whose very name it was punishment to him to pronounce.

He had done all this for Lydia whom he could neither regard nor esteem.

Her heart did whisper that he had done it for her.

275

Lissa Trevor

But it was a hope shortly checked by other considerations, and she soon felt that even her vanity was insufficient, when required to depend on his affection for her—for a woman who had already refused him—as able to overcome a sentiment so natural as abhorrence against relationship with Wickham. Brother-in-law of Wickham!

It was painful, exceedingly painful, to know that they were under obligations to a person who could never receive a return. They owed the restoration of Lydia, her character, every thing, to him. Oh! how heartily did she grieve over every ungracious sensation she had ever encouraged, every saucy speech she had ever directed towards him. For herself she was humbled; but she was proud of him. Proud that in a cause of compassion and honour, he had been able to get the better of himself.

Elizabeth penned a letter to Mr. Darcy and sent it off with a messenger to Pemberley. She tried her best to be as subtle as she dared.

My dear Mr. Darcy,

You parted in such haste that I was unable to give to you a small token of my gratitude for the lessons you imparted. Should our paths cross again, I would be most willing to accept whatever punishments you thought fit for my digression.

Sincerely and with great esteem of your character,

Miss Elizabeth Bennet

Chapter 30

About a month later, the housekeeper at Netherfield had received orders to prepare for the arrival of Mr. Bingley, who was coming down in a day or two, to shoot there for several weeks. Mrs. Bennet was quite in the fidgets. She looked at Jane, and smiled and shook her head by turns.

Jane had not been able to hear of his coming without changing colour. It was many months since she had mentioned his name to Elizabeth; but now, as soon as they were alone together, she said:

"I saw you look at me to-day, Lizzy, when and I know I appeared distressed. But don't imagine it was from any silly cause. I do assure you that the news does not affect me either with pleasure or pain. I am glad of one thing, that he comes alone; because we shall see the less of him. Not that I am afraid of myself, but I dread other people's remarks."

Elizabeth did not know what to make of it.

As the day of his arrival drew near, Jane said,

"I begin to be sorry that he comes at all. It would be nothing; I could see him with perfect indifference, but I can hardly bear to hear it thus perpetually talked of. My mother means well; but she does not know, no

277

one can know, how much I suffer from what she says. Happy shall I be, when his stay at Netherfield is over!"

"I wish I could say anything to comfort you," replied Elizabeth.

Mr. Bingley arrived. On the third morning after his arrival in Hertfordshire, she saw him, from her dressing-room window, enter the paddock and ride towards the house. Jane resolutely kept her place at the table; but Elizabeth, to satisfy her mother, went to the window—she looked,—she saw Mr. Darcy with him, and sat down again by her sister.

Had he received her letter?

"There is a gentleman with him, mamma," said Kitty; "who can it be?"

"Some acquaintance or other, my dear, I suppose; I am sure I do not know."

"La!" replied Kitty, "it looks just like that man that used to be with him before. Mr. what's-his-name. That tall, proud man."

"Good gracious! Mr. Darcy!—and so it does, I vow. Well, any friend of Mr. Bingley's will always be welcome here, to be sure; but else I must say that I hate the very sight of him."

Jane looked at Elizabeth with surprise and concern. To Jane, he could be only a man whose proposals she had refused, and whose merit she had undervalued; but to her own more extensive information, he was the person to whom the whole family were indebted for the first of benefits, and whom she regarded herself with an interest, if not quite so tender, at least as reasonable and just as what Jane felt for Bingley.

The colour which had been driven from her face,

returned for half a minute with an additional glow, and a smile of delight added lustre to her eyes, as she thought for that space of time that his affection and wishes must still be unshaken. But she would not be secure.

"Let me first see how he behaves," said she; "it will then be early enough for expectation."

She sat intently at work, striving to be composed, and without daring to lift up her eyes, till anxious curiosity carried them to the face of her sister as the servant was approaching the door. Jane looked a little paler than usual, but more sedate than Elizabeth had expected. On the gentlemen's appearing, her colour increased; yet she received them with tolerable ease, and with a propriety of behaviour equally free from any symptom of resentment or any unnecessary complaisance.

"It is a long time, Mr. Bingley, since you went away," said Mrs. Bennet.

He readily agreed to it.

"Too long, Mrs. Bennet," he said. "I was hoping to have a moment to speak with your eldest daughter."

Before Jane had time for anything but a blush of surprise, Mrs. Bennet answered instantly, "Oh dear!—yes—certainly. I am sure Jane will be very happy—I am sure she can have no objection. Come, Kitty, I want you up stairs. Elizabeth entertain Mr. Darcy."

Mr. Darcy quirked an eyebrow at Elizabeth, who hid a wide smile with her hand. Oblivious, Mrs. Bennet hustled Kitty and Mary upstairs.

"Entertain me, Miss Bennet," he said and offered her his arm.

"We'll be out walking," Elizabeth said to Jane

who was quite beyond hearing her.

They made haste across the lawns. She led him to the barn and with a look to see that no one had noticed their destination, she said, "I apologize for the lack of gazebos here."

He gave her a stern nod that both terrified her and turned her knees to jelly. They stepped inside and the horses whickered at them.

"Mr. Darcy," Elizabeth began, "I am a very selfish creature; and, for the sake of giving relief to my own feelings, care not how much I may be wounding yours. I can no longer help thanking you for your unexampled kindness to my poor sister Lydia. Ever since I have known it, I have been most anxious to acknowledge to you how gratefully I feel it. Were it known to the rest of my family, I should not have merely my own gratitude to express."

"I am sorry, exceedingly sorry," replied Darcy, in a tone of surprise and emotion, "that you have ever been informed of what may, in a mistaken light, have given you uneasiness."

"Lydia told me of your generous gift."

"If you will thank me," he replied, "let it be for yourself alone. That the wish of giving happiness to you might add force to the other inducements which led me on, I shall not attempt to deny. But your family owes me nothing. Much as I respect them, I believe I thought only of you."

Elizabeth fell to her knees and began to unfasten his trousers, "Allow me to show you how thankful I am for you, Master."

"You needn't," he said and choked on his worlds when she boldly pulled him free of his restraining trousers and licked his tip. "After our words the last time we met, I cannot fathom you would do this willingly.

Elizabeth was too much embarrassed to say a word, so she let her actions speak for her. Taking him fully in her mouth, she held him deep in the back of her throat and untied the lacings on the front of her dress.

Mr. Darcy attempted speech, but after she bobbed her head in slow languorous movements, so he nearly slipped out and then she darted forward until the head of his cock touched the back of his throat. In the end, he wound her hair around his hand and enjoyed her eager sucking sounds.

Had Elizabeth been able to encounter his eye, she might have seen how well the expression of heartfelt delight, diffused over his face, became him; but, though she could not look, she could listen, and he told her of feelings, which, in proving of what importance she was to him, made his affection every moment more valuable.

There was too much to be thought, and felt, and said, for attention to anything other than the thick feel of him slicking into her mouth..

"Elizabeth, my emotions are too near the surface to prolong this. I will spend myself down your throat." He tightened his grip on her hair and held her tight against me. "You will accept me?" Mr. Darcy used his Master's voice so the question was more of an order and she moaned her assent. Shortly thereafter, his hips thrust once, pushing him deepest. For a moment there wasn't any air, but she swallowed and gulped. Mr. Darcy hauled her to her feet and covered her mouth, still splattered with his issue, with his own.

The kiss was burningly fierce, and Elizabeth gave herself up to the hard possession in his arms that quickly divested her of her dress and chemise.

"When I got your letter, it taught me to hope," said he as he lay his jacket in the hay loft., "as I had scarcely ever allowed myself to hope before. I knew enough of your disposition to be certain that, had you been absolutely, irrevocably decided against me, you would never had written to me."

Elizabeth coloured and laughed as she climbed up the ladder. "Yes, you know enough of my frankness to believe me capable of that. After abusing you so abominably to your face, I could have no scruple in abusing you to all your relations."

He held her hips so she didn't climb any higher. Mr. Darcy ran his hands across her milk white shoulders, down the elegant curve of her spine, and finally over the rounded curves of her buttocks. "What did you say of me, that I did not deserve? For, though your accusations were ill-founded, formed on mistaken premises, my behaviour to you at the time had merited the severest reproof. It was unpardonable. I cannot think of it without abhorrence."

"We will not quarrel for the greater share of blame annexed to that evening," said Elizabeth. "The conduct of neither, if strictly examined, will be irreproachable; but since then, we have both, I hope, improved in civility."

" Your reproof, so well applied, I shall never forget: 'had you behaved in a more gentlemanlike manner.' Those were your words. You know not, you can scarcely conceive, how they have tortured me;—

though it was some time, I confess, before I was reasonable enough to allow their justice. That won't get you out of your punishment, though," he said.

She shivered delicately.

" You thought me then devoid of every proper feeling, I am sure you did. The turn of your countenance I shall never forget, as you said that I could not have addressed you in any possible way that would induce you to accept me." He ran his riding quirt over her back and then laid it across her buttocks with a quick snap of his wrists.

"Oh! do not repeat what I then said. These recollections will not do at all. I assure you that I have long been most heartily ashamed of it."

He slapped the braided leather against her again. Heat replaced the sharp pierce of pain, and Elizabeth was wet to the point of distraction. Mr. Darcy laid a third lash across her.

"You're skin is so white and delicate," he said, kissing the red weal that had popped up. He trailed his tongue over the mark and ended with a sharp bite on a meaty part of her cheek. "I am pained that our harsh words could have separated us forever."

"Think only of the past as its remembrance gives you pleasure," Elizabeth said shakily, trying to breathe through the new sensations.

"Climb," he ordered.

While still hazy from the pleasure pain, Elizabeth put one foot on the next rung.

"Stop," he said. He slid the handle of the riding quirt across her exposed folds. The leather had a knobbed surface that both soothed and inflamed her. Spreading her legs wider, she allowed him a greater range that had her rocking against it as she sought her pleasure. He tapped it up against her and while it didn't have the sting of the lash, it was a knock that had her moaning.

"More?" He asked and wiggled it so it probed her bud with hard taps that had her thighs closing on it as she rubbed the knobs by gyrating her hips against it. Frustrated, she fingered the spot she needed. Mr. Darcy removed her fingers, placing them in his mouth while he sucked the juices off them. He pleasured her with the crop until she sighed out her satisfaction.

"Let me see you lick your cream off this," Mr. Darcy pushed the leather into her mouth. He narrowed his eyes in a dark possessive leer when she hollowed her cheeks to suck the leather handle.

He tweaked her nipples, loving the way they reddened at his touch.

"Painful recollections will intrude which cannot, which ought not, to be repelled. I have been a selfish being all my life, in practice, though not in principle. As a child I was taught what was right, but I was not taught to correct my temper. I was given good principles, but left to follow them in pride and conceit. Such I was, from eight to eight and twenty; and such I might still have been but for you, dearest, loveliest Elizabeth! What do I not owe you! You taught me a lesson, hard indeed at first, but most advantageous. By you, I was properly humbled. I came to you without a doubt of my reception. You showed me how insufficient were all my pretensions to please a woman worthy of being pleased."

"I am greatly pleased, Master," she said as he pinched her nipples causing that pain pleasure spurt she was beginning to crave. "Please me more."

"Have you then persuaded yourself that I should?"

"Indeed I have. What will you think of my vanity?"

"I think you will make me a fine wife, Miss Bennet, if you will have me."

Elizabeth turned on the ladder to embrace him. "Oh yes, if you will still have me."

He buried his face in her belly as she stroked his hair. "Step higher," he instructed. "Have a care with your footing."

Elizabeth stepped higher on the ladder and Mr. Darcy continued to lavish her with kisses and nibbles on her curves. One more step and his tongue was all over the downy curls of her mound. The last step had her sitting on his jacket at the top of the loft, with his face nestled intimately between her legs. His tongue licked her from one end to the other, darting against that bud.

Her cries were urgent, and he reached into his pocket. "Lean forward," he ordered. When she complied, he attached a clamp on one nipple.

"Oh," Elizabeth cried out. It hurt. But his fingers plunging inside her had her gasping through it and as she was enjoying the friction of him sliding over her, he had a second one on.

"Hurts?" he asked.

She nodded, looking down at the chain that hung between her breasts.

"Good," he said and went back to ravishing her quim with licks and soft sucking bites. "You are mine, now, Elizabeth. Mine."

Elizabeth felt everything more. The pain in her

backside from the lashes, the heavy piercing weight on her nipples and Mr. Darcy's fast tongue and fingers were just too much. She cried his name and gave into him again. He was her Master. He would see to her pleasure. Forgive her when she erred. Protect her. Marry her. He would be her husband.

Boneless from ecstasy, Elizabeth allowed herself to be tossed up so she was on her hands and knees at the top of the loft. Mr. Darcy was behind her and inside her, pumping hard and fast, as if he couldn't bear a moment outside her body a moment longer.

"Sweet, beautiful Elizabeth," he muttered, his fingers digging into her backside and the red angry marks on them.

"Take me, Mr. Darcy," she cried out. "I am yours."

His body was pistoning inside her, stretching her filling her. How she missed his body invading hers! In the gazebo, in the barn, would they be married quickly so she could enjoy the marriage bed. She threw her head back in joy, happy to have such a strong, powerful lover. A man she could fight with and he wouldn't be frightened away. The love she had for him was near to bursting from her chest.

"My Darcy," she sighed as oblivion nearly took her as the sheer force of his orgasm brought her over again.

He pulled her on top of him. "I know you prefer walking my dear," he said. "But I want you to ride me."

"I have no breath to do so."

He pulled the chain and her nipples pulled painfully and stretched. Elizabeth whimpered even as her body quickened in desire again.

"Shall I ever get enough of you?" she said straddling him as he eased back inside
her.

"No," he said with a trace of the arrogant man she first met.

Elizabeth rocked astride him, the fire in her breasts egging her on. Whenever she
slowed or paused to catch a breath from the throbbing pulse of him inside her, he pulled on the chain as if it were reins and her body strummed back to life with the jolt of pain that she could no longer differentiate from the pleasure.

He slapped her buttocks as she was nearing her pleasure.

"Again," she groaned out in a voice she didn't recognize as her own. "Spank me, Mr. Darcy."

He obliged, laying his large hand across her until she was shrieking like a wild thing, bouncing without decorum or sanity until the wave of pleasure crashed over her and left her spent and panting against his neck.

She was barely aware of him, finishing as they were kissing passionately. Swallowing his grunt of satisfaction, she tasted herself on his tongue and never felt more connected to another human being. His cock, his tongue and his fingers were inside her and that sweet oblivion hit her as she drifted off on a wave of pleasure.

Elizabeth forced her eyes open what seemed to be moments later when Mr. Darcy urged her to dress herself before her father came out with a rifle for him.

She giggled. Wincing at the stiff and sore body parts, Elizabeth accepted his help down from the loft and into her clothes. He took off the chain and pinchers from her nipples, slipping them back into his pocket.

They walked back to the house, close enough to feel the heat from the other's body, but not touching.

"Do I have hay in my hair?" she asked, plucking a few strands from him.

"Surprisingly no."

"I wonder if Jane and Bingley have noticed our absence?"

"I would highly doubt it. They were probably engaging in the same thing we were."

"You're terrible," she said, swatting him. "My sister is pure. How did you get Bingley to come and offer for her? Or am I assuming the look I saw in his eye?"

"You are not. On the evening before my going to London," said he, "I made a confession to him, which I believe I ought to have made long ago. I told him of all that had occurred to make my former interference in his affairs absurd and impertinent. His surprise was great. He had never had the slightest suspicion. I told him, moreover, that I believed myself mistaken in supposing, as I had done, that your sister was indifferent to him; and as I could easily perceive that his attachment to her was unabated, I felt no doubt of their happiness together."

Elizabeth could not help smiling at his easy manner of directing his friend.

"Did you speak from your own observation," said she, "when you told him that my sister loved him, or merely from my information last spring?"

"From the former. I had narrowly observed her during the two visits which I had lately made here; and I was convinced of her affection."

"And your assurance of it, I suppose, carried immediate conviction to him."

"It did. Bingley is most unaffectedly modest. I was obliged to confess one thing, which for a time, and not unjustly, offended him. I could not allow myself to conceal that your sister had been in town three months last winter, that I had known it, and purposely kept it from him. He was angry. But his anger, I am persuaded, lasted no longer than he remained in any doubt of your sister's sentiments. He has heartily forgiven me now."

Elizabeth longed to observe that Mr. Bingley had been a most delightful friend; so easily guided that his worth was invaluable; but she checked herself. She remembered that he had yet to learn to be laughed at, and it was rather too early to begin. In anticipating the happiness of Bingley, which of course was to be inferior only to his own, he continued the conversation till they reached the house. In the hall they parted.

Chapter 32

On returning to the drawing-room, she perceived her sister and Bingley standing together over the hearth, as if engaged in earnest conversation; and had this led to no suspicion, the faces of both, as they hastily turned round and moved away from each other, would have told it all.

Elizabeth noted their mussed clothes and hastily put together clothes. Their situation was awkward enough; but hers she thought was still worse. Not a syllable was uttered by either; and Elizabeth was on the point of going away again, when Bingley, who as well as the other had sat down, suddenly rose, and whispering a few words to her sister, ran out of the room.

Jane could have no reserves from Elizabeth, where confidence would give pleasure; and instantly embracing her, acknowledged, with the liveliest emotion, that she was the happiest creature in the world.

"'Tis too much!" she added, "by far too much. I do not deserve it. Oh! why is not everybody as happy?"

Elizabeth's congratulations were given with a sincerity, a warmth, a delight, which words could but poorly express. Every sentence of kindness was a fresh source of happiness to Jane.

"I must go instantly to my mother;" she cried. "I would not on any account trifle with her affectionate solicitude; or allow her to hear it from anyone but myself. He is gone to my father already. Oh! Lizzy, to know that what I have to relate will give such pleasure to all my dear family! how shall I bear so much happiness!"

"He has made me so happy," Jane continued, "by telling me that he was totally ignorant of my being in town last spring! I had not believed it possible."

"I suspected as much," replied Elizabeth. "But how did he account for it?"

"It must have been his sister's doing. But when they see, as I trust they will, that their brother is happy with me, they will learn to be contented, and we shall be on good terms again; though we can never be what we once were to each other."

"That is the most unforgiving speech," said Elizabeth, "that I ever heard you utter. Good girl! It would vex me, indeed, to see you again the dupe of Miss Bingley's pretended regard."

"Truly, she made me feel as I was chasing her, the conceit!" Jane said and looked around surreptitiously. "She has a very high opinion of her charms."

"I noticed," Elizabeth rolled her eyes. And then unable to speak of anything else,

she opened her heart to Jane, unable to keep her own good news any longer.

"You are joking, Lizzy. This cannot be!— engaged to Mr. Darcy! No, no, you shall not deceive me. I know it to be impossible."

291

"This is a wretched beginning indeed! My sole dependence was on you; and I am sure nobody else will believe me, if you do not. Yet, indeed, I am in earnest. I speak nothing but the truth. He still loves me, and we are engaged."

Jane looked at her doubtingly. "Oh, Lizzy! it cannot be. I know how much you dislike him."

"You know nothing of the matter. That is all to be forgot. Perhaps I did not always love him so well as I do now. But in such cases as these, a good memory is unpardonable. This is the last time I shall ever remember it myself."

Miss Bennet still looked all amazement.. "My dear, dear Lizzy, I would—I do congratulate you—but are you certain? forgive the question—are you quite certain that you can be happy with him?"

"There can be no doubt of that. It is settled between us already, that we are to be the happiest couple in the world."

Jane and Elizabeth spoke happily of their loves and the future. A great while later, Mr. Darcy and Mr. Bingley returned. Bingley rushed over to Jane and kissed her cheek.

Mr. Darcy leaned in to Elizabeth and said, "Go to your father, he wants you in the library."

She was gone directly.

Her father was walking about the room, looking grave and anxious. "Lizzy," said he, "what are you doing? Are you out of your senses, to be accepting this man? Have not you always hated him?"

"I do, I do like him," she replied, with tears in her eyes, "I love him. Indeed he has no improper pride. He is perfectly amiable. You do not know what he really is; then pray do not pain me by speaking of him in such terms."

"Lizzy," said her father, "I have given him my consent. He is the kind of man, indeed, to whom I should never dare refuse anything, which he condescended to ask. I now give it to you, if you are resolved on having him. But let me advise you to think better of it. I know your disposition, Lizzy. I know that you could be neither happy nor respectable, unless you truly esteemed your husband; unless you looked up to him as a superior.

"He is my one true Master," she said.

"Well, my dear, if this be the case, he deserves you. I could not have parted with you, my Lizzy, to anyone less worthy."

To complete the favourable impression, she then told him what Mr. Darcy had voluntarily done for Lydia. He heard her with astonishment.

"This is an evening of wonders, indeed! And so, Darcy did every thing; made up the match, gave the money, paid the fellow's debts, and got him his commission! You have my blessing, my dearest child." He kissed her fondly on both cheeks, and

as she quitted the room said, "If any young men come for Mary or Kitty, send them in, for I am quite at leisure."

Chapter 33

Jane and Bingley were married first and spend a few months at Netherfield before deciding the close proximity to her mother was a detriment rather than an advantage. By the new year, they were ensconced near Pemberley.

Elizabeth and Darcy were married next, and Elizabeth was overjoyed to take his sister Georgina under her wing. By watching her beloved older brother and his new bride, Miss Darcy was able to see that a marriage should be more than money, but love and respect.

Lydia hinted outrageously for an invite to Pemberley, but out of respect for her husband, Elizabeth put her sister off by sending her funds from her own accounts. In that way everyone was happy.

Kitty had convinced Mary to go into the village with her and both of them were shaping up quite well under their aunt's tutelage.

Charlotte and Mr. Collins continued their bi-weekly trips to Lady Catherine's and through Charlotte's sweet words, and even sweeter tongue, eventually Lady Catherine accepted the fact that her favorite nephew eschewed her daughter to marry Ms.

Bennet.

Mr. and Mrs. Bennet, for the most part, had the home to themselves more often than not and Mr. Bennet settled his wife's nerves at every available opportunity.

Eventually, Netherfield was purchased by another eligible bachelor and the parties started up again, but that is another story without the Bingleys or the Darcys. For both of them found wedded bliss.

It was at Pemberley one evening after dinner. Georgina had played a concerto with such talent it brought tears to their eyes. After Georgina had said goodnight, Elizabeth pulled down on the secret wall sconce and followed her husband into their dungeon.

She undressed and held still while Mr. Darcy lovingly put her hands in restraints over her head and attached the clips that she had grown so fond of on each of her nipples. He waited until the sharp pain became an aching pleasure before making sure she was wet and ready for him to insert the glass jeweled plug. He had made it especially for his wife as a wedding present. The top of it was a flawless ruby that burned and sparkled like the fire in Elizabeth's eyes.

He began by flogging her lightly on her calves and thighs, taking time to kiss her and caress the smooth curve of her backside.

"Why are you smiling, dearest?" Mr. Darcy said.

"I am the happiest creature in the world," Mrs. Darcy said.

He raised an eyebrow, "Truly you could have waited until I was inside you to tell me thus."

Elizabeth chuckled. "Perhaps other people have said so before, but not one with such justice. I am happier even than Jane; she only smiles, I laugh."

And after she laughed, he made sure she was as satisfied as she was happy.

The End

About the Author

Lissa Trevor has her stilettos firmly entrenched in the romance community. A frequent reader at Manhattan's Between The Covers events, Lissa also created an erotic story template for Coliloquy's ValEntwined promotion that allowed readers to download a personalized ebook starring themselves and their significant other. Her novella Wild Oats, features a time traveling, wild night of fulfilling sexual fantasies that the heroine was too afraid to experience the first time around. You can find her at http://lissatrevor.wordpress.com/

Made in the USA
Charleston, SC
17 May 2013